TERROR AT G-20

Terror at G-20

A Kate Dawson Mystery

John L. Flynn

OPEN ROAD
INTEGRATED MEDIA
NEW YORK

This edition published in 2023 by Open Road Integrated Media, Inc.
180 Maiden Lane
New York, NY 10038
www.openroadmedia.com

TERROR AT G-20

PROLOGUE

Thirteen-year-old Mylee swayed back and forth uneasily on the balls of her tiny feet in the towering stiletto heels, as she and the five other, young girls were herded together into a group, like cattle, and forced to climb a narrow set of steps to the top of a platform by several ushers in ill-fitting suits, brandishing high-voltage cattle prods. At the top, Mylee and the others were then shoved, one-by-one, through a set of red, velvet drapes with gold trim onto a makeshift stage, and coerced into walking down a long runway that was surrounded on either side by face-less businessmen, leering at them from the shadows of the dark-ened hall.

Each of the girls was naked, except for a number that hung around her neck, high-heel shoes, and a small thong, which was little more than dental floss that covered her pubic hair. Most moved slowly, tentatively, each step measured as if they were stepping through a minefield instead of walking the length of a high-fashion runway.

At the end, each woman hit her mark on stage and was illu-minated by bright stage lights that made her more visible and aesthetically pleasing to the men who had gathered in the hotel

3

ballroom as potential bidders. Each woman then turned, some more skillfully than others, and headed back down the runaway to wait their turn behind the red-velvet drapes, to be called again and sold.

Wearing the number 133, Mylee staggered to the end of the runway last, one foot clumsily placed in front of the other, and finally stood on her mark, terrified, feeling as if her head was about to explode. She was not a runway model after all, but a simple girl from the country.

She had never even seen a runway before that morning when, during dress rehearsal, the ushers had used fear and intimidation along with liberal doses of electric shock to teach Mylee and the other girls how to walk from one end to the other as models. Now, as the tears began to stain her porcelain-like features, she gathered up her small breasts, and cupped her hands over each nipple, humiliated by the ordeal, trying to hide her shame from those who peered at her from the darkness. She then bowed her head, and began the long walk back down the runway, moving her lips in silence, praying, wishing herself away to oblivion. Mylee had no way of knowing that she was already teetering on the edge.

The frightened, young girl was the product of two cultures, one Asian and the other American. While she had the undeniable, physical appearance of other Thai women, with her long, silky, black hair and slim, firm, petite body, Mylee struggled every day to hide her Western side. That was the one way she bore her mother's shame.

During the years that her mother, Dara, had studied veterinary science at a small clinic in Bangkok, she paid her own way by working as a hostess at a popular night club. One night, two U.S. sailors on leave who had had too much to drink caught Dara in the alley closing up shop after work and brutally raped her. Fearing that she would be labeled as a whore who worked in one of Thailand's many brothels, she kept silent about the rape. Cleverly, Dara hid her pregnancy until the very last moment, and then gave birth to Mylee in the northern province of Lamphun where her step-brother labored as a farmer.

She left her daughter with him to be raised on the farm in anonymity, and returned to complete her studies in Bangkok. But it didn't take long for the locals to recognize just how different Mylee was from the other girls. They even managed to convince her uncle that she had great value to those in the Western world. So, at age seven, he sold her virginity to a Westerner who was passing through the village for the price of a goat. And then, at age twelve, he traded Mylee to a pimp for a small sum and the promise of more cash to come from her "work" in the highly lucrative Asian sex trade.

Mylee grew to hate her Western heritage. Almost every day, she scrubbed her skin until it was nearly raw to hide its creamy, white luster. She painted her eyes to hide the fact that they were round, not slanted. She bound her feet in white linen until they were blistered and bloody in order to keep them small and petite. She hot-ironed the curls in her hair on an ironing board, and practiced walking with her shoulders bowed slightly so that no one would see that she was actually two-to-three inches taller than the other girls.

As she continued down the runway and through the red-velvet drapes in front of her, she hung her head low with shame. Not only did she feel totally humiliated by the line-up in the ballroom on the fourth floor of the InterContinental Hotel, but Mylee also hated and despised everything that was "white." She prayed that she could blot away her whole existence. Ironically, her split heritage was exactly what appealed to most of the bidders, as they waited for Lot 133 to be auctioned.

"Fifty thousand dollars," shouted the Saudi prince who sat to the left of the stage with several other Arab businessmen, wearing traditional robes and guthras as head coverings. The ceremonial dagger that he wore on his hip was encrusted with rubies, diamonds and other expensive gems. Excitedly, he reached up and adjusted the *agal* or black "rope" that held the red-and-white-checkered cloth in place on his head, and then smiled at the beautiful, fourteen-year-old girl who stood alone on the stage. He had made up his mind to buy her as a concubine, to live with him in his grand palace along with his six wives and dozen or so other concubines and children.

"Thank you, sir," the auctioneer remarked in very formal English into the hand-held microphone, nodding his head with respect to the Saudi delegation. He then turned to his assistant, and barked out several words in Chinese, ordering him to coerce a smile from the young girl that was on the selling block. His assistant nodded, to one of the ushers who, in turn, waved a cattle prod at her.

Miao Yin complied with a mouthful of pearly whites.

"Fifty thousand dollars is bid for this lovely Asian flower."

Several of the hundred-odd spectators at the auction, who were seated on folding chairs around the runway and in the center of the room, grumbled their objections at the large bid, but didn't say anything more.

Those that had real money to spend, like the Saudis or the Wall Street types, kept the monthly auction of sex slaves truly a lively event, while the others who may have been recent lottery winners or were born trust-fund babies started the bidding low and, more often than not, went home empty-handed. They pretended to be high rollers and extravagantly tipped the beautiful, bikini-clad hostesses who moved along the aisles on either side of them, serving watered-down champagne. But in the end, most were little more than that certain type of Western man who was attracted to young, submissive Asian women. They tended to be older, unattractive, white men with few, if any, social skills. Most had struck out in life trying to win the heart of the prom queen but found it easier to pay for sex rather than develop a relationship with a woman they were only mildly attracted to. A bearded man, who had gone prematurely gray in his late thirties, sat among them, his pockets stuffed with cash from his life savings and a light saber prop clipped to his belt. Beyond their ranks, on either side of the fancy ballroom was the overflow of spectators, some of them seated, some standing, others leaning against the period antique furniture that defined the elegant InterContinental Hotel. They were the curious, the bored, and the unwashed masses that got off watching naked women paraded on a stage.

"Can I hear sixty thousand dollars?" the auctioneer pressed his audience for an increase to the existing bid. He looked around the room, making eye contact with some of the high rollers who had real money to spend. "Will you say sixty thousand? Can I say sixty thousand?" Purposely, he paused again, building anticipation, giving his high rollers one last chance to bid.

"Fair warning and last call then . . . Sold! To Prince Faisal bin Mohammed in the second row."

As Faisal stood up and clutched his hands together over his head in a victory pose, bathing in the admiration of both his friends and foes alike, the auctioneer turned slightly and, with a subtle nod of his head, signaled for the next girl. His assistant pulled the red-velvet drapes aside, and beckoned for Mylee, the next girl in line, to step forward and follow him down the runway to the auction block where she, too, would be sold. But she refused to budge an inch. Her head remained bowed, her body rigid, and her lips chapped, frozen mid-sentence in silent prayer. The harder the assistant tried to pull her into place, the more determined she was to stand her ground.

Finally, after he had failed to coerce her, he stepped out from behind the drapes and shrugged his shoulders in defeat. The auctioneer turned from his feeble-minded assistant to look at the young girl who stood, like an ice sculpture, solid and unmoving, as the drapes fell back into place. He had dealt with her kind before. There was at least one, in every third or fourth auction, who dared to defy his authority. And, he knew there was only one way to deal with them.

Very quickly, the auctioneer ordered the bikini-clad hostesses to fill everyone's glasses with more champagne, and proposed a toast to the Saudi prince's good fortune. "Congratulations, Prince Faisal, on such a hard-fought victory! You have outbid all of your competitors," he declared into the microphone, raising his glass in the air. "May Allah bless your union with Miao Yin with many, strong sons."

Faisal touched the fingers of his right hand to his lips and forehead, and twirled them twice in the air as a sign of respect for the auctioneer. "Shukran Jazilan! [Thank you, very much]," he replied in Arabic.

The auctioneer smiled broadly, his face belying his actual feelings.

Moments later, while most of the men in the audience were clanking glasses and toasting each other's health with watered-down champagne, the auctioneer turned back around to the stage. He stormed down the runway, and flung open the red-velvet drapes, like an avenging angel. Then, even before the drapes had managed to close fully behind him, the auctioneer kicked Mylee full-force in the lower abdomen, and she doubled over, clutching her stomach in pain. He kicked her again where she lay, and then with the cruel efficiency of a predator, he kicked her a third time. When his rage had finally subsided, he looked down at her, not in pity but in shock at what he had done. That look of "Oh, Shit!" registered on his face, as the auctioneer realized the potential damage he had inflicted on one of his most valuable assets. His cold, lifeless eyes turned away from her, and he quickly summoned three of his ushers to get Mylee back on her feet.

"How dare you attempt to defy me!" the auctioneer bellowed in Thai, standing over her like a great, mythical ogre. He grabbed her chin. "You little cunt, I own you. I OWN YOU!" The words did not seem to have had any effect on Mylee. She stood rooted to the spot. "Didn't you hear me? I own you!"

Mylee gave no sign of having heard. She stared at him, searching his face for a sign, some symbol that he was at the very least human, but only dead eyes stared back at her with a complete lack of emotion or empathy.

When the stark reality of her situation finally caught up to her, she twisted and turned, struggling to break free of her captors, but it was to no avail. She was simply no match for them, particularly in the vice grip of the three, large ushers who easily outweighed her by a thousand pounds.

She tried resisting, clawing at them and nipping at them with her teeth. But the more she struggled to break free, the tighter they clamped down on Mylee, her fragile limbs gripped like a wishbone between competing rivals.

"You shame me!" she cried out in disbelief in her native Thai language, spitting up blood.

"You bring shame to yourself, your family," the auctioneer replied, inches from her face, his foul breath causing her to wretch as the smell of garlic and raw onions filled her delicate nostrils. "The contract that I made with your uncle, when

9

you were just twelve-years-old, is a perfectly legal and binding document. It gives me exclusive rights to trade, barter or sell you to the highest bidder in a public auction. Furthermore, I have the right to lease you to one of the local brothels, and collect ninety percent of your earnings. I also have the right to terminate your miserable existence, if at any point in time you displease me. You have no rights! You are nothing more than property to me. So, you are instructed to hold your tongue and do as you're told."

Mylee looked up at him, her eyes ablaze with anger. "I'll not perform as your trained monkey."

"You will do what I tell you to do, or you will not leave this room alive," he said coldly, with a sense of finality, choosing a very formal version of Thai to communicate his last message to her. "And when I have finished feeding your remains to my pet piranha fish, I will destroy your uncle's farm, butcher your step-brothers and sisters, stake your worthless uncle to an ant hill, and see that your mother spends the rest of her life in a brothel, fucking lepers until she herself becomes one."

"Only the gods have power over me," she replied, still defiant.

The auctioneer shook his head. "No. You're wrong. I am god. I have the power to grant you life or end your existence right now. This moment! You must choose, and choose wisely."

With that, he nodded at two of his three ushers, and they began to pull on her arms with enough force to separate the tendons in each arm from the rest of her body. The auctioneer knew they'd never succeed in actually dislocating her shoulders, but he realized that she wouldn't. The fear alone should force her back in line.

Mylee screamed out in pain, a terror-stricken cry that echoed through the ballroom. Two ushers continued their tug-of-war, but before they could inflict any permanent damage, the auctioneer interceded. He wasn't about to have such a valuable commodity damaged. Scared, perhaps, but not damaged.

"Do you want them to continue?" he asked her, turning his back on the young woman as his men continued to ply their torture. "I will not ask you again, but rather will turn a deaf ear to your cries of mercy as they tear you apart. Is that what you want? A horrible, painful death? Or the chance to live, perhaps bathed in fine oils and dressed in rare silks?"

Mylee gasped for breath as she stared at him for another moment, unyielding. She couldn't have answered, even if she wanted to. In addition to feeling as if she was being pulled apart, literally limb from limb, by the two goons, a third usher's strong hands had clamped down on her windpipe, and the woman's eyes were bugging out.

Her face turned to blood-red.

"Master!" yelled one of the other slave girls in Thai, on her knees, tugging at the seam of the auctioneer's European trousers, shaking all over. "For the sake of our ancestors, stop! You're going to kill her."

"Please, Master," another one cried out, "do not kill Mylee."

"Spare her life!" young Miao Yin wailed, scared shitless, and followed the chorus of voices pleading with him to spare the young woman's life.

The auctioneer seemed not to care. But the fact was that he had already made up his mind to spare her life. He just didn't want her to know. He appeared blind to everything except the fearful, florid face in front of him. He then felt the smooth and calming notion of his own divinity wash over him like a fresh breeze. The room and all the other people in it were far away from him. The only thing that mattered to him was his absolute control.

Then, abruptly, he was wrenched back to reality by the simple but reluctant nod of Mylee as she gave into him.

"Let her go," the auctioneer said. And with a wave of his hand, the ushers loosed their grip completely, and Mylee doubled over, hacking and gagging, lying on the stage floor at his feet. He leaned down, and whispered to her—his voice was low and measured, and meant only for Mylee to hear—he didn't want anyone to know that there had been an attempted mutiny in the ranks of the slave girls, and certainly not from someone as young as her.

"Now, clean yourself up, and be ready when I call for you."

Her eyes narrowed, flashing loathing like a torch.

"I hate you!" she croaked back, her throat pulsating with pain, raw, gasping for air.

The auctioneer smiled, but there was no sense of amusement in his eyes. "Yes? Is that true? Well, you're going to make me a lot of money, my dear, and that's the only reason why I let you live." He paused a moment to stroke her flesh. "You're going to bring in over a hundred thousand dollars."

Mylee flinched at his touch, as if once again she had been slapped across the face, and turned her back on him.

Calmly, he stood, carefully readjusting the smile on his face, and confidently emerged from behind the redvelvet drapes. He strode the length of the runway, and returned to the microphone. He then looked down at his notes, at the lot number 133 that had been circled on the page, and nodded at his assistant. Mylee held her stomach as she emerged from the red-velvet drapes, and started down the runway.

"Lot 133. Ah, yes!" the auctioneer said, pretending to read through the special notes that accompanied each of the lot numbers, whether they were his property or not. As the owner of this particular lot, he was fully acquainted with its pluses and minuses, but he tried not to show any personal bias towards the lot for fear that he would unduly influence the bidding. "A superb example of femininity and grace, representing one of the oldest bloodlines in Thailand, with just the right dash of the modern world, this lovely, high-spirited, thirteen-year-old woman will enhance any collection."

Tears were pooling in the corners of Mylee's wide brown eyes as she placed one foot clumsily in front of the other, her tiny feet lashed to high-heeled shoes, like stilts that she could barely stand in, let alone walk. Blindly, she staggered all over the runway carpet, mortified and disgraced by her nakedness. What made matters worse to her was listening in dishonor as the men barked dollars back and forth, bidding for the right to be her next master.

When she reached the end of the runway, Mylee could not see her mark through the flood of tears in her eyes, and would have walked right off the edge of the stage had it not been an usher who kept her safe.

"Forty thousand dollars is offered. Thank you, Mister Sheridan," the auctioneer continued. "Forty thousand is bid, say forty-five, go forty-five. Forty-five is bid, now who'll say fifty thousand? Fifty thousand dollars! Thank you. Fifty thousand. At fifty thousand, say fifty-five. Bid the fifty-five thousand. Not enough for this choice piece. Can I hear fifty-five, selling at fifty-five thousand? Sixty thousand, you say? All right, I have sixty thousand dollars bid. Make it seventy thousand—seventy thousand dollars there. Now seventy is here, seventy-five is bid. Seventy-five thousand, I'm bid. Who'll say eighty thousand? Do I hear eighty thousand? Thank you. Eighty thousand dollars is the bid. Do I hear eighty-five thousand?"

All at once, Mylee clutched her stomach, and stopped dead in her tracks, a strange look on her face. The pain in her lower abdomen was overpowering, but the young woman fought back the urge to double-over and maintained her stance. Instead she smiled strangely at the auctioneer, a weird, knowing smile, and took one final step toward him. Then she collapsed to one knee, and finally slammed into the floor.

Mylee whispered something so low and softspoken that the auctioneer had to bend down until his ear was nearly resting on her lips.

She murmured her last words, "Oblivion, at last . . ."

CHAPTER ONE

Several hours later, Mylee's body was still sprawled on the makeshift stage when Kate Dawson walked into the ballroom of the InterContinental Hotel, and pushed her way through the people gathered at the crime scene. Her long blonde hair had been pulled into a ponytail; her blue eyes were dark and puffy from a lack of sleep. She'd donned comfortable jeans and loafers, a casual, button-down shirt haphazardly tucked-in and a light-weight windbreaker. She stared hard at the body, a slab of meat that had once contained all the hopes and dreams of a young woman's life. It was hard for Dawson to imagine a more tragic sight, particularly when she considered that her daughter—had she survived that fateful bullet which took her life—would have been the same age as Mylee, thirteen. Two beautiful, young girls, with a whole lifetime of promise ahead of them, cut down even before they could become women. She looked at the body again, as if photographing it with her mind, and then turned away, shaking her head, looking at the crowd of homicide investigators that filled the room. The crowd was so much smaller than she had ever seen before.

Slowly, somewhat methodically, Dawson moved through

the elegant ballroom, taking in every last detail, using her eyes to record everything, so that later she wouldn't have to rely on crime scene photos to remind her of what she had seen. First, she walked by the coroner's crew who were searching and probing the body, with the Chief Medical Officer. Then she walked past the forensics team who was unpacking a small piece of electronic equipment that would scan the room for clues. She sidestepped several plain-clothed detectives, including William Clark and Mikhail Jawara, who were conferring with some of the witnesses and hotel security. It had been their bad luck to pick up the call when they were just going off duty. As the cover officers, they had spent most of the wee hours of Monday morning collecting statements from the people who had been there. Finally, she came upon two crime scene boys who were working the room for trace evidence.

"How's it going, boys?" she asked, crouching down next to them.

"Not bad," one replied, looking over at her. "I'd much prefer to be home safely in bed with my wife than out on a cold night like this one. It's flu season, you know, and if I'm not mistaken, there are a lot of people out sick."

"Yeah," the other one answered. "It seems like we've been doing a lot of double shifts to cover for those out sick."

Dawson nodded. "I wondered why the turn-out was so light," she commented. She spoke softly, just soft enough for them to have heard her, but loud enough not to be rude. "Keep up the good work, boys."

Even though Kate's star had been on the rise with the capture of the "Angel of Death" serial killer and the indictment of the President and her staff for conspiracy to commit murder in the death of a Fox News reporter, most people didn't have a high opinion of the San Francisco Police Department. A Gallup poll, taken over the weekend, had found that the Department's approval rating had plunged to its lowest in the last fifty years. Less than twenty-nine percent of those sampled as a part of the poll rated the Department highly, while a whopping seventy-one percent of the people polled were critical of its roll in protecting the City. The local media, with its very liberal agenda, blamed the SFPD for putting the personal interests of its officers before the safety of the citizens they protected. But the issue was not as black-and-white as the press portrayed it.

Due to recent budget cuts, not only were police officers required to supply their own handguns, but they were also obligated to bring their own ammunition and keep their weapons clean and in good repair. For most officers, this was a huge expense that they simply could not easily afford. A nasty dispute between some of the more liberal members of the City Council and members of the police union over these "unreimbursed job expenses" had led to the first-ever "sick-out" last Wednesday when a large percentage of police officers and detectives called out and stayed home rather than report to duty. By Friday, nearly half of the Force, complete with their support staff, had also called out sick. Their protests were born out of frustration and desperation, but not everyone saw it that way. Fearing another police protest might wreak havoc on Monday, the Mayor had ordered every cop in the City to report to duty first thing in the morning under threat of suspension and dismissal. That deadline was just a few hours away, and as she glanced at her watch, the last thing that Kate wanted to see was another "sick-out."

"What was the cause of death, doctor?" Dawson asked, after she had completed a full circuit of the crime scene.

Edgar Brogan greeted her with more unwelcome news. The Chief Medical Examiner stood up wearily from the body as she approached, and sighed deeply. His cheeks were rosy red and windblown, like he had been spending most of the time during the "sick-out" on his sailboat in the bay rather than at the ME's office. "She was poisoned, probably cyanide," Doctor Brogan reported. "But unlike most poisons, like arsenic, cyanide does not go down unnoticed. It's better known as a strong, bitter poison; noticeable when swallowed. If she died of cyanide poisoning, she may have ingested it herself."

"Are we talking suicide, doctor?" she asked, looking at the body which had been roped off by Brogan to safeguard others from getting too close.

"That's my preliminary finding," he replied, flatly.

"I'm still going to run a standard toxicology screen back at the lab to check for common exposures to narcotics and carbon monoxide, but that bloody froth that dribbled out of her mouth is a dead giveaway. I'd be surprised if the tox-screen came back with any other finding but cyanide poisoning."

Kate swallowed hard. "How did she die, Edgar?"

Brogan folded his arms across his chest. "Cyanide poisoning has a wonderfully precise lethal action. As a form of *histotoxic hypoxia*, it disables the body's ability to metabolize oxygen cell by cell, a kind of chemical suffocation that sets off a spreading cell-death meltdown in the body. Victims gasp desperately for breath, trying to fill their lungs, but find themselves unable to use the oxygen. Loss of consciousness is preceded by general weakness, headaches, dizziness, and confusion. As the organs start to die, the victim exhibits muscle tremors. They stagger and finally collapse. My guess is that the young woman ingested the poison, and was dead from cardiac arrest, within a matter of moments."

"But that doesn't tell me the 'why,' doctor. Why would a healthy, normal, young girl, like Mylee, take her own life?"

The Chief Medical Officer shook his head, and smiled. "I wish

I could tell you, Kate. You want to know the how and the when, I've got you covered. But there are certain questions that science simply can't answer. I suppose that's the reason why some of us still turn to God for answers to those deeper questions."

Dawson smiled back at him. "Thanks, Edgar," she said, glimpsing her boss, the head of the Homicide Bureau, out of the corner of her eye.

James Roberts looked uptight and tense, irritable from the wait his lead detective had extracted from him.

But as he was the one who had called her in the middle of the night and insisted that she take charge of the investigation, he could hardly complain if Dawson took a few extra minutes to acquaint herself with the crime scene. The Lieutenant was a big, hulking man who carried the weight of his office around with him, like most cops carried sidearms. He was known as a bureaucrat's bureaucrat, and played the game better than most. In fact, Roberts was the real reason why the Homicide Bureau consistently topped all of the other departments with a prosecution rate of eighty-two percent (or better). He just wasn't a very good detective himself. He was such a slave to the day-today routine of the job that he lacked imagination, which was where, Dawson reasoned, most good investigative work happened. They had butted heads so often over this very same issue that she had actually started calling him a pragmatist, the rarest of God's creatures, also known as a person with all four feet on the ground.

Dawson watched him fret for another moment, then decided to put Roberts out his misery. "Okay, people. I want to know exactly what happened here," she demanded, the lead detective's words summoning everyone to attention.

As if he had been switched on like a light switch, William Clark started reading from his notes. "According to witnesses, the deceased—known simply as Mylee—was one of six Thai national girls being auctioned off to the highest bidder as a sex-x-x s-s-slave . . . sex slave," he stuttered, having to repeat it for clarity. "Apparently, auctions of this kind are held regularly, about once a month, for 'members only' at upscale venues like this one."

"They must have left my name off the guest list," Mikhail Jawara joked, but Clark did not pay his partner any mind.

"How come I've never heard of this?" Dawson asked, with a frown.

Clark shrugged. "Vice has been trying to close these down for years, but the promoters are very clever with how they advertise their shows for 'entertainment purposes' only. They get all the proper permits. They break no apparent laws because they're not 'actually' selling sex slaves, even if they are, and they're very well-connected downtown. I've heard the Mayor's attended more than one."

"Go on," she ordered, with a look of disgust.

"After the first girl was sold to a Saudi prince for a record $50,000, Mylee was supposed to be the next girl on the auction block, but there was some kind of problem," Clark continued his narrative. For someone with an eidetic memory for recalling all manner of facts and details, he kept extensive notes that could have easily formed the basis for a half dozen mystery novels. "She was either unwilling or unable to proceed, and that held the auction up for a good five or ten minutes."

"Well, what was it? Unwilling, or unable?"

"I don't know, Kate, and no one else seems to know either."

"I've interviewed about half those eyewitnesses for Clark," Jawara interjected, "and the only thing that they would all agree on was the likelihood that Mylee and the auctioneer had a dust-up backstage."

Dawson shook her head as if to clear it. "Are you kidding me? Do you know what they were fighting about?"

"No idea," Clark confessed, with a shrug.

"Nada," Jawara added.

"But when she finally did emerge from behind the curtains, Mylee was holding her stomach, walking kind of funny."

"Walking funny? Shit, no! That woman had been beaten up," Jawara said, correcting his partner. "She could hardly keep one foot in front of the other. She looked like she was completely disoriented."

Clark elbowed him in the ribs. "I was just getting ready to report that."

"Christ, Clark, when are you going to learn to cut to the chase? This isn't fuckin' *Murder, She Wrote*, you know," Jawara insisted.

"Well, guys, what was it?" she pressed, growing impatient.

"According to the eyewitnesses, it looked like Mylee had been beaten up pretty badly," Clark reported, notes in hand. "She was disoriented, and could barely walk down the runway straight. When she reached the end, she just collapsed."

"More like, fell flat on her face," Jawara concluded.

"I said that," William Clark added.

"No, you didn't."

"Were there any bruises on the body, Dr. Brogan?" Kate asked.

The Chief Medical Examiner looked at the body.

"Negative," he replied. "There are no obvious signs of blunt force trauma. If she was struck in the lower abdomen, it's possible the broken blood vessels beneath the surface of the skin may not have had the time to form into a definite indicator of damage. But then, just remember that bruising does not always indicate injuries sustained deeper within the body, such as in the chest cavity and around the lungs. I'll have a much better idea once I've conducted a complete autopsy back in the lab."

"You still think it was suicide?"

"Mylee died of cyanide poisoning," Brogan replied, after a moment's hesitation. "Now whether it was suicide or the deliberate act of someone attempting to kill her, I cannot say for any degree of certainty. Cyanide continues to be a favorite poison for professionals as well as amateurs alike. A single tablespoon of potassium cyanide will kill 90% of the forty-three people who ingest it, or about thirty-nine people, in two hours or less. But it is a bitter substance, and anyone who ingests cyanide will taste it. It wouldn't be my drug of choice."

Confused, William Clark turned back to his notes.

"Has Mylee's death been officially ruled a homicide?" he asked, thumbing back through the pages. "Or are we still working under the assumption it was suicide?"

"That hasn't been decided, Clark," Dawson said, with a frown.

"Why would anyone want to kill a sweet girl, like Mylee?" Clark asked. "She was barely thirteen-years-old."

Jawara objected. "How do you know she was so sweet? You never met her. She may have been a real bitch on wheels! Why do we always give the pretty ones a pass? For all we know, she may have been evil incarnate, and there was a long line of people who were anxious to see her dead."

"You're such a cynic, Mikhail," his partner concluded.

"I'm a realist," Jawara corrected him, "and whoever poisoned her was willing to sacrifice thousands of dollars in potential revenue in order to put her down. For what it's worth, my money's on the guy who held her pink slip."

"And what if you're wrong?" Clark asked. "What if Mylee was so humiliated by the circumstances of her life—the whole degradation of being sold as a sex slave—that she chose to end her life, rather than face a lifetime of shame?"

Dawson got between them. "That's enough speculation, gentlemen. I need you to be focused on the facts in the case, not idle speculation."

"Okay," Clark replied.

"You're right, Kate," Jawara added.

While Dawson continued to work the evidence, her boss clung to the edges of the crime scene, running interference like a perfect offensive lineman. He kept several noisy reporters out of the ballroom, and with the help of several police officers, maintained a proper cordon around the witnesses. He also served as the perfect liaison official with the front desk and other hotel officials. James Roberts stood in the door, with his arms folded across his chest, and his eyes swept the room, a commander of all that he beheld. So, when a tall, handsome, African-American man tried to push his way through the entrance to the ballroom, with badge in hand, Roberts glowered at him. The look eloquently said, *You'd better not piss me off.*

"I'm the agent from—" the stranger started to say.

"Yeah, I know who you are," the Lieutenant interrupted him, with a dismissive tone of voice. "You think that Justice Department badge is gonna get you a free lunch or something down here?"

"No," he replied. "Maybe just a little professional courtesy?"

Roberts smirked, and it took all his police officers could do to stop themselves from laughing out loud at the stranger. "In a city with half of its officers out on strike three days before hosting the G-20 International Summit next door at the Moscone Center. You gotta be fucking kidding me."

"All right. Forget courtesy. How about just being professional?"

"Look, I've dealt with you self-important pricks from Justice before," Roberts replied, shooting him one of his patented steely looks. "You talk a big game about professionalism and cooperation when you need something from us, but the minute my men do your dirty work, you hightail it back to Washington, and take all the rewards. Well, that's not going to happen this time. This is my crime scene and my investigation. If, and only if, I allow you to join this party, things are going to be done my way, or it's the highway, bub."

"Whaddya think they're going to say in D.C. when I call and tell them the brass is refusing to cooperate with me?" the stranger asked, threatening him.

"I don't really give a fuck," the Lieutenant replied.

"Why don't you call them right now, wake up a few of those assholes, and find out?"

"I don't need to wake anyone up," he said, with his trump card. "I just need to make one phone call to pull all the federal funding for the State of California. Funding for roads, hospitals, Head Start—you name it."

Roberts grunted. "You wouldn't dare."

"Your boys can dust down that entire crime scene, and they're not going to know any more than what I know already."

The Lieutenant scratched the stubble of beard that was growing on his face, and then reached up to adjust the small, horned-rim glasses on the end of his nose as if to bring the microscopic image of the Justice Department agent into focus. "So, what are you? Some kind of psychic?"

"No," he replied. "I just don't need the results of a forensics investigation to tell me this girl's death was part of a case I've been working on for several years; actually, part of a much larger, ongoing investigation that we've been conducting into human trafficking. You know, Justice tends to be pretty thorough with its work."

"Agent Whatever-the-hell-your-name-is, don't start believing your own press," Roberts cautioned him.

"The Department of Justice doesn't do anything unless it's politically expedient to do so."

"I take my orders from the Attorney General," the agent said flatly.

"Then you're a bigger fool than I thought you were," Roberts said, signaling a couple of his men. He pulled them to one side, and whispered several orders. He then turned back to the man from Justice. "Now, you want a front seat at the party, fine. Knock yourself out. I'll even send the Attorney General a fuckin' commendation for your assistance with my murder case. But the minute I hear a single word about jurisdiction or your taking control of the investigation, I'm going to bust your ass all the way back to Washington. Is that clear?"

"Crystal," he replied.

"Toomey and Loomis, kindly escort our new 'friend' to Inspector Dawson," Roberts instructed his men. "Make sure, he doesn't get lost."

Flanked by two burly officers who towered over him by a foot, the agent was escorted into the elegant ballroom. He was middle-aged, perhaps thirty-five or forty, and well-groomed, with a neatly trimmed goatee and shaved head. He wore an expensive suit, a three-button one-piece that was just a touch too fashionable to identify him as a police detective, but not trendy enough for court or the Wall Street crowd. He appeared to have an edge to him, a swagger and confidence that belied a man who lived his life, one day at a time, with a semi-automatic pistol at his side. But his street-smart, urban toughness seemed to be at odds with the sensitivity that shown through his eyes. Unlike his burned-out counterparts, that sense of feeling revealed a man who wore his heart on a sleeve.

He walked up to the makeshift stage, and gently pulled aside one corner of the blanket that covered Mylee's body. He was visibly moved.

"Did you know the deceased?" Dawson asked, glancing at the two police officers who escorted him before turning her gaze on him.

"No, not really," he said, shaking his head. Tears had pooled up in the corners of his eyes, but he did not shed a single tear. "She had been part of an ongoing investigation that the Justice Department was conducting into human trafficking, but I never knew her real name. She was always just #4, out of the six women we were tracking."

"Mylee," she said.

"My-lee?" he repeated awkwardly.

After she pulled the corner of the blanket back into place, Dawson dismissed Toomey and Loomis, and looked long and hard at the handsome stranger. While her curiosity about him was fleeting, at best, she had been more than satisfied by the view. It wasn't every day that a well-dressed man walked into her life, and gave her pause. But Kate knew better than to trust him. Her last beau had been an agent with the Department of Justice, and he not only exploited their relationship for political gain, but also broke her heart when he stole secret microfilm she was protecting. She never forgave him his deceit.

"I don't know if that was her real name, but that's the name they called her," she added.

"Were you here when it happened?" he inquired, politely.

"No, I'm afraid not," she replied, gazing at him. "I was called about an hour later by the head of the Homicide Bureau, and asked to take over the investigation. So, like you, I'm a relative latecomer to the party."

"What do you know about her death?" he asked, meeting her gaze.

Dawson shrugged lightly. "We're not really sure. Eyewitnesses claim that she had a scuffle with the auctioneer, and then, a few moments later, collapsed to the floor and died, but to what extent the scuffle contributed to her death, we just don't know yet. The Medical Examiner thinks its cyanide poisoning, but no one really knows if she ingested the poison on her own, or was force-fed the poison by someone, looking to kill her."

He closed his eyes for a moment, as if imagining Mylee's violent demise, and then squeezed back tears.

"How can I help you?" he said, at last.

"Why don't we start with introductions?" Kate asked solicitously. "My name is Kate Dawson, and I'm an inspector with the San Francisco Police Department."

"Gregory Morris," he said, shaking hands with her. "Special agent, Department of Justice."

"Agent Morris, what can you tell us about your investigation?"

"Not much," he replied, with a shrug of his shoulders. "It is still ongoing, but what I can do is talk to you in very general terms. Perhaps even provide the framework for what must have transpired here tonight."

Dawson nodded. "Okay, anything you share with us will be helpful."

"Human Trafficking is a billion-dollar-a-year business," Morris said, speaking directly to Kate but also making eye contact with several of the other detectives, "that is controlled not only by the criminal gangs but also large cartels that operate with military-like precision in nearly every corner of the world. They operate right out in the very open, and are unafraid of the sovereignty or military might of any nation. In fact, in many third-world countries, they offer the only real order those nations have seen in decades. It is estimated that some three hundred thousand women and children are traded every week on the black market by these groups, and each trade builds more wealth and power for them. But make no mistake, this isn't something that's happening 'over there.' The Asian sex trade, for example, is very real, and if you think it's just limited to Southeast Asia, then you've got a rude awakening coming at you. The sex trade is in every major city in the United States and Canada. In upscale venues, just like this one, which cater to Wall Street types, dotcom millionaires, and even Saudi princes. It is a trade that includes not only sex, but pedophilia, human slavery, and even organ harvesting. With hundreds of thousands of women and children being brokered on the open market, this is human slavery on a scale that hasn't been seen since the Pharaohs first enslaved Jews to build the Great Pyramids in Egypt."

"I had no idea it was that big or as far-reaching," Dawson confessed, taking a moment to digest everything that he had said.

Furiously, William Clark was taking notes. "Agent Morris, you stated the 'trade' not only included sex but also organ harvesting as well," he repeated, almost word for word. "Exactly how does that work? They couldn't possibly have the resources or medical expertise to maintain a large enough pool of organs for transplant."

The Justice agent stared at Clark, without expression. "Each year, tens of thousands of those who are held by the cartels are tissue typed, and then routinely killed once a matching recipient in Europe or the United States is found for their organs," he said, as a matter of fact. "Their precious kidneys, livers, and hearts are sold on demand and transplanted at enormous profit to overseas patients, who can afford them. All they have to do is keep their 'donors' alive long enough to be profitable to them."

"That's really cold, man," Jawara commented, eyes sullen.

"I'd say they were the lucky ones," Morris added.

"At least they don't have to suffer a lifetime of humiliation and abuse. They just have to wait a few months, while chained up at a prison camp, to be freed of all of their cares."

"I'd like to know why this isn't better reported," Clark said.

"Most Americans don't have a clue," Morris replied, with a snicker, "and honestly, wouldn't care if they did know all of the facts. They live in their safe, cookie-cutter, gated communities, shop at Wal-Mart or Costco on the weekends, and drive their little darlings in SUVs to the Kiddie Academy at the corner. Their shallow lives remain untouched by the world around them. That is, until a child goes missing or the pretty blonde next door disappears. Then, suddenly, their whole world comes apart. The last trace of their loved ones are the names and photos that show up on the sides of milk cartons, but by then, it's way too late to save them. Their loved ones have already been swallowed up whole by a billion-dollar-a-year business that only sees them as a commodity to be sold or traded. Not a human being at all."

Dawson nodded. "Of course, I've seen it happen time and time again. They're completely disinterested, until it happens to them. Then, when it's their own loved one at stake, they push the panic button, and turn to government agencies, like the Department of Justice or the F.B.I., to do something about it."

"There's very little that we can actually do," he said, with a sigh, "except file a report and hope for a miracle they're found."

"But what I don't understand," she objected, "is how the Asian sex trade found its way to our shores? I was under the belief, like most Americans, that the lawlessness was confined to the third-world toilets of Southeast Asia."

Morris replied, "Thirty-five years ago, there was a thriving sex industry in Thailand that catered primarily to the U.S. military and 'sex tourism.' Visitors to Bangkok could satisfy any kind of sexual pleasure or perversion, as long as the price was right. If you wanted a virgin, no problem. Pimps in the local bars sold virgins for $500 a pop. If you were looking for a light-skinned Thai girl from the northern region of the country, the brothels of Patpong Road and Soi Cowboy in Bangkok's red-light district were teaming with them. If you happened to be a known pedophile from the States who sought to buy a teenaged boy or girl, even children, you were welcomed with open arms as long as you had money to spend. Most people just looked the other way, or paid Thai police to look the other way. In time, prostitution became such an important part of the gross national product of Thailand, the Thai government's Interior Ministry enacted special legislation that protected those who profited from the sex trade. No one seemed to care about the victims, the young women and children who were raped or killed as a part of the industry. Profit was all that mattered, and soon other countries were trading sex for profit. In India, exotic women from the Himalayas were brought to Calcutta and other cities for their perceived beauty. Chinese nationals seeking a better life for themselves and children crawled through the malaria-infested jungles of Laos and Burma to reach Kuala Lumpur, Malaysia, only to discover they were sold or trapped into working the sex trade in some of the border towns. Expansion by the criminal gangs and cartels into the other nations in Southeast Asia, including Vietnam, means higher profits and greater demand for more product."

"Christ almighty!" Dawson swore.

"Aren't they concerned about HIV/AIDS and other diseases?" Clark asked, turning to a new page in his notebook.

"No, not really," Morris replied. "The cartels have an excellent record at policing their prostitutes for drugs and sexually-transmitted diseases. Women and children who are diagnosed with HIV/AIDS or herpes are summarily executed to reduce the likelihood of an epidemic, while the others with curable diseases are isolated from their peers to give antibiotics a chance to clear everything up."

"You've gotta be fuckin' kidding me," Jawara added.

"I wish that I was," he remarked.

Clark said, "I guess they take their business pretty seriously."

"That isn't the half of it," the Justice agent continued. "Today, while the sex trade still exists in Thailand, trafficked girls, especially the pretty ones, do not necessarily end up in the brothels of Bangkok. Pimps and other shady characters bargain for their ownership and services, demanding nothing less than their full loyalty. Some of these women are kidnapped, others are sold off by their parents and relatives, while still others are orphans. Most of them are traded, as many as seven to ten times, between pimps and criminal thugs. The lucky ones move into a world that is far more hidden and far more sinister than they could ever possibly imagine. They are taken to internment camps, which have been built deep in the jungle, where they are caged like animals and trained as sex slaves, then sold off to the highest bidder. Their pimps dress them in fine clothes, which are stolen from Chinese shipments bound for New York or Paris, and the girls end up here, on runways just like this one, in cities across the country."

Kate shook her head, in utter disbelief. "I guess I just don't get the whole thing," she confessed. "In a city like San Francisco, where women outnumber straight men ten-to-one, why would a man spend his life savings to buy a young, Asian girl? He's got his pick of women at any age, including Asian women. So, what's the big deal? Why are men so infatuated with these Asian women? Is it because women from Asian are more subservient than Western women, or is it because they make easy sex slaves?"

"I wish I could give you a simple answer, Inspector," Morris replied, "but it's a great deal more complicated than you can imagine."

"Really?" she asked, with a dumb look on her face.

"According to everything that I've learned, most men prefer them to Western women for reasons that go well-beyond their ready submission," the Justice agent reported, as he began counting down the top-five reasons on his right hand. "For one, Asian women are hardworking and faithful, two qualities that men are naturally hard-wired to like—"

"I could say the same thing about your average cocker spaniel," she quipped.

"The physical appeal of Asian women is undeniable. Their perfect teeth, their long, silky jet-black hair, their slim, firm, petite bodies, and their graceful manner all belie their social status," Morris continued, pointing out two additional reasons, "and they are not only attractive in their twenties, but also in their thirties, forties and fifties—unlike white women."

"There's plenty of fat, unattractive Asian women, too!"

Morris half-smiled. "Asian women tend to possess a sense of innocence that makes men curious to know more about them. And finally, they make perfect wives."

"Don't you mean 'slaves'?"

"Wives," he repeated himself. "Beyond everything else, they have strong family values and love to cater to the man."

"The perfect, little Geisha."

"Yeah, something like that," he replied.

Kate Dawson looked like she was going to be sick to her stomach. "You really know how to boost a woman's ego, Morris," she complained, holding her head.

"The way you talk, women like me should be adopting stray cats and taking up a spinster's rocking chair instead of trying to find true love on Match.com. You do realize there are still a few of us Western women out there that are looking for husbands and companions, and have no desire whatsoever to compete with the likes of them."

"I meant no offense, Inspector. I was really talking more in generalities, based upon my observations, and not making a critical statement about—"

"So, what about the sex?" she asked, abruptly interrupting him. "Are Asian women really sex-crazed and willing to do anything to gratify their men in the bedroom? Do they really want to 'love you long time'?"

Dawson had finally asked the one question that all of her detectives wanted answered.

Morris was blasé, brushing off her query. "Sex doesn't have the same meaning in the Far East that it does to us Westerners. I mean we've built up this whole mystique about sex, whereas Asian women view sex as just another form of affection, like kissing and hugging. They're far more proficient at sex than Western women, and leave absolutely nothing off the table. I suppose that's what makes them so desirable to Western men. They will do anything to please their man, and not feel guilty about it later. If he wants to have a threesome with her hot girlfriend, she'll do everything to make it happen, while most Western women would be on the phone with their attorney discussing a divorce."

Clark had opened his notebook. He said, "I've read articles, written by so-called 'bitter' Western women, who believe that guys into Asian girls aren't 'strong' enough or 'man' enough to handle a 'real woman.'"

"I won't dispute that because I have met plenty of Western

women who actually dislike their counterparts in Asia," the Justice agent replied.

He thought about Clark's point for another moment, and then looked over at the crowd of men who had come to leer at naked sex slaves and were now considered accessories to murder. They were sitting in a roped-off section of the ballroom, isolated, under arrest; Kate's neighbor Lenny was among them. Most were nervous, fretful, and even apprehensive as they waited, and watched, and listened. Morris regarded them, for an instant with disdain, and then added, "During my travels to Thailand, I've also encountered a certain type of Western man who is attracted to Asian women. He tends to be older, socially awkward, unattractive, white and, yes, let's not mince words, creepy! Take a look around, and you'll see that stereotype is well-represented here. This is the real reason why human trafficking and the sex trade exists. For these men, and millions of others just like them."

Jawara had heard enough. "Suppose you cut off the money source? Wouldn't you stop the sex trade cold?"

"That would be a good first step," he conceded, "but the problem is education. Until people realize the global consequences of their actions, there's always going to be some guy who thinks he's above the law and the sex workers who yield to him."

"We should castrate the lot of them," Dawson muttered, without realizing she had actually spoken out loud. Angry with herself, she shook her head. "Sorry. This whole thing makes me think of my own daughter being forced to have sex with some dirty old man. It just doesn't sit right with me, at all. In fact, it makes my skin crawl!"

"You don't have anything to apologize for, Kate," Jawara assured her.

"We were all thinking the same thing," Clark added.

"Thanks, guys. This is just very unsettling to me," she replied.

After a moment of silence, Clark picked up his pencil, and opened his notebook back up. He asked, "So, are Western men really 'the ticket to a better life' for these Asian women? Or is that just another myth?"

Morris shook his head. "No, not at all. Pimps working the system exploit their girls' weaknesses by telling them stories about a better world where people with money live, but it's done for the most cynical of reasons. To extract the best possible sexual performance out of them. Girls living in these third world countries have no real idea about America, just what they've seen on television or been told by their pimps. They think *Dallas* and *Dynasty* are real places, and for all intents and purposes, their pimps reinforce that fantasy by telling them exactly what they want to hear."

"'Telling them exactly what they want to hear,'" Kate repeated his last words to herself, over and over, until she saw a glimmer of truth in them. She didn't have to hear any more from him. A burning anger was building in the back of her brain, and, from the hazy cloud of unknowns related to Mylee's violent death to the intense attraction she felt for the Department of Justice agent, one thing was becoming increasingly clear, Gregory Morris might have been an extremely knowledgeable man when it came to details about human trafficking and the Asian sex trade, but he had not been forthright about his investigation. Morris hadn't given them anything of real value that they couldn't have discovered on their own. He had merely told them exactly what they wanted to hear, while he had gleaned most of the important details from their own investigation. Dawson felt like she had been sold out.

For the next twenty minutes, or so, she kept Morris at a distance. She listened to him talk to her detectives and waited patiently for him to finish. She then watched him shake hands and exchange final pleasantries with the team. Finally, as he made his way for the door, she caught up with him in mid-stride.

"Wait a minute, Morris," Kate said, betraying nothing. Her face was as set and hard as an ancient ceremonial mask. "You're not leaving, are you? It's early still."

He glanced down at his watch, and replied, "I'm still on Eastern Standard time, Inspector. For me, it's very, very late."

"Okay, then give me five minutes."

"Five minutes?"

She nodded, without expression.

"All right," Morris conceded, turning to listen to her. "Five minutes."

Dawson stared at him blankly. "For the last hour, I've been trying to make up my mind about you," she said, sounding like she was all business. "On the one hand, you breeze into my crime scene with a badge from Justice, offer to help us, and then spin a narrative that partially supports the evidence. But then, on the other, you're not very forthcoming about your own investigation. In fact, you're actually evasive with your answers. If I didn't know any better, and I don't, I'd say you were deliberately trying to derail my investigation."

"And just why would I do that?" he asked, with one eyebrow raised.

"I don't know," Kate confessed, shaking her head.

"Maybe there's some larger issue at hand that you don't want us to find out about. Perhaps a State Department official who got caught with his pants down? Or maybe it has something to do with military payoffs to one of the cartels for helping to destabilize an unfriendly nation? Whatever it is you're trying to cover-up, I will find out. I'm not afraid of the Department of Justice."

"You sound paranoid, Inspector."

"Paranoid? Probably. But you know what they say? Just because you're paranoid doesn't mean they aren't still out to get you."

"And who would 'they' be?"

Dawson side-stepped his question. "You weren't actually looking for Mylee, were you? You had someone on the inside that tipped you off about the auction? Just what was your purpose in coming here tonight? Disinformation?"

Gregory Morris shook his head. "I'm not permitted to comment about an on-going investigation."

Kate's eyes never left his face. "You're looking for the ringleader, aren't you? The one they call "the auctioneer"? And those other five girls? What's in it for you, Morris? A big, fat promotion, so that you can buy that row house in Georgetown and walk to work every day? Or do you get a kick-back directly from one of the gangs?"

"Now, you've gone too far!"

Morris pushed by her. He walked out of the ballroom through the double doors, without a backward glance.

Two hours later, as the third hour of the investigation dragged on, Kate Dawson walked towards the back of the ballroom with one of the uniformed officers, and singled her friend Lenny out from the group of men that was under house arrest. Dawson didn't waste any time in reading his name from the top of a list.

"Mister Provolone, we'd like you to come downtown and answer some questions for us."

He stared at her for a long moment, a slight smile on his lips. "Are you arresting me?" he asked, as the officer pulled him out of the chair.

"If that's the way you want to play it," she replied, all business.

"Just out of interest, are we talking the whole thing?" he stuttered, suddenly nervous. "You know, Miranda rights, handcuffs, the one phone call?"

"Just like in the movies, buster," the police officer remarked, guiding him out of the make-shift cordon, and then forcing him to stand in front of the Inspector.

"Will that be necessary, Mister Provolone?" Kate asked, nose-to-nose.

Lenny hesitated for a moment, as if on the verge of a panic attack, and quickly swallowed down several deep gulps of air. His face was pale, like a white linen shroud. "No, I don't think that will be necessary."

"Then let's get going," said Kate, as she escorted him from the room. "I'm due in court in a couple of hours, and you're not going to make me late."

They had driven a few blocks from the InterContinental Hotel before Dawson finally broke the silence. She leaned forward in the driver's seat of her BMW 5.25i, and looked over at her friend while she continued driving. "Lenny, just what the hell were you doing going to that slave auction?"

"Having fun," he replied, with all of the innocence of a child. "I go to the slave auctions once or twice a month. It's all just in fun. You know, a way to blow off some steam, and hang with your buddies."

"You've got your pockets stuffed with cash," Kate said, pointing at the ten and twenty-dollar bills hanging out of his pants pocket.

"Just tip money," Lenny said, with a shrug.

Dawson swallowed hard. "You must think I'm really stupid."

"Honestly, Kate. I don't know why you're so upset. It's no big deal."

"No big deal? Why don't you try explaining that to poor, little Mylee?" she said, her eyes focused on the road.

"Who?"

"The woman who died."

Provolone looked down at his feet. "I didn't know that was her name, but she was my favorite. Lot 133. A real dream-boat!"

"The number she was wearing around her neck matched a list of six names we found lying next to the podium," Kate reported. "Lot 133 was a Thai national, and she was only thirteen-years-old."

"Thirteen?"

"Yes, thirteen," she repeated, with an angry tone of voice. "Your dream girl was just thirteen! Men who get involved with little girls, Mylee's age, are called pedophiles. Do you have any idea what the average jail sentence is for a convicted pedophile? Eleven years, but here in the State of California, we add a little bit extra to the sentence. We start with 'Chemical castration,' which is also mandated for all sex offenders, so that the sexual appetite is completely squashed."

"What has that got to do with me?" Lenny asked, playing dumb.

Dawson got right to the point. "You can stop pretending that these so-called 'slave auctions' are anything but real. This is not some new form of adult entertainment, or some new-fangled strip-show. Those six women who were paraded around on that stage tonight were being auctioned off as sex slaves to the highest bidder. And if Mylee hadn't died during the auction, each and every one of those little girls would have ended up a nameless victim of some sexual predator more than twice her age. The really tragic part is that there are millions of women and children around the world, just like them, who are hope-lessly enslaved by gangs that trade in human flesh. They live in dark places—in brothels and bars, brick factories, fishing boats and slums—and rarely see the light of day."

Lenny Provolone shook his head. "How was I supposed to know? I read a blog online about a new service that helped guys like me meet cute, young girlfriends for between $20–50,000. That seemed like a reasonable price to pay. After all, lots of people pay matchmakers to find them suitable matches."

"Christ, Lenny, you're already dating my best friend."

"I like Rosa Romano. We have a lot of fun together, but I'm just not attracted to her the way I am with younger women."

"Yeah, yeah, I remember. You said something about 'saggy tits and wrinkled skin,'" Dawson quoted him verbatim.

"I prefer younger women, and I'm not going to allow you make me feel guilty about my personal preferences," he replied, defensively. "There are plenty of men out there who only date younger women."

"Just keep telling yourself that, if it helps you sleep at night," she said, trying to reach him on some level. "But the real reason why you don't like women your own age, and prefer little girls, is that they wouldn't deal with your emotional immaturity for one second. Little girls aren't as discerning."

"Thanks a lot."

Kate pulled her car to a stop at the intersection, when the light turned red, and glanced at her passenger in the adjacent seat. "Well, right now, my friend, there's the body of a thirteen-year-old girl headed to the morgue who would still be alive today if it weren't for you and men like you."

"You can't put that one on me," Lenny said, indignantly. "I didn't have anything to do with her death. I love women. I'd never hurt one."

"You don't get it, do you?" Dawson persisted, pulling away from the traffic light after it had turned green. "Young girls, strippers, prostitutes, sex slaves, you don't really care about women, do you? You act like a gentleman, pay lip service to liking women. The bottom line is that you're nothing but a misogynist."

Lenny had a pained look on his face. "Now, you're just being cruel."

"No, I'm being honest with you, and don't you think it's time you started being honest with yourself?"

"I haven't got a clue what you're talking about," he replied, folding his arms across his chest. "I told you once already that I wasn't going to allow you make me feel guilty about my personal taste in women. That should be enough."

"I can see we're not getting anywhere with this conversation," she said, taking a deep breath and letting it out between clenched teeth. "In fairness to Rosa, I really do think you owe her the truth. You need to tell her that you enjoy her company and that she's a lot of fun, but you're not interested in her romantically."

"That's really none of your concern," he said, curtly.

"Christ, Lenny. I'm only looking out for my friend. If situations were reversed, I'd say the same thing to her."

Lenny sat silent, brooding.

They rode for another mile, and then Dawson turned into Bayside Village Apartments on the south side of town, near San Francisco's hip, trendy neighborhood of South Beach. She pulled into a parking spot near their building, and turned off the engine of her car. Finally, she climbed out of the driver's side, and grabbed her briefcase from the back seat, while Lenny fumbled with the lock.

She looked at him, trying to find the gentle, kind friend that he had been to her, but only saw what appeared to be a stranger. "Look, it's really late, and I've got to be in court in a couple of hours. Why don't we just table this discussion until later, when we're both better rested, and talk about it some more then?"

"Whatever," he said, stumbling out the door of the car.

"Listen, could you do me a favor?" Kate asked.

Provolone's shoulders slumped as fatigue and despair washed over him. "What do you want? I've just about run out of favors."

"Could you send me a link to that blog site?" she said, without waiting for him to fully respond to her question. "You know the one that promises to find you a girl for $50,000. I'd like to ask Clark to follow up on it."

He turned his back on her, and headed towards the stairs. "Yeah, sure, whatever," he muttered, over his shoulder.

She stood there on the parking lot, looking apprehensively at him for a moment longer, and when she realized that he wasn't coming back, she walked alone to her apartment. It had been a long night.

CHAPTER TWO

At eight fifty-five on Monday morning, Kate Dawson scrambled down the third-floor corridor of the Hall of Justice building, and stopped outside Courtroom #5. She tucked a stray strand of hair behind her right ear, checking herself as she walked past the darkened windows of the offices lining the hall. To be presentable for the judge, she was more formally dressed, adding her Versace blazer to cover her piece. No one would have mistaken her for an attorney, particularly when she had to read the docket on the door in order to make sure she was in the right place: "Nine a.m.—Bail hearing in the State of California versus Jonathan Prinze."

With a sigh of relief, Dawson entered the courtroom through the rear door, and looked around briefly to get her bearings. She hadn't been in Courtroom #5 since they completed the renovations to the south end of the building earlier in the year, but the room didn't look all that different from her recollection of the place.

At the back, where she stood, the gallery was one-quarter filled, mostly with the usual reporters, curious spectators, and other interested parties. They sat on pew-style benches made out of a dark, mahogany wood that looked like they belonged in an old Episcopal church rather than a modern courtroom. With all of the advances in modern technology and ergonomic furniture design, she was surprised they were still using benches that had been made over a century-and-a-half ago. At the very least, they could have provided bench cushions or some other form of padding. As she completed her scan of the gallery, Kate was surprised to see Gregory Morris sitting in the last row. The fact that he had nothing to do with the Bail hearing was unsettling to her.

Dawson turned away from him, and walked toward the front of the courtroom, glancing to her left at the Defendant's table. Gina Victor, a former district attorney and friend, was at the defense table, talking with her client, a black lawyer, and a couple of interns. She had always thought that Gina was a very sexy, youthful woman, but the more Kate examined her hip, puckish style, the more she realized that her former friend had abandoned all of her principles in order to put her sexuality out there as a weapon to disarm juries. She was no longer the refined district attorney that she once knew; had, in fact, morphed into a woman that Kate no longer recognized. Then, of course, there was Jonathan "Jack" Prinze. Back in the day, Gina would have never represented a scumbag like him, but with Prinze's face plastered on every newspaper in the country for allegedly killing his pregnant secretary, she was enjoying a notoriety that she had never experienced before in her short career as an attorney. Even if she lost the case, Kate figured that Gina's next paycheck was bound to be in the seven figures. Dawson looked at the silver-haired, multimillionaire in his fifties who was handcuffed in an orange jumpsuit, and wondered if she was sleeping with him, too.

Just then, as if he had heard her thoughts, Prinze looked up at Kate, and caught her glare.

Without a second glance, she continued walking along, past the jury box, which was empty, and stopped at the District Attorney's table. Assistant DA Luke Wilson, already seated, was studying notes on a yellow legal pad.

Dawson leaned on the lectern between the two tables, where the lawyers would argue their case before the judge, and said, "Hello."

Wilson turned toward her. "How are you holding up?" he asked.

"I'm okay. Maybe a little tired, but I'm ready to go."

"Any idea where Matt Balardi is?" the Assistant DA asked, checking his watch against the clock that hung in the court-room. "He *is* the investigating detective on record."

Kate shook her head. "No, but I'm sure Matt knows how important this bail hearing is. The two of us spent three months putting this case together. I can always stand in for him as the lead detective."

"Well, let's just hope he doesn't have the flu," Wilson added.

"He'll be here."

Through the front door, the Bailiff entered the courtroom, and Dawson followed him with her eyes as he crossed in front of the judge's bench and the witness stand. He stood next to the desks where the court clerk and court reporter sat. Some spectators, knowing the routine, started to get to their feet. "All rise," he said.

The rest of those gathered in the courtroom slowly got to their feet as the judge in a plain black robe entered through the front door, and sat down behind the desk. Hot upon the heels of her arrival, a soft wave of murmurs flowed throughout the courtroom, like ripples on a lake, as people began to take notice of their new judge. Even the Assistant DA got in on the act as he leaned over to Kate.

"We've got a new judge," he whispered, with a surprised look. Dawson was dumbfounded. "I can't believe it."

"Where the hell is Zumbo?"

"No clue," she replied. "Maybe he's out sick with the flu?"

"Ladies and Gentlemen, criminal court is now in session," the Bailiff announced. "The Honorable judge Luisa Hernandez-Lopez presiding. All persons having anything to do with this court draw near, give your attendance and you shall be heard. God save the City of San Francisco and the great State of California." The Bailiff looked up at the great seal of jurisdiction and the flags of the United States and California, respectively, behind the judge, and nodded his head in satisfaction.

The judge settled into her seat, and then looked up at the people who were gathered in the courtroom. "Good morning, everyone. Please be seated," she said, as a matter of fact, all business. She waited until everyone was seated, then said, "Due to an unforeseen conflict of interest, Judge Salvatore Zumbo has recused himself from this case. I've been brought up to speed. So unless the State or Defense wishes to object, let's proceed with the bail hearing. The State may present arguments—"

Luke Wilson, the Assistant DA, got to his feet. He walked over to the Defense table, looked at them, appraisingly. He then turned back to the judge, and with great effort, took a deep breath and exhaled. "Your honor, under California Penal Code 12-70.5, a defendant charged with a capital offense may not be granted bail when proof of his or her guilt is evident. DNA evidence not only puts Jonathan Prinze at the crime scene, but also proves that he had sex with the victim within an hour of her murder."

There were a few whispers from the courtroom.

"Your honor," he continued, "the defendant, Jonathan Prinze, is a man of unlimited financial means who has mocked the authority of this court and brazenly violated the terms of an earlier bail agreement. He has proven beyond all reason that he is an extreme flight risk. Therefore, the State moves that the defendant be remanded to the custody of the court for the duration of these proceedings."

"Duly noted," the judge remarked. She was now sitting at the bench, wearing her reading glasses. Papers were spread out in front of her. "Anything else, counselor?"

"Not at this moment, your honor," Wilson replied.

"Very well," Judge Luisa Hernandez-Lopez said, with a nod. "Ms. Victor, does the defense wish to rebut?"

"Yes, your honor, we do," Gina replied. She picked up a yellow legal pad from the Defense table, and approached the lectern in the center of the courtroom.

"The State's arguments to deny bail to my client are chock-full of half-truths and convenient omissions from which they offer no real evidence against my client. Only baseless conclusions. Let us consider CPT 12-70.5, for just a moment. The statute expressly prohibits bail when, and I quote this directly from the statute 'the presumption of guilt is great.' And yet the State has failed to produce a shred of *prima fascia* evidence connecting my client to a crime or even shown that a crime was even committed."

For an instant, a few murmurs disrupted the provisional silence in the courtroom, but the judge simply hammered them away with her gavel.

"Now, as to the assertion that my client is a violent criminal and, therefore, a menace to society and not worthy of bail, I would like to know exactly what evidence the Prosecution has found that would back up their point," she continued, glancing at the Assistant DA.

"His personality? The Defense is prepared to stipulate that

Jonathan Prinze, on occasion, is a petulant, self-involved, ego-maniac—"

"To what end, Ms. Victor?" the judge asked, almost bored.

Gina shrugged her shoulders. "The point I'm trying to make here, your honor, is that even though Mr. Prinze is an asshole with an abrasive personality that does not make him a murderer. But that's exactly what the Prosecution would have you believe. They don't have any substantive evidence against my client so they're putting his ruthless, and sometimes boorish, reputation on trial here instead. Had they done any additional research, beyond what has been written about my client in the tabloids or the blogs, or spent any time investigating his background, they might have found out that Jack happens to be one of the most generous, most loyal persons that has ever owned a Fortune-500 company. With no history of criminal behavior, and not one incident in his past of violence, ever, he is the model of a perfect, taxpaying citizen. So, for Mr. Wilson's claim that Prinze is a dangerous felon and a threat to the public, at large, I find it to be a ludicrous, irresponsible assertion—"

Rising to his feet, the Assistant DA broke into the conversation, "I object."

"Overruled," the judge replied.

"As for the minor infraction the State claims demonstrated a disregard towards law enforcement or the authority of this court," Victor added, with a slight smile, "or that he is a flight risk, I respectfully ask the court to consider that Jonathan Prinze has a multi-million-dollar company that employs over five hundred workers in this city, and appeared in court this morning as instructed. Therefore, the Defense requests that Mister Prinze be released on his own recognizance, without bail."

Judge Luisa Hernandez-Lopez looked over the top of her glasses. "All right, thank you, counsel," she said, flatly, without emotion. She examined several of the pieces of paper in front of her, and then thought long and hard about her decision. "Jonathan Prinze, I am reinstating the bail at $1,000,000, and the court will retain your passport. You may not travel beyond the limits of San Francisco, Marin, and San Mateo counties. Is there any part of my order that is unclear to you, Mister Prinze?"

Prinze had risen to his feet, and was standing right next to Gina Victor at the Defense table. "No, your honor. Your order is crystal clear."

"Furthermore," the judge added, "you will be fitted with a GPS ankle bracelet, and if you wander one foot beyond those limits, no excuse in the world will keep me from throwing your ass back in jail. That's all. You're dismissed." Hernandez-Lopez signed off on a couple of papers the Bailiff had handed her, and then, without any fanfare, she stood up at the bench and quickly exited through the front door.

Elated by the judge's decision, Jonathan Prinze turned to a police officer who was leaning against the empty jury box, and raised his shackled wrists in the air.

The cop sauntered over, unlocked the handcuffs, and released the chain and shackles on his ankles that had bound Prinze as a county prisoner. Almost immediately, he walked around to his attorney, and gave her a polite hug. He then reached out to the black attorney and the two interns at the Defense table and shook their hands.

"Thank you," Prinze said, his eyes bright with mirth.

Victor studied his face for a long moment, then said, "Wipe that smile off your face, Jack. Half of the reporters in the State of California are in this courtroom, and they came here to chronicle the fate-filled story of an innocent man falsely accused of murder. Not a criminal mastermind who had just beaten the system."

"Do you really think I care?" he replied, glancing around as the light-bulbs and digital flashes caught his image.

"Perception is reality," she reminded him.

At that instant, he caught sight of Dawson and smiled, whispering a few words to his attorney. Gina Victor looked up. She followed the direction of his gaze, looking at Dawson and smiling at her former friend, her eyes full of amusement and contempt. Then she finally looked away. The two of them continued to talk clandestinely with each other, but Jonathan Prinze's stare never left the police inspector. He seemed to be fixated on her, as if memorizing every last detail.

Naturally, Dawson was aware he was staring at her. She shook hands with Luke Wilson, the Assistant District Attorney, and walked away from the table. She then wandered through the courtroom, biding her time, checking the place out. She exchanged pleasantries with several people she knew, making the rounds, always aware of his attention. Dawson was at once repelled and fascinated by the playboy. She couldn't believe that the court had taken such a lenient approach with him. He had already proven his contempt for the legal system by meeting his buddies in Lake Tahoe for the weekend without permission. And now, he seemed to be sticking his finger in the eye of the Prosecution that had argued to ground him without bail. He seemed to be playing a game with all of them where the rules simply didn't apply to him. Kate Dawson seemed to lose sight of him in the sea of reporters and interested bystanders and onlookers just as she reached the rear door to the courtroom, but that's exactly where he was waiting for her.

The silver-haired, man in his fifties, wearing the orange jumpsuit, stood between her and the door. He pretended to be surprised to see her, but like everything else about Jonathan Prinze, nothing was as it seemed. He looked long and hard at Kate, and looked away feigning disinterest. Then he looked at her again, more deeply. His steely, blue eyes unsettled her. They were wide but knowing, and as they swept over Dawson like beams of light, she felt naked, like he could see right through her.

"I think we may have gotten off on the wrong foot," Prinze said evenly, closing the gap between them.

He wouldn't or didn't want to acknowledge anyone in the room but Kate. Even though there were many others vying for his attention with their cameras and small, digital recorders, he stayed focused on her. "I'm really a nice guy."

"I guess that's a matter of opinion," she replied.

"You see, you've already made up your mind, and you don't know a thing about me," he said softly but loud enough to be heard by Kate. His eyes never left her face.

"What's it going to take for you to stop looking at me as some hardened killer and see me as a man wrongfully accused of murder?"

Dawson shook her head slowly, deliberately. "I'm really the wrong person to ask about that, Mister Prinze."

"Really, why is that? What happened to 'innocent until proven guilty'?"

"You can't be serious," she answered, a hint of incredulity. "After all, I'm part of the team that's working with the District Attorney's office to put the man who killed Alicia Summers on death row."

Jonathan Prinze leaned into her, crowding her space, his eyes boring deeply into hers. "And you think that man is me?"

"It's not important what I think," she replied, refusing to play. Kate stood toe-to-toe with the State's number one suspect. "I wasn't there. I didn't see what happened the night she was murdered. I can make an educated guess, but in fairness, it's all about the evidence. And right now, the overwhelming physical evidence points directly to you."

"Do you think it's possible you made a mistake?"

"Possible? Yes," she responded curtly. "Likely? No."

"Evidence can be wrong, sometimes misleading," he suggested, with an unctuous smile. "You're too good of a detective not to consider that."

"A compliment?"

Their eyes were locked now, as if they were trying to see into each other's skulls. Prinze was the acknowledged master of the mind fuck, but Kate had learned enough to acquit herself well. Tension crackled between them, like a short in an electrical box. Finally, he blinked first. "Inspector, you should really take the time to get to know me. You're going to like me once you realize I'm just a regular guy."

"I doubt it," she said, with a nod. "I already know a lot about you, and I don't much care for the man that I know."

"You mustn't let a little thing like murder get in the way of our happiness."

There was a moment, a long moment of silence.

Kate stared at him without any kind of emotion, a blank slate.

"Are you hitting on me, Mister Prinze?" she asked, without curiosity.

He was blasé, brushing off the query, as if he were brushing cookie crumbs away from his state-mandated, orange jumpsuit. "Maybe, or maybe I was just trying to imagine how empty your life must be, Inspector, without a real man in it. But what difference does that make?"

Prinze reached out, and stroked the side of her face. "I can see how conflicted you are about the whole thing. You're very attracted to me, but you're also honor-bound by a code of justice that won't let you feel the kind of primal urges that you're feeling when you get close to me. Duty can be a harsh mistress."

"Primal urges," she repeated, the two-word phrase stuck midway in her craw. "I suppose you know a lot about primal urges?"

"Yes, of course. Particularly in women."

"Is that the line you used on Alicia Summers?"

Prinze's smile had turned upside down. "No, I didn't use a line at all with her. Alicia was in love with me the first day we laid eyes on each other at my corporate headquarters downtown. She had been a naïve, young literature student at the University of San Francisco, with her head in the clouds. I suppose my singular, erotic tastes must have seemed a bit intimidating for her, at first, but she gradually took to them. She was so desperate to get close to me, and I'll admit that I wanted her, too—but only on my terms."

"I'm beginning to understand."

"What about you, Inspector? Care to explore your primal urges?"

"The only primal urge that interests me is murder," Kate said, flatly. "Specifically, why a man would murder his secretary, the mother of his unborn child, and then work so hard to hide the fact that a murder had taken place."

There was another pause, a long moment of awkward silence, as Prinze regarded her expressionlessly.

He had become acutely aware of the flurry of activity around him, and backed away from her ever so slightly.

The small gap was suddenly filled by members of the media shouting questions at him.

"You shouldn't play this game," Jonathan said, at last, over the din.

"Why not?" Dawson said, "I like this game."

53

Prinze shook his head. "It's not going to come out the way you want. You won't learn anything from me. I don't confess any of my secrets just because a beautiful woman happens to turn my head."

"I'm more than just a beautiful woman."

"I know," he said, acknowledging her statement.

"But you'll never learn anything I don't want you to know." Kate smiled thinly at him. "Yes, I will."

"No, you won't. You're simply not in my league, Inspector."

"But I've already learned so much already."

"Consider that a gift," he replied, a sour look on his face. The reporters had already overwhelmed him, and they were threatening to swallow him whole. "That's why they call it 'the present.'"

His defense attorney, Gina Victor shoved her way through the crowd of reporters, and then literally pushed her client through the back door. In moments, Victor was hard at work doing a fast repair job on her client's image.

She stood with Theodore Long in the corridor outside of the courtroom, apologizing for him and restating the reasons why she considered him to be an innocent man.

Prinze wasn't paying much attention. He smiled a faraway smile as he watched Dawson exit the courtroom.

He continued to watch her as she walked slowly down the corridor of the Hall of Justice.

Just as she reached them, Victor was saying, "My client deserves the same protection under the law as any person who has been accused of a crime. He should not be penalized for his wealth." She stood poised, cool, in complete command of herself, as she rattled off her talking points to the press. In turn, they were respectful, drinking down the Kool-Aid that she served them like mindless cult members. The well-educated woman had a way of commanding an audience that few, except perhaps Kate, had ever seen. She enjoyed seizing and holding the spotlight like a young, Hollywood starlet.

Dawson looked sharply at her old friend, and smiled, but Gina Victor was too ensconced in her impromptu news conference to acknowledge her in any way. She continued walking down the corridor, but slowed her pace. Kate was curious about what she'd say, and listened carefully as the rhetoric mounted. In fact, she was so focused that she completely missed someone calling her last name. When she heard it again, she stole a glimpse over her shoulder, and saw that Greg Morris had followed her out of the courtroom.

"Dawson!" he cried, trying to get her attention.

She ignored him, her gaze fixed on Victor. She looked at the defense attorney with something that resembled respect. In reality, Kate had always admired her friend, but in the last few years, she had also come to despise her as well. She still despised her. It was truly a first for her. Admiration and scorn, all bundled together in a neat package for a woman she once called her friend.

"Dawson, for Christ's sake, didn't you hear me calling you?" Morris asked breathlessly, as he scrambled to her side.

"No," Kate replied, turning her gaze to him. He was breathing heavily. "For a field agent, you ought to be in better shape."

"What would you know about it?"

"I dated a Justice agent for more than a year," she explained, as the memories of her ex-boyfriend washed over her temporarily. "He had the perfect body, but then again, he really worked at it every day."

Morris shrugged. "I suppose this 'superman' has a name?"

"John Prescott."

"The name sounds familiar," Morris replied, thinking about

him. "But then again, I've been on assignment in Southeast Asia for the last couple of years. I haven't exactly had access to the latest in Nautilus fitness equipment."

"But you can barely breathe," she reminded him.

"I can hear you wheezing just walking down the corridor."

"Cut me some slack, Dawson," he said, returning her stare. "I just gave up a five-packet-a-day smoking habit."

"Nasty habit," she said. "How's not smoking?"

"It's fucked," said Morris shortly.

They held each other's eye for a moment longer, then Kate looked away. She turned back to Gina Victor and her client. She listened for a few minutes, then concluded the press conference seemed to be winding down. Finally, Dawson said to the Justice agent, "What do you want, Morris?"

"I need your help," he replied.

She snorted. "You've got to be kidding me."

"No, I'm very serious."

Kate Dawson smiled thinly. "I've already been fucked over once by the Department of Justice. What makes you think I'd be stupid enough to crawl back into bed with them? Besides you ain't got nothing I want."

"You want the same thing that I do," Morris said, with a shit-eating grin.

"Really? And what is that?"

"You want to catch these bastards, and put 'em behind bars, so that they won't be able to hurt another innocent, like Mylee."

"I don't need your help for that," Dawson growled.

"But what if I told you I had a line on the one they call 'the auctioneer'?" he asked, with an opening move that was worthy of a grandmaster in chess. "Maybe even the five other girls they were auctioning that night?"

Dawson's eyes narrowed in suspicion. "Bullshit. If you really had a line on them, you wouldn't be bringing it to me."

"I would, if I needed the resources of your department."

"So, that's what it is," Kate concluded, as she continued down the corridor with Morris trailing a step or two behind her. "You want the SFPD to do all the dirty work, so that you can go back home, clean as a whistle, and take all the credit. That's not going to happen on my watch, if I have anything to say about it."

Morris shook his head. "You're wrong. I don't give a damn about the credit!"

"Well, that's a first."

"I've been tracking this cartel for over two years now, and they've always managed to stay one or two steps ahead of me. I'd like to be in a position where we're actually ahead of them for once, and I can grab the son-of-a-bitch ringleader."

Dawson shrugged. "Why don't you just go back to your buddies in D.C., and get them to write you a big, fat appropriations check?"

"Because by the time I do that," Morris reasoned, like a reasonable man, "my suspect would've already blown town, and I'll end up with butt-kiss."

She was silent for a moment, still wasn't buying it.

"Besides your people are already here, right now. It might take me days or wecks to mobilize a task force."

Dawson swallowed hard, barely restraining her resentment. It was a bitter pill for her to swallow, but the justice agent was right. If they had waited too long, their chief suspect might have slipped right through their fingers. They continued walking in silence, and stopped right outside the Homicide Bureau.

"I suppose you're right, Morris," she said, at last.

"We would be better off working together, but I'm still not certain if I trust you."

"Well, I don't trust you either," he replied.

"So, what do you say? Do you wanna to pool our resources?" Dawson asked, more of a rhetorical question, but he understood exactly what she meant.

Morris nodded. "It could have its compensations."

"Professionalism?" she suggested, with a raised eyebrow.

"Agreed," he responded, affirmatively. He thought about it for another moment, and then added, "Understanding?"

"Possibly," she replied, with a shrug.

"Cooperation?"

"Maybe."

"Trust?" asked Morris, going way out on the proverbial limb.

"Out of the question," Kate said, finally. "Trust is the one thing you're still going to have to earn from me, Morris."

"I need a cigarette," he said, tired.

"I thought you quit."

"So, I'll quit tomorrow."

Dawson reached into her slacks and fished out a key. She threw it to him. "You'll find some cigarettes in the top drawer of my desk. Third row, on the left," she said, heading off in the opposite direction. "I'll meet you in the parking garage, near the entrance."

"Where are you going?"

"I still have to square all of this with the Lieutenant," Kate replied, over her shoulder as she walked into her boss' corner office.

Twenty minutes later, Kate Dawson pulled her BMW 5.25i out of the Hall of Justice, heading east on Bryant Street, with Gregory Morris in the passenger seat.

She made the left at Third Street, and drove past the Moscone Center. They both could see dozens of city workers busy installing banners announcing the G-20 Summit or erecting barriers that would be used to control the flow of traffic, but not a single cop was on duty.

Dawson shook her head as she made the slight jog in the road, and then turned left at Geary. When she reached Grant Avenue, she turned right and headed north to Bush Street.

They had driven a few blocks from the Hall of Justice before Morris finally broke the silence. He leaned forward in the passenger seat of her BMW, and looked over at her while she was driving. "My biggest fear is the Tongs," he said, with a degree of reverence in his voice.

"We don't want to run afoul of them, but at the same time, we've got to be prepared for the fact that "the auctioneer" may be hiding out among them. My last confirmed sighting was at an opium den a few hours ago."

"Tongs? That's ancient history, Morris," Kate dismissed his fear, with a smirk. "These days, the only tongs you're going to find in Chinatown are the cooking utensils that are used in a Chinese restaurant."

"When I was in Southeast Asia, the Cartels hired certain Tong groups as enforcers and armed them with AK-47s," the Justice agent reported. "They were highly effective in dispensing with local militia groups and hired mercenaries."

Dawson directed her car down along Grant Avenue, taking the shortest route that she knew to Chinatown. "Okay, I'll admit that the City had more than its share of run-ins with the Tongs. At one time, they ran protections rackets, gambling, opium distribution, and prostitution, and were more deadly than any of their Mafia counterparts in Chicago or New York. But that was the 1940s and 50s," she explained. "Today, the Tongs are, for the most part, members of Chinese benevolent associations. They provide essential services for Chinatown communities, such as immigrant counseling, Chinese schools, and English classes for adults. They care for their members and their respective communities, and are really not that unlike the Freemasons or the Knights of Columbus."

"The Hip Sing Tong is a member of organized crime, and has been involved in drug-trafficking in Chicago, Seattle, and San Francisco. In fact, a recent drug raid in Portland, Oregon, turned up the largest stockpile of heroin in the world. You may have been lulled into thinking that the Tongs are little more than a charitable organization. But the fact of the matter is that they have made in-roads into every major city in the U.S."

"Now who's the one sounding paranoid?" she asked, with a thin smile.

Dawson rolled to a stop at the curb and put the car in park. She leaned out the car window, and looked backwards down the street.

The Gateway Arch, or Dragon Gate, on Grant A venue at Bush Street, the only authentic Chinese gate in North America, marked the entrance to Chinatown.

Unlike similar structures, which had been built on wooden pillars, this iconic symbol conformed to Chinese architectural standards that required stone masonry from base to top and green-tiled, pagoda-shaped roofs in addition to wood as the basic building materials. A pair of Chinese guardian lions, traditionally believed to provide protection, stood guard on each side. Called "Shi" in Chinese or "Foo Dogs" in the West, they were a common sight in front of Chinese Imperial palaces, Imperial tombs, government offices, and temples. They seemed to warn casual visitors that beyond the Dragon Gate lay a completely separate world—an enclave that still retained its own customs, languages, places of worship, social clubs, and identity. A land that time forgot.

Chinatown was the largest base of Chinese culture and style, outside of native China itself, in the world.

While casual visitors often sought to become immersed in the ancient and cultural heritage of the Asia world, with its herbal shops, temples, Chinese restaurants, pagoda roofs and dragon parades, a far more sinister world had developed in the back alleys, opium dens, brothels and sewers that ran beneath the street. The first Tong in America originated in San Francisco in 1874, when the word "tong" initially meant "parlor." Merchants who were concerned about their businesses met in parlors to discuss ways to defend themselves against the brutal treatment they received from the white inhabitants of the city. Their merchant's protective association developed into an organization known as a "tong," with men who were hired to protect the less fortunate. Eventually, the unseen enforcers of the Tong not only became powerful enough to sell "protection" to the newer merchants but also established illegal gambling halls. Success in extortion and gambling led to other illegal activities, like opium distribution and prostitution. Like the Mafia, the tongs came to control everything within the eight blocks that made up Chinatown.

Recent immigrants and the elderly chose to live within the confines of "little China" not simply because of the availability of affordable housing and their familiarity with the culture, but also because they knew they would be safe and protected. The casual visitor to Chinatown never saw what existed below the surface. For them, organized crime didn't exist, and the Tongs were part of a fairy tale parents told their children. Instead they saw a quaint, little world of crowded streets with old-fashioned, little Chinese people in their traditional dress, busy restaurants, market stalls, tacky replica décor, mass-produced souvenirs, and bright, candy-colored lanterns that littered every possible space. But to the residents, they still lived in a world that had been spared the ravages of time and now only existed within those eight blocks.

She took the car out of park and made a wide U-turn, wheeling the sedan to a halt in front of a building on the opposite side of the street. Dawson parked on Grant A venue, facing south, and the two of them stepped out of the car. They walked nearly halfway around the BWM 5.25i, and stood on the sidewalk, looking back at Bush Street.

"We'll be far less conspicuous if we park here," Dawson said, closely checking out her surroundings, "and then walk in through the gate, like a couple of tourists."

"I'll follow your lead," he replied, anxious to get the show on the road.

"Now, if only the Big Bus was here."

Morris raised an eyebrow. "The Big Bus?"

Kate looked down the street, and smiled. She then reached over, and took his hand in hers. "The Big Bus," she whispered to him, as a large, red, double-decker, open-top bus pulled into the intersection.

A Chinese woman, carrying a small baton, led a group of English tourists from their tour bus. Both Dawson and Morris saw them climbing down the stairs, and seized the opportunity to enter the gate somewhat anonymously. They quickly blended in with the group, keeping pace with their leader. The Chinese tour guide walked right through the Dragon Gate, like she had belonged there, and stopped in the center of the plaza, where her group formed a semi-circle around her. A few of them took pictures, while the majority of them stood around patiently, waiting for her to resume her guided tour, speaking softly among themselves. Dawson and Morris waited, and listened.

The Chinese tour guide smiled at them, a pleasant but formal smile. "In 1852, a serious crop failure in Southern China affected more than half of the farms in the country, and caused a nationwide depression that impacted nearly everyone, regardless of social status. The rumor of 'gam saan' or 'mountain of gold' in California prompted many Chinese men to abandon their failing farms in order to make the perilous journey to the Americas. They mostly came from Peking and Canton, and were illiterate, but the promises of riches beyond their imagination fortified their resolve. Their gold-rush fever was as intense as any in America, and they left their wives and families behind to pursue a dream of wealth," she stated, entertaining the tourists with her tale of the first Chinese settlers to the United States. "They worked long hours and days for many years, helping in the gold mines and building the railroads. Chinese miners tended to live in groups and work claims the Americans had abandoned. They were very frugal and saved every penny they earned. Many were homesick for the world they had left behind, but rather than returning home to China, they brought their families to America. They built this beautiful Chinatown, and lived happy and productive lives."

Morris leaned over to Dawson. "Less than one percent of those who came to California, as a part of the Gold Rush, ever became rich," he reported in a low, quiet voice. "The merchants who sold prospecting tools and other goods to the miners were the ones who truly profited from the discovery of gold at Sutter's Mill."

"That's pretty sobering news," she replied.

"Very few Chinese women came to the States before 1880, but many of those who did served as prostitutes in the whore houses in San Francisco. Upon arrival, they were examined and sold for between $300 and $3,000 to brothel owners or wealthy

Chinese seeking a mistress. You might just say that was the very beginning of the Asian sex trade."

With a genuine look of surprise, Kate said, "I don't remember reading about that in any of my history books."

"Those that write the history books rarely tell the truth. They filter the facts through their own prism of beliefs, and what remains is but a shadow of the truth."

"You sound more like an academic, Morris, than a Justice Department agent."

"Let's just say, I've spent a lot of time researching this topic," he confessed, without revealing anything.

At that moment, the Chinese tour guide said, "Okay, you will now have forty minutes to explore the city. We will leave from this spot at fifty-minutes past the hour."

"Bloody good," one English tourist said, directing his comment to Kate.

"I wonder if there's a decent pub nearby?" another one inquired, his words directed at the agent.

"Steady, Bunky, the pub can wait," the tourist's wife remarked. "I want one of those cute little elephants for my collection."

"Of course, dear."

"Jolly good sport, dear," Morris said, affecting an English accent as part of his cover, but she never heard his comment.

As the English tourists had begun to disperse, Dawson stepped away from Morris, and started clicking off several photographs of the plaza with her cell phone.

First, she focused on an ornately-designed wooden sign, lit from the bottom, which featured a red dragon. The red dragon, which was carved in deep relief, wrapped around from the top of the sign, the right side, and to its bottom, where it was partially immersed in a black pool of water.

Written in the usual Chinese restaurant-style script, the sign read: "The Dragon of the Black Pool/Cantonese Cuisine." Then, Kate snapped a couple of shots of a Buddhist temple with its ornate pagoda-shaped roof.

Next, she turned to the Gateway Arch, and snapped several photos of each of the "Foo Dogs." She seemed to think they were emblematic of Chinatown, and they deserved to have an honored place in her collection of photos. Finally, as she focused her camera for the next photo, she zoomed the telephoto lens on that of a garbage truck as it poured trash from a dumpster into its hull. She hesitated a moment, and missed her photo of the garbage truck. But when she refocused the tiny lens on her camera, Dawson caught site of Jawara, face dirty, and wearing a tarnished, grey jumpsuit which was the standard uniform of a city sanitation worker. She watched him as he jumped on-and-off the truck, collecting trash in garbage cans up-and-down the street. Near a dark alley, he jumped off, but did not get back on.

"C'mon, dear," she summoned him.

With Morris in tow, she continued working her way down the street, playing the role of tourist. She paused in a couple of the open shops, and glanced though the Asian trinkets that had all been manufactured in Taiwan. At one shop, she haggled with the shopkeeper over price, and in another, she discussed how perfect one of the items was to bring home as a souvenir for their "son." They browsed through each of the shops, and at the end of the street, pretended to read the menu outside a Chinese restaurant. When they were both satisfied they weren't being watched, one-at-a-time, they slipped down the dark alley and out of view.

"Jawara?" Dawson whispered, just loud enough to be heard.

"I'm here, Kate," replied the African-American detective, appearing out of the darkness, like a specter back from the dead. He was black from head to toe with filth.

Kate threw her arms around his shoulders, and gave him a brief but friendly hug. He was one of three men that she numbered among her closest friends. Then she took a step or two back, and introduced him formally to her new partner. She said, "Morris, this is Mikhail Jawara, Detective, San Francisco Police Department."

"Yes, I remember seeing you last night," the justice agent said, with the look of familiarity on his face.

He shook hands with Jawara, and then absentmindedly wiped the dirt from Jawara's handshake on his pants.

"What's with the jumpsuit?"

"I'm undercover," Jawara replied, with a laugh.

He pulled a handkerchief out of his pocket, and offered it to Morris, who declined. "Clever disguise, don't you think? Black man in a sanitation outfit. Who would have ever guessed that I was a cop?"

Gregory Morris shrugged. "I hate to say it, but it suits you."

"Thanks a lot. That makes it even worse," he added, wiping away some of the dirt from his face and hands with the clean handkerchief. "I suppose if the strike lasts much longer I won't have to look far for a new job."

"So, Roberts took my advice?" Kate asked, smiling.

"Hook, line and sinker," Jawara said, putting the handkerchief away in his pocket. "After we wrapped up the crime scene last night, the Lieutenant sent Clark and me here to keep an eye out for the one they call "the auctioneer." He figured this would be the one place where our number one suspect would be able to hide out in plain site without being seen. An Asian hiding out in Chinatown."

"Good thinking," Morris commented, still trying to wipe his hand clean. "So, you didn't really need my help."

"It was my idea," she interjected, with a shake of her head, "but I'm sure Roberts made it sound like it was the latest in a long line of brilliant deductions of his own making. Seemed like a pretty good bet."

"Can't say that I like the timing all that much," Jawara added. "Clark and I were just going off shift when we answered the call at the InterContinental Hotel."

Dawson nodded, then looked around. "By the way, where is Clark?"

"He's doing a high-wire act over on the next block, trying to rundown a cable outage that Pacific Bell arranged for us. You'd never recognize him with the hard hat. I think he really likes it. Be prepared to start calling him 'Spiderman.'"

"What have you learned?" Kate pressed him.

"Every business in Chinatown has been operating today, except a Chinese laundry two blocks over," he reported. "They've been opening their doors for the last thirty years at 6 am to take in laundry from the locals and those commuters who drop off on their way to work. This morning, they didn't open their doors at all, and they've been closed for several hours. Rumor has it, there's an opium den in the basement."

"That fits," Morris said, trying to contain his surprise. "The one they call "the auctioneer" has an opium habit, and I doubt if he'd be able to go for more than a few days without a fix. That's got to be the place."

Dawson decided it was time to get moving. "It looks like we gonna pay a visit to the local laundry."

"I'll keep a look-out for you," Jawara said, "and send in the cavalry, if things start to look dicey."

"Okay," she replied, "but don't go blundering in there, unless we really need your help."

"Understood. Good hunting."

With their guns drawn, Kate Dawson and Morris inched their way down the dark alley that was sandwiched between the slop shop and the Chinese laundry. They approached a steep stairway and started down, heading into a black abyss that resembled the mouth of a cave.

They passed down steps, which had been worn hollow in the center by a ceaseless tread of drunken feet, and stopped short of the bottom. Kate heard the distinctive sound of a door creaking open, and waited with Morris in the shadows. Just ahead, they saw an Asian man, with a yellow, pasty face, drooping eyelids, and pin-point pupils, stumble out of an open door. He meandered from right to left, trying to keep his balance, and walked right by them without a word. They waited until he climbed the steps to the street level, and then continued to the door.

By the light of Dawson's cell phone, she found the latch, and pushed the creaking door fully open. They made their way into a long, low room which was thick and heavy with brown opium smoke. Bunk beds lined the room with terraced upper and lower wooden berths, much like an army barracks.

Through the gloom, she and Morris could glimpse the bodies of men lying in strange and fantastic poses, bowed shoulders, bent knees, heads thrown back, and chins pointing upward, with here and there a black, lackluster eye turned upon the newcomers. Out of the dark shadows, they saw glimmering, little red circles of light—now bright, now faint—as the burning poison waxed or waned in the bowls of metal pipes. Most of the patrons lay silent, but some sat cross-legged muttering to themselves, while others talked together in a strange, low, monotonous voice, their conversation coming in gushes, and then suddenly trailing off into silence, each mumbling aloud and paying little heed to the words of the man next to him. Dawson was immediately reminded of the Arabic restaurants and bars in San Francisco that catered to a certain clientele that smoked Hookah pipes as part of their culture and traditions, but she had to remind herself that was tobacco, not opium.

At the farthest end of the room, she spotted a tall, thin older man, sitting on a three-legged wooden stool.

His jaw was resting upon his two fists and his elbows upon his knees, staring off into the oblivion created in a small brazier of burning charcoal. He didn't seem to notice them or care that they were there.

A sallow Chinese attendant scurried through the open door, grabbed a pipe and a supply of the drug, and beckoned Dawson and Morris to an empty berth.

"Please . . ."

"Thank you, we're not here to stay," Kate said, doing her best with sign language to make her meaning clear.

"We're actually here, looking for a friend," Morris added, trying to describe the auctioneer.

The Chinese attendant listened to the two of them, as if he spoke English, then shrugged his shoulders and shook his head, indicating he did not understand them at all. Again, he held out the pipe and opium, and beckoned them to a small berth. "Please . . ." he repeated, the only word of English he knew.

They turned away from him, and walked down the narrow passage between the double rows of sleepers. The vile, stupe-fying fumes of the drug filled the air with its sickly sweet odor of poppies, distilled with bitter liquor.

The potent smell caused both Dawson and Morris to wretch. Fearing that one or the other or both of them might succumb to secondary, opium high, they took turns holding their breath or holding their hands over their nose, as they searched the room for their suspect. They looked carefully at each of the sleepers, but the distinguished-looking auctioneer was not among the poor wretches they passed.

As Dawson passed the tall, thin man by the brazier, she felt a pair of eyes on her back, and heard a low whisper, "I know where you can find your friend."

The words fell quite distinctly upon her ear, and as she turned, the old man came into view. He didn't say anything, but made a slight motion for Dawson to approach him. She moved towards him very slowly, and as she glanced down at him, the old man's dull eyes stared back at her, empty and lifeless. He looked like he was one hundred years old. His back was bent with age, and his face was very thin and wrinkled, with doddering, loose lips. The nails on his boney fingers had turned black, and his skin had not only yellowed but turned brittle, like parchment paper. She kept waiting for the skin to break off, and reveal his skeleton beneath.

"Your friend is behind that door," he said, like sandpaper over wood, pointing at a door at the back of the room.

Cautiously, Dawson surveyed the closed door, and said, "Thank you." Then, with Morris at her side, she edged toward the closed door, weapon out, finger on the trigger, ready to fire. Dawson turned the handle about half way with her left hand, then she and Morris burst through the door and into the room beyond. She wasn't expecting to see anyone, much less the auctioneer standing there waiting for them, but had anticipated some kind of trap.

So, when the door flew open, she only caught a glimpse of her suspect, dressed elegantly in Western clothes. He was conferring with several others wearing more traditional Chinese garb. In that instant, she struggled to get the words out, "You're under arrest," but they became frozen in time and place, much like her finger on the trigger of her gun. Both she and Morris were suddenly aware they had made a mistake, but that thought glimmered for only an instant just before they were both struck unconscious by some sophisticated jujitsu blow by their captors.

Kate Dawson sat slumped in a chair, her hands tied behind her back, as she gradually stirred to consciousness in a brightly-lit, business office, with all of the equipment, furniture and amenities of a Fortune-500 company. The ancient land of Chinatown had been replaced by a more modern, mechanized one. As she looked around, groggy, with blurred vision, she saw that Morris was slumped over, tied to the chair next to hers.

He was still unconscious, but he was still breathing, showing signs of life. In front of her, Lo Pan, the Chinese Godfather himself who had united all of the Tongs under his ruthless leadership, sat silently, staring at her with his dark, piercing eyes. He was dressed in a black, three-piece business suit, with a black shirt and tie, like a Chinese version of Donald Trump. The white-haired Lo Pan was flanked by two of his men. On the one side was a stocky, long-haired Chinese man with a well-grown Fu-Manchu mustache. He was dressed all in black as well, with a red sash tied around his waist in place of a belt. In his hands, he carried two large, butcher knives that reflected the expression of pure hatred on his face. On the other side was a younger, Chinese man, tall and well-groomed in a neat dark suit, with a yellow sash slung over one shoulder.

In his hands, he carried a MAC-10 machine pistol, and his face also held an expression of unmitigated hatred.

"What the hell's going on?" Dawson demanded, pulling at her bonds. "I'm a Homicide inspector with the San Francisco Police Department. I demand to be released from these bonds immediately."

"You will be released in time," Lo Pan replied, soft spoken, totally indifferent to her demands on him.

"No, that's not good enough. You'll release me and my partner right now," Dawson commanded, raising her voice several octaves. She pulled again at her bonds, only with a great deal more force than before. "I don't know who the hell you think you're dealing with here, but I've got an extremely low tolerance to bullshit. I represent the people of San Francisco as a duly sworn officer of the law."

"You have used the word 'hell' twice now," the white-haired, old man observed. "We Chinese have many Hells. In fact, there are as many as eighteen in the common tongue. 'Diyu' is the realm of the dead where souls are taken to atone for their earthly sins, and is a maze of underground levels and chambers. It is very loosely based upon the Buddhist concept of Naraka.

Punishment also varies according to belief, but most legends speak of highly imaginative chambers where wrong-doers are sawn in half, beheaded, thrown into pits of filth or forced to climb trees adorned with sharp blades."

"Is that so?" she said, "Well, the only hell that interests me is the one that finds you and my suspect burning for all eternity."

Lo Pan shook his head. "We Chinese have never embraced your Judeo-Christian concept of hell. Instead we believe in the healing power of atonement. Most legends agree that once a soul has atoned for its deeds and repented, he or she is given the Drink of Forgetfulness by Meng Po and sent back into the world to be reborn, possibly as an animal or a poor or sick person, for further enlightenment."

"I guess if that helps you sleep at night," Dawson added. She tugged again at the rope that bound her to the chair, but it was pretty solid.

"What helps you sleep at night, detective?"

She looked at him squarely in the eyes. "Knowing that I've been successful in putting away scumbags like you."

"You persist in trying to provoke me, detective," Lo Pan observed, with a smile that he had to manufacture.

"I have made no threats against you or your partner. I could have had you killed in the basement of the laundry."

"And why didn't you?" she said, cutting him off.

"I thought you less stupid," he replied, annoyed.

"Unfortunately, I misjudged you. You are just a stupid policeman."

"Woman," Kate corrected him. "Police woman."

"You will find no criminal element here. In Chinatown," he replied softly, ignoring her obvious attempt to anger him. "This is a community built upon the labors of hardworking, law-abiding individuals and families. We are a simple, peaceful people who cherish simplicity and peace above all things."

Dawson snorted, but her eyes never left him.

"Hardworking, law-abiding citizens don't run around tying up police officers."

"You are the one who brought violence and destruction."

"We were tracking a suspect," she tried to make her actions clear. "We know that he has been hiding out somewhere within the city."

"We do not harbor wanted criminals here," Lo Pan said, flatly.

"The one they call "the auctioneer" is here."

Lo Pan rose slowly, almost majestically, from his chair. He folded his hands behind his back in a contemplative state, and paced back and forth between the two men who served as his personal bodyguards. Finally, after a moment or two, he stopped. "Do you know the expression, 'China is here'?" he asked the detective.

"No," she replied.

"It means that China, especially our ideals, our beliefs, our cultural heritage, is all around us here," he explained, in simplest terms. "When we built Chinatown in the 1850s, we Chinese not only brought our families here but China as well. Today, over one hundred thousand residents live within the twenty square blocks that form this city. The fact that Chinatown is the most densely populated urban area west of Manhattan in all of the United States speaks to our peoples' desire to live together in peace and harmony. Unlike so many, lesser communities, we Chinese have struggled together to survive the Gold Rush, racial discrimination and unrest, the Bubonic plague, the 1906 earthquake, and the nationwide depression of the 1930s to build a community that is the most vibrant in all the world."

"And the Tongs?" Kate asked, eyeing his two bodyguards.

Lo Pan nodded. "They serve the community in ways that you will never understand, but do so with the blessing of all those who live here."

Dawson decided to try a different approach. "The man I seek is not a member of your community. He is an interloper. He is someone who has come in from the outside, but I fear he is the one who brings violence and destruction."

"What is your purpose for hunting this man?"

"He is wanted for questioning in the death of a young Thai girl?" Kate responded, keeping her answer simple but accurate.

"Where did this death take place?" the Chinese man asked.

"At the Hotel InterContinental. In a fourth floor ballroom."

"What has this death to do with us?" he asked his third question in a row. "The Hotel InterContinental is not a part of Chinatown."

"We have it under reliable sources that he fled here for asylum."

Lo Pan had heard enough. Once he returned to his desk, and sat back down in the center chair, he signaled to his guards to untie them, and said, "You'll be taken to the Dragon Gate, and released outside of the city. I'd advise you not to return."

"I'll be back," she replied, very determined.

"Only this time, I'll be armed with a search warrant that empowers me to search through every nook and cranny of your perfect, little world here until I find my suspect."

"A search warrant would be worthless and complicated," Lo Pan replied, with total confidence.

"You'll find nothing we don't want you to find."

"In addition to my suspect, I'm also looking for five young women that he may have been traveling with," Dawson added, still probing for his weak spot. "We believe these girls may have been abducted from their families in Southeast Asia, and sold into slavery without their consent as part of the Asian sex trade."

Lo Pan regarded the detective with his dark, piercing eyes. He said finally, "We do not condone the sex trade. It has brought us nothing but misery and disease, but we also have no interest in what happens outside of the confines of Chinatown. We must remain unconcerned with the affairs of others beyond our borders."

Dawson didn't have to hear any more. There was a red-hot anger building in her brain, as Lo Pan's two bodyguards roughly untied her bonds and those of Agent Morris. From the casual, almost insensitive way they had treated Mylee's brutal murder to the wholesale sex trade, one thing was becoming increasingly clear to her, life was cheap in Chinatown. And she suspected that few understood that notion better than those individuals who had built a wall around themselves for their family's protection. It might just as well have been the Great Wall of China, for all that it mattered. The one hundred thousand Chinese people who resided in that section of town were living over a powder-keg, and she knew it really wouldn't take much to ignite the fuse and blow them all to kingdom come.

As she and her partner were pushed and shoved and fast-walked out of Chinatown by the two Tong bodyguards, fury had been burning deep within her, white hot like a solar flare. But Kate Dawson betrayed nothing, her face as set and hard as the ancient stone faces carved on the side of Mount Rushmore. Morris was conscious, but just barely aware of his surroundings. He was little more than a rag-doll in the arms of his captor. He felt his body in motion and his legs moving but only with the help of his Tong puppeteer.

"Christ!" he cried, trying to shake it off. "I feel like I was hit by a Mack truck. What did they do to us?"

"I don't know," she whispered back. "Some form of kung-fu that renders the victim unconscious. Leave it to the Tong to come up with a head-cracker that—"

"You, no talk!" the one bodyguard shouted.

Their captors pulled them up short as a funeral procession entered the plaza, where she had stood just an hour or two earlier, taking photographs with her cell phone, and crossed to the other side. Eight men, dressed all in black with a yellow sash, walked along, carrying a casket on their shoulders. Behind the pallbearers, a single Chinese man marched close at hand, holding a photograph of the deceased, followed by about ten others, one of them being a ceremonial drummer. A single beat on his drum kept pace with the procession as the participants continued their slow march through the plaza.

The funeral procession took less than five minutes, but its odd spectacle had reminded Kate just how strange Chinatown was to the rest of the City of San Francisco.

Her guard shoved her through the square with little concern for her well-being. Dawson then went through the Dragon Gate without a backward glance as the tourists from another Big Bus entered the ancient city, with their tour guide.

Released by the two thugs at the intersection of Grant Avenue and Bush Street, she stood there for an instant in silence, but only for an instant. Anger had finally bubbled up to the surface, and exploded in a high-pitched scream.

"Christ, Dawson!" Morris shouted, shaky, still sobering up. "What the hell was that?"

"A war cry," she replied, after a moment of thought.

His ears were still ringing. "That just scared the shit out of me!"

"Good. I'm hoping they heard it, too," Kate said, with a satis-fied nod, as she looked one last time around the intersection. "Let's get the fuck out of here."

CHAPTER THREE

An hour later, Wang Chi, the one they called "the auctioneer," was seated comfortably in Lieutenant Roberts' office at the Hall of Justice, drinking Chinese tea, when Dawson finally strolled into the Homicide Bureau. As she surveyed the room with a cool eye, Kate was surprised to see him sitting there, rather than in lockup, but tried not to let the surprise show on her face. Her suspect was flanked by the Mayor's high counsel, a cute red-head in her thirties named Ellen Bloomfield, on the one side, and her boss James Roberts, on the other, and it was right about that moment Dawson realized that Wang Chi must have cut a deal with them for his cooperation.

Dressed in an expensive, hand-tailored Armani suit, black t-shirt, and Italian soft-leather shoes, Chi looked more European than Asian. She didn't think he was a particularly tall man, but his larger-than-life presence seemed to fill the entire room. Dawson completed her visual sweep, and then sat down opposite her boss.

"Had I known our chief suspect was going to waltz right into police headquarters and surrender himself," Kate Dawson said, with an edge to her voice, "I wouldn't have spent the morning hunting him down in Chinatown."

Lieutenant Roberts looked sharply at his detective, but didn't say anything. Bloomfield caught the glance, and looked suspiciously from his face to hers. "Did I miss something?" she asked, almost ready to pull up stakes.

"No, not at all," he replied. James Roberts appeared as if he was about ready to kiss Bloomfield's ass as part of an elaborate apology, then thought better of it and contented himself with short explanation instead.

"Inspector Dawson has been busy this morning, working on a joint task force with agents from the Department of Justice and other government agencies. She doesn't know that Mister Chi had agreed to come in and talk with us on his own, and is no longer considered a suspect in the unfortunate demise of that thirteen-year-old girl, Mylee."

Bloomfield nodded her head. "Lieutenant, I just want to make this one point is very clear for the record.

My client is not waiving his right to diplomatic immunity by coming forward and agreeing to speak with you and your staff today. Under the Vienna Convention on Diplomatic Relations of 1961, all diplomats possess a form of legal immunity that ensures they are given safe passage, and are not susceptible to lawsuit or prosecution under the host country's laws. As a member of the Chinese delegation in standing, Mister Wang Chi holds a diplomatic passport, and has been granted certain privileges and immunities to ensure that he may effectively carry out his duties without penalty or prosecution."

"I know what diplomatic immunity is," Roberts growled.

Bloomfield ignored him, her gaze fixed on the female detective. She looked at Kate with disapproving eyes. She finally said, "And you, Inspector? Do you understand international law and the conventions that prevent diplomats from being legally sued or prosecuted under the host country's laws?"

"Yes, I do," Dawson replied. She thought about it for a moment, and then added, "I also know that diplomats can still be expelled from the United States if they are suspected of any kind of criminal behavior."

"Well!" Bloomfield exclaimed, with an element of surprise and sarcasm. "The things you learn in night school!"

Lieutenant Roberts took out a handkerchief, and mopped his brow. The windows were sealed shut, and it was starting to get warm in his office with all the bodies.

"Just get on with it, Bloomberg, before I lose my patience."

"It's Bloomfield," she replied, annoyed.

Kate reached for her leather attaché. She pulled out a small, manila folder, and opened it on Roberts' desk. She glanced down at the papers, reading through some of the eyewitness accounts of Mylee's death, and said finally, "Would you state your name for the record, please?"

"Wang Chi," the Chinese man replied.

"What is your occupation, Mister Chi?"

"I work as a—"

Bloomfield cut him off in mid-sentence. "My client is . . . sort of . . . an entertainer. He performs the role of emcee or master of ceremonies at large, public and social events. To say anything further would violate the trust my client has forged with many large companies, both here and abroad, that he represents," she said in a clipped, no nonsense tone of voice. "Let us just move on, shall we, Inspector?"

"Ms. Bloomberg, I have more than fifty signed affidavits from witnesses who attended last night's event," Dawson said, extracting the affidavits from the small, manila folder on the desk and holding them in her hand, "that identify Mister Chi as an 'auctioneer,' not an 'emcee.' Are you saying all of these people are wrong?"

"Bloomfield."

Dawson raised her eyebrows into question marks.

"I beg your pardon."

"My last name is Bloomfield, not Bloomberg," she corrected the police detective, and then took the signed affidavits out of Kate's hands. Ellen Bloomfield rifled through several of them, and finally handed the whole group of papers back. "And yes, I do believe your witnesses have misidentified the role that my client was playing at last night's event. Mister Chi was the master of ceremonies, not an auctioneer. He clearly wasn't authorized or licensed by law to sell any goods or services at public auction, but now I'm beginning to think that some of your witnesses may have mistaken my client's parody of slave auctions as the real deal. The whole gist of last night's event was to have fun, while drinking watered-down champagne and looking at pretty girls. Like a *Saturday Night Live* skit."

"That was no comedy sketch!" Dawson objected, seizing the affidavits from her hands and slamming them down on the table. "Several of the men we booked last night had thousands of dollars in cash stuffed in their pockets!"

"Impossible! What morons!"

"So, for the record, none of these girls were for sale?"

"No, absolutely not!"

Dawson glanced over her notes. "According to eyewitness accounts, an Arab dressed in his traditional garb paid $50,000 for one of the girls."

"It was all part of the show," she replied, after a glance at Wang Chi.

"Do you suppose we could talk to him?"

Chi shrugged. "I do not know his name."

"You don't know much about anything, do you?"

"My client was the master of ceremonies for this event,"

Bloomfield stated, with a deliberate "huff" in her voice, "not the casting director."

She then pulled another sheet out of the folder. It was a business flyer offering to hook up some sad sack with a beauty queen. Price: $35,000. Location: InterContinental Hotel. "And what do you make of this?"

"Disgusting!" Bloomfield commented. "The lengths to which some people will go to impugn my client's character."

"Then you're saying that it's not true?" Dawson asked, putting her on record.

"Absolutely, not!" the red-headed attorney replied, angry. "Mister Chi is a first class entertainer and emcee. To suggest anything else is utterly ridiculous! Now, shall we move on, or must I terminate this interview?"

"Did you know the young woman who died? Mylee?" Dawson asked Wang Chi.

"As I told Lieutenant Roberts, I had just met Mylee earlier that day," Chi replied, acknowledging Roberts' presence in the room with a nod. "She was one of the new girls. I had not worked with her before, but she seemed so very eager during dress rehearsal to learn the routine that I gave her my personal attention."

"Personal attention? What kind of personal attention?"

"Oh, you know, Inspector," the Chinese national replied, without saying anything. Then, when he realized that Kate was looking for something specific, he started rattling things off that he might have done, with a physical exaggeration of each. "I showed her how to walk down the runway, like a model. I showed her how to hit her mark and strike a pose. I showed her how to act sexy, and how to play the audience for sympathy."

"Did you have sex with her?" Kate asked, simply.

"What?" Wang Chi responded, totally caught off guard.

"I asked if you had sex with her."

Bloomfield objected, "What kind of question is that, Inspector? My client is a respected, upstanding member of the showbiz community, and has been a top entertainment personality for more than a decade in his own country. To insinuate that he had sex with one of his showgirls is simply outrageous!"

"I wasn't insinuating anything, Miss Bloomberg," said Dawson.

"Bloomfield."

"I am merely pursuing a line of questioning here, and I meant no disrespect of any kind to Mister Chi," she replied, all business. "But then, let's be totally honest here. You and I both know that we can't go a week these days without hearing about some celebrity or political figure who is involved in a sex scandal. Bill Clinton. Kim Kardashian. Prince Andrew. Bill Cosby. Miley Cyrus. Bob Barker. Tonya Harding. Hulk Hogan. Even JFK. The list goes on and on. I'd like to rule that out as a motive."

Ellen Bloomfield leaned over to her client and whispered something in his ear. The Chinese national nodded, with a grin.

"Did you have sex with Mylee?" Kate repeated her question.

"No," Chi answered, as the grin on his face grew into a smile. "I have no interest in women . . . sexually. I am a homosexual. I prefer men, especially young, teenaged boys when they are available."

Dawson swallowed hard. That was the one answer she hadn't expected to hear, unless he was lying to her.

All at once, she was angry, pissed off for breaking the number one rule of all interrogators: Never ask a question that you don't already have the answer to. She felt like such an amateur in front of the Mayor's high counsel.

Quickly, she searched through her notes on the case, and scrambled to put together her next question.

"What about boyfriends? Rivals?" Kate stammered, trying to get it out.

Wang Chi smiled. "I've had sex with a lot of boyfriends and rivals. Who exactly did you have in mind?"

"Don't answer that," Bloomfield instructed Chi.

She then looked at Dawson, while she addressed her comments to Roberts. "Lieutenant, my client agreed to come down here today to assist with your investigation. He did not come here to have his integrity questioned or his reputation besmirched by one of your detectives."

"Dawson, what kind of question was that?" Roberts asked, annoyed.

"Sir, I was asking the question about Mylee, not Mister Chi," she replied, as beads of sweat formed on her forehead. "I wanted to know about her boyfriends or rivals."

"Okay, then carry on," the Lieutenant said sourly.

Kate Dawson took a deep breath, as if that along could help bring her back into focus, and turned to Bloomfield and her client. "Mister Chi, do you know if anyone who might have had it in for Mylee?"

"No, Inspector," he replied, "and as I told you before, I barely knew her. She was a new girl that I had met earlier in the day."

"Was there any rivalry between the girls? Any enmity? Jealousy?"

"No, none that I could see."

Kate shrugged her shoulders. "I don't suppose I could talk with one of them?"

"No, but then, they weren't my responsibility either."

"So, if I wanted to set up interviews with each of the girls, who would I talk to? Where would I find them?" she asked, playing innocent.

"I wouldn't know, detective."

Dawson glanced again at her affidavits. "Several of my eyewitnesses report there was some kind of altercation just prior to

Mylee's death. It happened backstage, but some think you may have been directly involved in the squabble."

"Nonsense, I am the consummate performer," Chi stated proudly. "I raise my voice, but never my hands to discipline my cast."

"Did you raise a hand to Mylee? Hurt her in any way?"

"No, of course not!"

"What kind of questions are those?" Bloomfield asked. "My client has already said that he was not part of any altercation with the young woman."

"Miss Bloomberg, I am merely trying to get to the truth of the matter."

"Bloomfield."

Dawson continued, "I have evidence that suggests Mylee was severely beaten and then poisoned moments before her death."

Wang Chi's eyes widened. He looked shocked and was utterly speechless.

"What is the nature of your evidence?" she demanded.

"Our forensics investigators have gone over the body with a fine tooth comb, and found evidence of internal contusions on the body which are consistent with an individual being struck or kicked in the lower abdomen repeatedly," Dawson reported. "According to eyewitness accounts, it looked like Mylee had been beaten pretty badly. For when she emerged from behind the curtain, she was clearly disoriented, and could barely walk down the runway straight. When she reached the end, she just collapsed."

"And the cause of death?" Bloomfield asked.

"Our chief medical examiner, Edgar Brogan, has determined that Mylee was likely poisoned, probably cyanide."

Once again, Ellen Bloomfield leaned over to her client and whispered some words in his ear. Wang Chi replied, and the two exchanged several glances and a few more, frantically whispered remarks.

Dawson waited for them to finish. "We'd like to obtain your client's permission to have him tested for exposure to cyanide," she said finally.

"Out of the question!" Bloomfield replied.

"Now, just hold on a minute," Kate said. "Mister Chi isn't being charged with a crime. We'd just like to rule him out as a suspect."

Bloomfield started packing up her briefcase. She appeared to be very agitated, but tried to mask her true feelings. Dawson could see that hiding her emotions was second nature with the mayor's head counsel.

"I can see now that this interview was nothing more than a fishing expedition, an attempt to embarrass my client with material that has no relevance whatsoever to your investigation into that poor girl's death," she stated, full of sound and fury. "When I get back to my office, I intend to file a formal complaint on the part of my client, and notify the Chinese embassy about Mister Chi's poor treatment by the San Francisco Police Department. This City values its international partners, and may require a formal, written apology from the Chief's office in order to set this matter straight."

Dawson had had enough with Bloomfield. She stood up, walked around the table, and got right in her face. "You know, I've had my fill of political operatives, like you, that are constantly running around apologizing for my country to third-world toilets like his that urinate on our flag and enslave its populace behind a bamboo curtain of lies and deceit. We may sometimes make mistakes, and pretty big ones at that, but the last time I checked, we were still the land of the free and the home of the brave. We're the good guys. Just remember that, you pinko bitch, the next time you need a cop to save your ass."

"Well, I never . . ." Bloomfield started to say.

"It's about time you started," Kate said, cutting her off.

Wang Chi was suddenly out of his chair, and standing toe-to-toe with Dawson. His hands were poised to strike swiftly and without mercy, but Roberts moved between them before anything happened.

"All right, that's enough," the Lieutenant said, a great big hulking mass. "Counselor, I'd say that this interview is officially over. Time for you to collect your client, and get out of here before things get ugly."

"Mister Chi, we're leaving," she cautioned her client.

Wang Chi's features hardened with the look of contempt. "You Americans are all the same. You read too many comic books and eat too many fast foods, while we in the East grow stronger every day, feeding our minds the wisdom of Sun Tzu. *The Art of War* reminds us to subdue our enemy without fighting."

Dawson stared right into Chi's face. Her eyes were on fire. "The immortal Stan Lee reminds us in *Fantastic Four #1* that 'It's clobberin' time!'"

Kate stood her ground, the fingers of her right hand curling into a fist. She wanted to punch that smug Chinese bastard right in the nose, and for an instant, she was ready to follow through with her fist, but then she thought better of it. She studied Wang Chi's face for a long moment, then looked away. She had already made her point.

"Your client has quite a temper," Dawson said to her.

Bloomfield ignored her. "Well, this is far from over! When the Mayor hears about this, he'll be demanding both of your resignations."

"Always a pleasure, Miss Bloomberg," Lieutenant Roberts

said, as he crossed the room and sat back down in his chair. He picked up a random folder from his desk, and pretended to read its contents, holding it close to his face. He had had enough of her for one day, and couldn't wait for her to leave.

"It's Bloomfield," she said, at last, walking away.

She steered Wang Chi toward the exit and the busy corridors beyond.

"There'll be another time and another place, Inspector," Chi whispered, over his shoulder.

Dawson nodded. "Count on it."

The two cops watched them leave, then turned back to each other. "Don't they make a lovely couple?" said Kate.

"You'd better watch that mouth of yours, Dawson," he warned her. "One of these days, it's going to get you into a lot of trouble."

"C'mon, Lieutenant, you didn't buy all that bullshit they were shoveling, did you? He's no fuckin' emcee. He's the auctioneer. He was selling those girls off to the highest bidder, and Mylee must have done something that pissed him off. So he killed her. How much clearer could that have been?"

Roberts shrugged his very large shoulders. "So what? Even if he did kill her, he's also a member of the Chinese delegation, with diplomatic immunity. We couldn't touch him, even if he gave us a signed confession."

"Diplomatic immunity be damned, I'm still gonna bust his ass," she replied.

"Not on my watch, detective," the Lieutenant reminded her who was still in charge. He took a deep breath, as if that alone would extinguish the irritation he felt towards his one and only female inspector. He let the air out slowly, through clenched teeth. "In fact, I'd rather you have nothing more to do with this case."

"Lieutenant!"

"I'll assign Clark, who knows how to take orders," he added, with a sense of finality, "and I'll find you a more suitable assignment."

"Lieutenant," she pleaded.

"That's all," Roberts said, and then repeated the words, "*That's all.*"

Dawson turned her back on him. She was already walking out his door.

Late in the day, Kate Dawson sat at her desk, rubbing her eyes. She was very tired. She hadn't gotten her requisite eight hours the night before, and blamed Wang Chi for her lack of sleep. In front of her, spread out on the desk, were photos of the crime scene, forensics reports, and other documents. She had been sorting through the material, and examining each piece, for more than two hours. The only piece of evidence she was still missing was the official coroner's report on Mylee's death.

Rosa Romano stopped by, carrying a bag from Starbucks, and rapped her knuckles on the edge of the desk to get Kate's attention. "I thought you could use a break, girlfriend," she said, handing her the bag. "That was coffee, extra lite with sugar?"

"You remembered."

"How could I forget? The first time I ever brought you coffee, I loaded it up with sugar, you know, the way I like it, and you spent the rest of the day, bouncing off the walls, on some kind of sugar high."

Dawson removed the coffee, and started rooting through the bag. "Yeah, I remember. But I'd be even more impressed if there was a sticky bun in here," she commented, and as if by magic, the sticky bun appeared.

"Awesome!"

"Sticky buns," Rosa replied, with a shrug. "Who knew?"

"You did good, girlfriend. Thanks," she said, biting into the sticky bun. As she chewed on the tasty morsel, Kate rolled her eyes with pleasure.

"I heard through the grapevine that you'd been removed from the case. Is there anything that I can do?"

Romano asked, sitting down on the edge of the detective's desk. She seemed to be genuinely concerned.

Kate shrugged. "I need the coroner's report. I'm hoping there's something in there that ties Wang Chi directly to the girl's death."

"I was just heading down there now," Rosa remarked. "You'll need to give me an hour or two to complete the coroner's report."

"Thanks, hon. You're the best friend I ever had."

All of a sudden, Dawson's cell phone rang, playing the first few notes of Eric Clapton's "Layla," and then it rang again. Since she was closest to the phone, Romano reached for it on the desk, and glanced down at the first screen that appeared. "Ah? You've got a hit on your profile at Match.com. He wants to meet you for dinner."

"Don't start," Kate said, gesturing for her phone.

"You know, it's really sad that you have to hire an electronic matchmaker on the Internet to find you dates," Rosa said, smiling, with her tongue firmly implanted in her cheek. "I mean I'd say you were a decent catch, but then—"

"*Decent catch?* Are you kidding me right now?"

"No," she replied, with a grin.

Dawson shook her head. "And this is coming from a woman who's dating a guy that thinks he's a character from *Star Wars*."

"Don't you dare make fun of my Lenny," Romano warned her, playfully. "He may be a little odd, but I always know where his heart is."

"Rosa, the thing is—" Kate started to tell her the truth about Lenny, but was interrupted.

"I want to know how it works."

Dawson shrugged her shoulders. "All right," she replied. "So you create a profile, post a recent photo or two, and put in your preferences. Then it comes back with all of your possible matches. I have three."

"Not bad," Rosa said.

"Not bad? Three is actually pretty good."

Rosa Romano read Kate's profile out loud, "'Attractive, athletic woman, thirty-nine, with graduate degree seeks gentleman in the high income bracket.'"

"All right. That's enough."

"I think, if I had been you, I would have added something about my tight, firm buttocks," Rosa said, laughing at her friend's expense.

"You're so funny."

"So, have you had much luck?"

"Not really," Kate confessed, looking down.

Rosa Romano, sitting on the desk next to Dawson, could feel her friend go limp, and all the life drain out of her body, like she had already thrown in the towel on love. The upbeat smile in her girlfriend's face had turned into a frown. Romano put a hand on her forearm, ready to give her friend an instant transfusion of life from her own blood.

"Can I make a friendly suggestion?"

"No."

"Maybe try lowering your standards just a little?" she said, without a beat. "No man wants to know that he's being targeted because of his income."

Dawson tilted her head to one side. "You're probably right."

"So, what about this cute stockbroker?"

"His name is Tom," she replied, with a half-smile.

"We're supposed to meet tonight at Ernie's Restaurant. At 7 pm."

"The restaurant from *Vertigo*."

"Yeah."

"So, what are you doing here, sitting around talking with me?" Romano asked, checking her watch for the time. "It's after 6 pm. You should be in a car, heading to Ernie's to meet this rich, handsome guy, and making plans to have lots of babies."

"Oh, Rosa," Kate said, about to cry.

Romano gave her a great, big hug. "Now go, before I get half a notion to switch places with you, and take this guy for myself."

"Tell you all about it, tomorrow," Dawson said, on her way out.

"I'm gonna hold you to that," Rosa replied, heading to the morgue.

Rosa Romano strolled down the stairs to the morgue on the basement level of the Hall of Justice, and listened closely as the echo of her footsteps finally caught up to her actual movements. The place was completely empty. She paused briefly at her office to throw her large purse, scarf and raincoat on the chair next to her desk, and walked right back out. She went to the end of the basement corridor, and walked through a double set of doors into the county morgue. The strong odor of formaldehyde, which hung in the air like an eighth grade biology class, no longer bothered her sense of smell, but she still enjoyed teasing others who found the smell particularly overwhelming. As the Assistant Medical Examiner for the City of San Francisco, she was trained as a forensic pathologist, and had conducted hundreds of autopsies in her eight years of service. For this particular shift, she was surprised that her diener wasn't there. He had left her a note, saying that he had already prepped the body for her and that there were no signs of any cyanide residue. But she was also annoyed that her autopsy technician had decided to call out sick for a second day in a row. He wasn't even a cop, but he was supporting the strike nonetheless—along with all of the others.

In the prep room, she quickly pulled on her coroner's sweats and white lab coat, and scrubbed up before donning her mask and goggles. She thought about the "chem" gear for an instant, but decided to move forward without it. After all, the diener's body would have been laying there next to Mylee's, if there had been a problem. Rosa then pulled on a pair of latex gloves. She didn't want to contaminate the body with any microorganisms from her hands that she might have carried in from the street, and had made the scrubbing-in process a familiar routine. The only thing Romano really objected to was the way the abrasive cleanser had left her hands after each scrub-in. They were rough and callused, and she had spent a fortune on moisturizers to treat them after each autopsy.

On her iPod, Romano loaded track #6: "Don't Fear the Reaper" from Blue Öyster Cult's 1976 album *Agents of Fortune*, and immediately began singing along with the band's lead guitarist, Donald Roeser. She sang, reaching some of the high notes in a range that was clearly above her ability, but she didn't mind. Rosa rarely got the chance to sing at work during the swing shift between 6 pm and 2 am because that's when most of the interns, autopsy technicians, and photographers worked.

But with most of them out on "sick leave," supporting the police union with their absences, Romano had the complete run of the morgue. She cranked up her voice, and wailed away.

Mylee's body was laid out on the stainless-steel table, with a simple sheet covering it. Rosa Romano pulled the sheet back, and glanced down at the petite young woman. She could see the dissection had already been made, and the body was prepped and ready for her examination. The familiar Y-shaped incision, which started at the top of each shoulder and ran down the front of the woman's chest to her sternum, was there, with the chest flaps pulled back for easy access to the chest cavity.

Just then, Rosa felt a tickle near her nose. But rather than reach up and scratch it—and thereby contaminate her gloved hands—she took hold of a sterilized probe, and scratched her nose with it. She quickly discarded the probe, making certain it did not affect her autopsy in any way.

One by one, Romano removed Mylee's internal organs, weighed them and measured them before placing them neatly in two rows on stainless steel trays. She divided them equally into four groups on the table. The body block, which was often used to elevate the chest cavity for dissection, was firmly in place, and made Rosa's job an easy one. She only had to make incisions behind the ears and over the crown of the head to remove the brain and examine the skull. Those would have been the last steps she made before completing the autopsy.

But as she looked down at the lower abdomen, Rosa Romano was troubled by the bruising that had formed on some of the inner tissue. She also noticed that the young girl had had surgery recently, for there was a small incision near the vaginal cavity that had healed with a fairly noticeable scar. The wound couldn't have been more than a few months old. Just as she was making that determination, the tickle to her nose returned. She moved her nose back and forth in an effort to shake it off. She then reached for a scalpel, and began tracing a line from the sternum to the vagina. Just below the epidermis, Rosa struck something that was hard like a bone. She knew the body's skeletal structure, like the back of her hand, and was literally stunned to find a foreign object buried just under the skin. Romano was determined to find out what the hell it was, while at the same time being distracted by her tickle. Then, all of a sudden, as she continued to probe the object, an explosive gas blew up in her face.

Romano put a hand over her mask, but by then, it was too late. She had already breathed in a lethal dose of the gas—a bitter poison that smelled of almonds.

Cyanide. Rosa staggered back away from the table, and collapsed to the floor, gasping desperately for breath. A bloody froth filled her mouth, and dribbled down her cheek. Within a matter of moments, she had gone into cardiac arrest, and was dead.

At exactly 7 pm, Kate Dawson stepped out of her car at the intersection of Jackson and Montgomery Streets, and walked the half block to the restaurant where she had agreed to meet Tom, the Stockbroker. Located at 847 Montgomery Street, Ernie's Restaurant was a popular landmark in San Francisco for over sixty years, and had earned many prestigious, five-star awards for its service and cuisine. Both the interior and exterior of the restaurant were re-created by Alfred Hitchcock as sets in the studio for *Vertigo* in 1958. In fact, the owners of the restaurant, Roland and Victor Gotti, appeared in the film as extras, and provided numerous props from the restaurant for the studio set. The restaurant closed in 1995, but was re-opened twenty years later by a fan of the film, looking for a once-in-a-lifetime dining experience.

Dawson thought Ernie's Restaurant was a rather posh restaurant to meet someone for the first time, but since Tom was such a big movie-buff, she reluctantly agreed. She found Tom sitting at the bar where Jimmy Stewart's character first met Madeline Ulster.

"It's a pretty sweet place, don't you think, Katherine?" Tom said, as he carried his drink from the bar to the table. The waiter helped Dawson with her chair, and then the stockbroker sat down, opposite her. "But I guess, only in retrospect, to movie-buffs like me. Most of the diners, eating here tonight, have no idea of the restaurant's history."

"I understand that Alfred Hitchcock brought his wife Alma here several times, and after one outstanding dining experience after another, he decided to immortalize the place in the film *Vertigo*," Kate explained, recalling details that she had read on Wikipedia.

Tom smiled. "Excellent, you just earned a bronze star. But Hitchcock actually didn't film the scenes here at Ernie's. He arranged for his production designer Henry Bumstead to reproduce the interiors and exteriors of the restaurant on the Paramount lot, so he wouldn't have to shoot around Ernie's customers."

"I'd heard that Hitchcock was somewhat of a control freak," she commented.

"That's not the least of it," Tom said, taking another drink. "When I had heard this place was up for sale, I went way out of my way to buy it. What happened is that I drove down all of the local buyers who were interested in the property by offering to pay Victor Gotti $50K above the actual sale price. I sold off several small start-ups that I had acquired for a song, and parlayed that money into $8 million. I did all of this by the time I was just twenty-seven, but of course, Thomas Sullivan had already earned his first million."

"How interesting," Dawson said, ordering herself a cocktail from the bar. She was actually not interested in how Tom had earned his money, and would have preferred to continue talking about Vertigo. "I had heard that Victor Gotti flubbed his line, during principal photography, when James Stewart enters the restaurant, saying 'Good evening, Mr. Stewart' instead of calling him 'Mr. Ferguson,' his character's name."

"Yeah, right, but that wasn't nearly as interesting as my putting together the rest of the money to buy this place," Sullivan boasted, as he continued to drone on about his wealth. "You have to understand that I was massively overleveraged, having stockpiled all of my money in this one start-up I held the pink slip on. I went from plus $8 million to minus $12 million over-night. I actually owed $12 million. You have never lived until you owe the bank $12 million. I will tell you something, no matter how much money I ever make, I will never feel richer than the day that I got back to zero."

"I can just imagine," she said, bored, taking another drink.

Tom shrugged. "Of course, the real trick to buying this place from the Gotti's was making them think I was a high roller with millions to spend, and then closing the deal with the $50K I started with."

"Bravo. That was a great story," she lied.

After he had finished ordering his meal, Sullivan sat back in his rich leather chair, and said, "Your profile says that you work for the City. What do you do? You're not one of those 'steno-girls,' are you?"

"I'm a cop," Kate replied. "San Francisco Police Department. Homicide Bureau."

"Oh, that's right. You're the ones out on strike. Something to do with getting the public to pay for your bullets."

"Is that a problem?" she asked, praying there would be one.

Tom Sullivan was silent for a moment. "So, you like carry a gun?"

"Yes," she replied simply. "Always a part of the job."

"Where is it?" Tom continued to probe.

"In my purse."

"Can I see it?" he asked.

She nodded her head. "Sure, but then, I'd have to shoot you," she replied, with a certain degree of levity, but the joke seemed to fall on deaf ears. Tom the Stockbroker wasn't interested in her.

When the first course of the meal came, she settled back in her chair, and listened to Tom drone on for another twenty-five minutes about how he had restored the restaurant to its 1958 décor, as if he had personally chosen all of the furnishings himself. Now that might have been truly interesting, particularly if he had had to search through antique shops in the older section of San Francisco, but all he did was write the check. His description of finding the right wallpaper, with its distinctive red pattern, took more than ten minutes alone.

To say the least, Tom Sullivan was the most boring man she had ever met. If the other two men on Match.com were anything like him, she might as well adopt a cat and take up knitting. This whole dating thing was clearly not worth the effort, not after tonight.

Kate was about ready to order another drink from the bar when her cell phone chimed and the text "Code 10-00 ('ten double-zero')" appeared in the text window.

In the lexicon of police emergencies, no two words or sets of numbers carried more weight or concern than the words "officer down," or code 10-00 ("ten double-zero"), for they often meant that a policeman had been shot down, possibly killed, in the line of duty. It was well-known, all throughout the United States and Canada, that police officers were a sentimental lot. They loved their families, attended church every Sunday, took care of their homes, and served their communities by offering the fullest measure of devotion. Nothing brought them together faster than the thought one of their own was "down." Without any thought or volition, she pushed her chair back and stood bolt upright as a reflex, looking down at the text.

"Tom, I feel bad about doing this to you," she said, holding the iPhone out so that he could read the text, "but I have to go. There's been an emergency."

"What about the rest of your meal? And our date?" he asked, with the look of surprise plastered all over his face.

"I've already seen how the rest of this movie ends," Dawson replied, kissing him politely on the cheek.

"Good luck with your search on Match."

"Hey, what does that mean? I thought we were having a good time."

Without a backward glance, she ran out of the restaurant, jumped into her car, and headed to Bryant Street.

At the Hall of Justice, Kate Dawson scrambled down several flights of stairs, and when she reached the basement, she ran down the hall past the coroner's office, and burst through the double doors into the morgue. She found the usual crime-scene circus. Maybe this one was little bigger, considering the victim was one of their own, with forensics guys everywhere and uniformed cops standing around as if they half-expected the criminal to return to the scene of the crime. As she reached the center of the room, Dawson found Lieutenant Roberts, Clark and Jawara, Gregory Morris, several uniformed officers, and a few of the crime-scene boys gathered around a body.

They parted as she approached to give her plenty of room.

She crouched down, looking closely, and could hardly believe her eyes. Rosa Romano lay dead on the cold, linoleum floor, a crimson-red foam upon her lips.

"Christ Almighty," Kate said, barely audible, and started crying.

Doctor Brogan gave the detective a moment with her grief, and then squatted down next to her. He reached over, and put his arm around her shoulder, like a father comforting his child. He said finally, "It looks like she was poisoned. Cyanide."

"What? How is that possible?" she demanded, her tearful eyes barely registering the hustle and flow of the crime-scene boys.

"I'm really not sure, but I'd guess there must have been some residual poison leftover in Mylee's body cavity that she hit when conducting the autopsy," Brogan responded. "I'll know more once I run a full test on both of the bodies."

Dawson did not appear to have heard him. She was in a state of shock, and her bright, inquisitive gaze had been replaced by an empty, vacuous one that seemed to look right through her colleagues, like they were little more than X-rays. Her hands trembled as she reached up to squeeze back the flow of tears. When she lowered her head, she shook it slowly back and forth and closed her eyes, hoping the nightmare would go away. But just as soon as she re-opened them, she saw Rosa Romano's dead body still lying there. She was visibly shaken, and everyone around her could see it.

The Lieutenant stood over her, confused and concerned. "Are you all right?"

"No," Dawson confessed, the rosy color in her face all but gone. "I don't think I'll ever be right again."

"I know that Rosa Romano was your friend," Roberts said, putting a comforting hand on her shoulder.

"Don't worry. We'll get whoever was responsible for this."

"She was more than just my friend, Lieutenant," Kate replied, a million miles away. "She was like a big sister to me who I could talk to about men and fashions. Rosa once told me that she loved me, but I didn't have the courage, particularly in those days, to tell her what she really meant to me."

James Roberts looked at his female detective. "I'm sure she knew."

"I just wish that I had told her," she said, her cheeks stained with tears.

Mikhail Jawara was sniffling back tears. "There wasn't anything we could have done, Kate."

"Jawara's right," Clark said, teary-eyed. "We don't always know when our time is up, but she would have wanted it this way."

"I know, fellas," she muttered.

"What the hell was Romano doing down here so late?" Morris asked, desperate for some answers, but totally unaware that the San Francisco Police Department's two medical examiners worked different shifts.

"Her job, you fucking dick head!" Kate screamed loudly, unaware that her sudden outburst had caught most of the crime-scene workers by surprise until she realized that everyone in the room had stopped what they were doing and were staring right at her. Gregory Morris was equally surprised. He put out his hand to touch her, to reassure her if he could, but she refused to be comforted.

She brushed him away and shivered.

"Kate . . ."

"What was she like?" Dawson completed the question that Morris was about to ask. She wondered how her friend would be remembered to the casual bystander who never met her. "Rosa Romano was the kindest person I ever met. She rarely said a cruel word about anyone, and if you needed something, anything from a hug to fifty dollars, she was always the first person standing there to give it to you."

"She sounded like a very special person," Morris replied.

Kate nodded. "We'll not likely see her kind again."

Flanked by Clark and Jawara, Lieutenant Roberts approached Dawson with caution. He took a deep breath, then said finally, "Kate, we've got a lot of work to do before most of us can leave here tonight. We know that Rosa was your friend and you wanna help out, but you're really not helping us. Why don't you let one of the patrol boys drive you home?"

"Go home, and chill out, Kate," Jawara said.

"We're gonna need you," Clark added. "So, why don't you just go home, relax, and get some rest."

Before Dawson could raise any objections, a young, rookie cop walked in through the double doors, and said, "I've got a car waiting for you, Inspector."

"Thanks, Lieutenant, for telling me straight," Kate said, gathering her things.

In the back of the rookie's squad car, Dawson's shoulders slumped as fatigue and despair descended on her, like a fresh blanket of snow over a field of spring flowers. She struggled to keep her eyes open and her mind alert, but at the first red light on Bryant Street, she fell asleep, and didn't wake again until the squad car was pulling into the parking lot at Bayside Village Apartments. She climbed out of the squad car, and headed for the stairs.

Jonathan Prinze was hunkered down on the first landing, wearing a pair of jeans and a flannel shirt, waiting for her. He said, "Hey . . ."

"Hey," she replied.

"I had to see you."

"You shouldn't be here," Kate said, walking up the steps with her head down, determined to get by him.

Even though her cheeks were stained with tears, she tried to put on a face that was all business. "You know the rules, Prinze. This is where I live, and is off-limits to you."

He stood up, and stopped her from taking any more steps. "I've been thinking about you all day, Katherine."

"Really?" she asked, with a raised eyebrow.

Dawson tried to get around him, first on the right side and then on the left, but her path was blocked. Annoyed, she folded her arms across her chest, and looked him straight in the eyes. "And I haven't thought about you once today, Jack. Isn't unrequited love a bitch?"

"C'mon, Katherine. You know that's a lie," Prinze said, with a smirk. "I saw you this morning outside the courtroom with that agent from the Justice Department. What was his name? Morris. I'll bet you spent the whole day telling him all about me."

"Actually, the subject never came up."

"I don't believe you."

"I don't give a shit whether you believe me or not."

Prinze smiled wryly. "Yes, you do."

Kate threw her arms up in the air. "Okay, you win! You're just too smart for me. I don't know why I bother trying to keep anything a secret from you. You always seem to know what I'm thinking."

"Sarcasm? Really, I thought you'd be above that sort of thing."

"But that is what you want to hear, isn't it?"

Dawson asked him, straight out. "Men like you are such control freaks. You don't really want to hear the truth.

You want to hear whatever suits the demands of your ego."

Dawson pushed her way past him, and continued up the stairs.

"Kate, you have me all wrong," he said, following after her. "You should really take the time to get to know me. The real me."

"That's never gonna happen," Dawson replied, over her shoulder. "You're a suspect in a murder case."

"And you're the lead detective in that murder case. I know. I know. We've been over this before," Prinze reminded her, with a smile that was nearly all teeth. He caught up to her at the next landing, and seized her shoulders, gently. "When are we going to stop playing all these roles, and just be ourselves?"

She shivered. It was hard to tell if it was from the chill in the night's air or the fact that it had been so long since a man had touched her. "I . . . I don't know. I just know I'm tired, and I need to get some rest."

"So, invite me up to your place, and I'll tuck you in," he said, playfully.

She shook her head, as if in disbelief. "You must really think I'm pretty hard up to imagine that I'd invite you into my apartment. Just why the hell are you here at this hour, Jonathan?"

"I heard about what happened," he replied, as the playful look on Prinze's face was wiped away and replaced instantly with one of sadness, regret. The look appeared to be a genuine one. "I'm really sorry, Kate."

"Sorry. Sorry about what?"

"Your friend Rosa."

Dawson was in no mood to play one of his sick, twisted games. She was rarely in the mood to play games.

"What exactly did you hear?"

"Well, you know how it is," he confessed, releasing her. "I have attorneys, and they have friends.

They talk with other attorneys down at the precinct, and they also have friends. Money buys you a lot of attorneys and friends. That's how I found out where you live and about when you'd be home."

"I wouldn't know about things like that. I've never had any money. I've only ever had one attorney, for my divorce. And Rosa Romano was my only real friend. I guess now that she's dead I don't have any friends either."

Jonathan Prinze shrugged. "I can be your friend, Kate."

"You don't really want to be my friend," she said, with a sour look on her face. "You just want to take me to bed."

"The two are not mutually exclusive, you know," he said, plying his charm. "I can be your friend, and I can also be your lover."

She glanced at the watch on her wrist, a knock-off Patek Philippe Twenty that she had purchased at the flea market for thirty-five dollars. "It's getting late. I've been up so long already my body thinks that it's Tuesday afternoon."

Prinze quoted a line of lyrics, written by Justin Hayward, for the Moody Blues song "Tuesday Afternoon."

"What did you just say?" she asked, totally surprised.

Jonathan Prinze laughed. "I was quoting from a song I heard last year at a concert at AT&T Park."

"The Moody Blues?"

"Yeah, that was the group," he said, with a nod.

"According to an interview I saw, Justin wrote "Tuesday Afternoon" while sitting in the middle of a field near his home in England on a beautiful spring afternoon," Prinze reported, sounding like a real fan. "I've always wondered what that would be like to just take a day off in the middle of the work week, and go out and sit in a field. But then, I remind myself that Hayward was working when he wrote those lyrics. He was creating a song for the 1967 album *Days of Future Passed*, a concept album chronicling a typical day in the life."

Dawson smiled. "So, you never did take that day off?"

"No, I never did," he said, pleading guilty. "As the CEO of a large corporation, I could never afford to take a day off, and sit out on a lovely field. Too many people depend on me every day for their livelihood."

"I know what you mean," she replied, with a sigh.

"I haven't had a day off in two years, and now, with the

'sick-out,' I don't dare take any time off. The City needs me to protect honest, hard-working folks from people like you."

Prinze looked wounded, shot through the heart, but it was mostly an act. "Hey, that's not a very nice thing to say, Kate."

"I call 'em like I see 'em."

"And here I thought we were making real progress."

"We are," she said, kissing him quickly, softly on the cheek. "But it's going to take a lot more than reciting song lyrics or telling me how the big corporate giant is so misunderstood by his employees. A woman wants to hear a lot more than that." Kate winked at him as she turned.

"Are you coming or not?"

He flashed his most dazzling smile. "I thought you'd never ask me."

They started up the third flight, climbing the dark, shabby stairs to her third-floor apartment. She went ahead of him, but remained silent, contemplative, as if she was hypnotized by some strange force that she could not understand. They stopped in front of her apartment, and she reached into her purse for keys. She then unlocked the door, and Kate ushered him into the small, studio apartment. She knew she might lose her job, but that was the furthest thing from her mind when she entered.

Dawson was silent for another moment or two, standing in the center of the front room, with her back to him. Then she turned around, and reached for him, grabbing him and kissing him urgently, hungrily. He responded by kissing her back, pushing her up against the front door, grinding his body into hers. He was hard and rough, but at that moment, she wanted him to be nothing more than hard and rough with her. Kate felt an animallike desire course through her veins, and a mean determination to have him. She reached up and grabbed him by the collar of his flannel shirt, and pulled him tightly against her.

"Don't stop—please, Jack—don't stop—" she shouted.

He didn't say anything back to her, other than a few, inarticulate grunts, but continued to press his advantage of size and weight against her. With her pinned against the door, he unzipped the fly to her slacks, and let them fall to the floor. He then reached down, and tore off her panties with one hand, ripping the flimsy fabric like it was tissue paper. Prinze quickly pulled the blouse from her shoulders, and then pushed his hands up under her bra, scooping out her breasts, like mounds of mouthwatering ice cream served in a cone at a summer picnic.

Then his lips closed over a nipple, sucking it into his mouth and nibbling softly.

He reached for her again, gathering her into his arms. She melted into them, kissing him hot and deeply.

Their bodies were pressed together firmly, using the back of the front door as their backstop. His hands were on her hard, first the breasts and then her ass, pulling her against him, their hips thrusting.

Her voice was raised with passion and ecstasy in anticipation of feeling him inside her. "Please, Jack . . ."

Like two ballet dancers, they pirouetted away from the door, and moved to the floor of the living room.

At first, she was on top of him, writhing on top of the bulge in his pants, and then he was on top of her, pressing down with all of his weight. He raised himself above her only long enough to pull open his flannel shirt and unzip his jeans. He then began thrusting into her, his cock buried deep inside, hips moving back and forth. She writhed under him, lost in the brute carnality of their lovemaking.

JOHN L. FLYNN

Kate arched her back, and ground into him, crying out loud, as he continued to thrust into her.

"Yes—yes—yes—YES!" she screamed aloud, and came.

Jonathan Prinze also came quickly, leaving him spent after only a few moments of their heated passion.

He rolled off her onto the hardwood floor, and laid next to Kate, staring at the ceiling as he fought to catch his breath. Now that it was done, she only had one thought that ran through her mind: How long was she expected to lay next to him, and pretend that their love-making had made any kind of difference? She still despised him and the cavalier way that he had murdered his secretary and their unborn child. Even though she was laying right next to him, she was unable to look at him or speak to him.

He put out his hand to touch her, to reach out to her, to reassure her if he could, but she refused to be comforted by him. She brushed his hand away, and curled herself into a ball, much like a fetal position.

"Kate, that was really incredible," he said, still breathing hard.

"I'm glad you think so," she replied, with a frown. Dawson turned away from him, her arms crossed across her breasts, as if hugging herself for warmth. Tears glistened in the corners of her eyes.

"The fuck of the century," he commented.

"I wouldn't go that far."

She struggled unsteadily to her feet, and gathered her clothes together around her, as if to cover herself up.

She felt totally embarrassed by her nakedness in front of Prinze, but took quick steps to remedy that. Kate drew her bra around her waist and snapped it shut from behind before hauling it around into place. She then draped the blouse over her shoulders and pulled her panties on, one leg at a time. "I can't believe I've been so stupid," she said to herself, shaking her head.

"What did you say, Kate?" he asked, looking up at her.

"I said I can't believe how stupid men are when it comes to sex," retorted Dawson. "It was just sex, nothing more."

"I thought it was the fuck of the century," he repeated.

"Well, it just goes to show that you need to get out more," she said harshly. "Expand your sample pool before you make ridiculous claims."

Jonathan Prinze was silent a moment. "Are you upset, Kate?" he asked. "I didn't mean to upset you by what I said."

"I'm not upset. I'm tired. There is a difference," she replied. "I've been up for over twenty hours, and I just need to get some rest."

"You don't have any coke, do you?" he said, looking around. "I could really use a good hit right now to wake me up."

"No, but I've got a Pepsi in the fridge."

Jonathan Prinze smiled at her again and shook his head slightly. "It's just not the same thing, is it, Kate?"

"I wouldn't know," she replied. "I don't do drugs."

"Never?"

"Never."

"The perfect little Girl Scout," he condescended.

"Do you have any cigarettes?"

"Your attorney told me you quit."

"Ah, so you have been checking on me?" Prinze asked, with a twinkle in his eye. "I really did think I had it beat, but I started again."

"You'll find some cigarettes in the top drawer of the cabinet near the door," Dawson growled, pointing to the front door. "Help yourself on your way out."

Dawson walked calmly to the bathroom, and closed the door tightly behind her. She then sat down on the toilet seat cover, and gathered her knees up tight under her chin, listening to

Prinze pull himself back together in the other room. After he was finally gone, she quickly locked and bolted her front door. She then climbed into the shower, turned the hot water on until it was nearly scalding, and scrubbed every inch of her body with a harsh detergent that she kept for cleaning the grungiest of clothes. Her skin was raw, scraped nearly to the bone, when she finally stepped from the shower. She pulled on a fresh pair of sweats, and gently slid between the sheets on her double-sized bed. The moment her head hit the pillow she was unconscious, and she slept uneventfully through the night.

CHAPTER FOUR

On Tuesday morning, the fifth day of the "sick-out," Kate Dawson had very little trouble parking her car in front of the Hall of Justice. Located at 850 Bryant Street, the Southern Station for the San Francisco Police Department was head-quarters for the Personal Crimes Division, which included Homicide. As she climbed the steps to the front door, Dawson paused for a moment to read the dedication plaque: "To the faithful and impartial enforcement of the laws—with equal and exact justice to all—of whatever state or persuasion—this building is dedicated by the people of this city and county of San Francisco. Erected 1958–1960." She had read the plaque a hundred times before, but for some reason, the words had taken on new meaning for her that day. Perhaps it had something to do with the "sick-out," or perhaps it was all about the death of her friend. She wasn't really sure.

By the time Dawson had reached the conference room, most of those who had gathered for the morning review of open cases were seated, and quietly discussing their assignments with the people seated next to them.

Thankfully, the meeting had not yet started. She entered

quickly through the door, and headed directly for the cantina. There, she poured herself a steaming cup of coffee, and added a couple of sugars and a shot of milk.

Kate also picked up a couple of donuts, and slid into an empty chair at the conference table. A handful of photocopied materials sat in front of her. What was left of the Homicide Bureau, those who had not called in sick that day, were assembled around the conference room table, including Clark and Jawara, Ramirez, Doctor Brogan, and much to her surprise Matt Balardi. Balardi had been among the first to call in sick, and had done so consistently throughout the strike. But Matt was sitting there, as big as life, drinking down his coffee and feasting on a donut. She liked to think he was there to pay his last respects to Rosa Romano and not because there had been a shortage of coffee and donuts at the Balardi house hold.

Lieutenant Roberts walked into the conference room, with very little fanfare, and took the center seat at the table. He was followed, close at hand, by Gregory Morris who closed the door behind him and sat down, next to the boss. Both men had a somber, almost dismal, look on their faces that communicated volumes to the others.

"Good morning," Roberts said, all business, with a perfunctory clearing of his throat. "I've decided to postpone your reports on all the open cases so that we can focus our attention on finding the person or persons responsible for Doctor Romano's death. We'll pick your open cases back up next week. But right now, I just want you to put everything you've got into finding her killer."

Matt Balardi raised his hand. "What makes you think she was murdered, Lieutenant? From what I could tell at the crime scene, she was careless, and bungled the whole examination like a third rate amateur."

"The note from her diener said the body was clear," Clark defended her.

Balardi continued, "She ignored standard protocol."

Kate Dawson swiveled around in her seat, and glared at her partner. *So, it was the donuts and coffee after all, she thought to herself. No friend of Rosa Romano's would have dared to say those things in this company, except Balardi.* It was little wonder why no one in the precinct liked him. He was not a very likable guy.

"You'll get your chance, Balardi," Roberts barked.

"I put a lot of time and effort into my open cases this week, and I'm pissed off that they're being shelved so that you can conduct this farcical 'dog and pony' show for the big brass. Rather than eulogizing her, sir, you should be citing Romano for reckless endangerment."

"Matt, you sick fucking bastard, that's a cruel thing to say," Kate admonished him.

"I wasn't quite finished," he replied, with a frown.

"The fact of the matter is that Rosa Romano would still be alive today, if she had stuck to standard procedure in conducting a post-mortem on the deceased. She should have worked closely with her diener, and if he wasn't available, brought in another diener from a different shift.

Then, upon the first sign of trouble, she should have followed the protocols that are required by the Centers for Disease Control in cases of this kind, rather than going off half-cocked with a scalpel in hand."

Edgar Brogan shrugged his shoulders. "I'll admit that Doctor Romano's methods were a bit unorthodox, but that's what made her a good medical examiner. She was always willing to think outside of the box."

"She took one too many chances, and now she's dead," Balardi concluded.

Dawson pulled him aside, and said, "What's gotten into you, Matt?"

"Nothing!" he snapped. "Maybe I've just gotten fed up with the hypocrisy of it all. Saint-sinner. Hero-fool. Beggarman-thief."

Roberts folded his arms across his chest, and his eyes came down on Matt. "I think we've heard quite enough out of you, Balardi, for one day."

"I've said my piece," he replied, still very angry.

"Then be good enough to keep that trap of yours shut," Roberts insisted. "We're here today to bury a hero and find her killer."

"You might as well get on with it then!"

The Lieutenant glowered at Balardi. The look so eloquently said, *You'd better not piss me off, if you know what's good for you.* He reached into the pocket of his jacket, and took out some prepared notes he had scribbled on a legal pad. He said, "Rosa Romano was a hero, in the truest sense of the word. As the Assistant Medical Examiner for the city and county of San Francisco, Doctor Romano faithfully discharged her duties for eight years with distinction. She earned two medals of commendation for services above and beyond the call of duty, and was honored once with the medal of valor when, during a routine murder investigation, she evaded a Russian assassin's attempts to kill her, while assisting detectives in bringing down all of those who were involved in conspiracy at the highest levels of our federal government. She was both a colleague and a loyal friend who gave completely of herself to this department. We are not likely to see her kind again, and the world is diminished by her loss."

They all paused for a moment of silence, even Balardi. In fact, the room was so silent that the sweep of the second hand on the clock sounded like a continual barrage of cannon fire off in the distance. After the moment of silence, several of the detectives stretched, while others returned to their coffee and donuts.

"One more thing," Roberts added, as he scratched the day-old stubble of beard that was growing on his face, "I've asked Agent Morris from the Department of Justice to stay on with us for a few days more to help out. With all the "sick-outs," we are short on manpower, and he does have special knowledge of the Asian cartels that we may be forced to deal with. Besides most of you have already met him or worked with him." He stood up, and looked around the room. "In terms of the work rotation and specific assignments, I'll meet with you individually at the conclusion of our meeting today, and we'll hash out the details."

"Congratulations, Morris!" Clark said, with all sincerity, leaning over the conference room table with an outstretched palm. "It'll be a pleasure to work with you."

Morris nodded. "Thanks."

"Welcome aboard, Agent Morris," Jawara said, holding out his fist. "I'm sure I've got an extra grey jumpsuit in your size for those undercover assignments."

"Much obliged," he replied, with a fist-bump.

Dawson nodded her head. "Good to have you with us, Morris. We could really use someone with your expertise."

"I'm looking forward to working with you again, Kate," he replied.

"Yeah, me, too."

Lieutenant Roberts pushed by Morris and his wellwishers, and reclaimed his seat at the center of the table.

He said finally, "I've asked the Chief Medical Examiner, Doctor Brogan, to say a word or two about the mysterious circumstances surrounding Doctor Romano's demise. I shouldn't have to remind you that none of this information is to leave this room. We consider the investigation into Romano's death as 'ongoing,' and the last thing that any of us would want is to have half-truths and innuendo leading the press to draw their own conclusions. There will be no rush to judgment in this case. We welcome your input, but also insist upon your discretion in keeping these details private. She was, after all is said and done, one of ours. Edgar, are you ready for us?"

The ME nodded his head, and walked down to the front of the room, with notes in hand and a thumb-drive.

He seemed poised, cool, in complete command of himself. "Last night, Rosa Romano died from exposure to cyanide gas while conducting a routine autopsy on the body of the young Asian girl, Mylee," Brogan explained, while powering up the conference room's audio-visual system. He then inserted the thumb-drive in the USB port, and clicked through several autopsy photos, settling on one which revealed a fairly noticeable scar near the girl's vaginal cavity. "Apparently, Rosa had just completed the standard post-mortem examination when she found this scar. It couldn't have been more than a few months old, but it didn't correlate with any known gynecologic or surgical procedure."

"Hysterectomy?" Dawson asked, looking up at the image. She had had a hysterectomy, and she well-remembered the pain in her lower abdomen.

"No."

"Myomectomy?" Ramirez guessed, mindful of his wife.

"No, but it does leave a similar scar."

"Pelvic organ prolapse?" Jawara asked, stumbling on the words. William Clark looked at his partner sideways.

"You just made that up."

"No, I didn't," Jawara said with a shrug, "My cousin from Baltimore had to have the procedure, and she said that it was really painful."

Brogan frowned. "No, not even close," he replied.

"But before the rest of you geniuses start trying to impress me with your knowledge of female anatomy, let me just say that I have ruled out every major and minor procedure, from a routine D&C to endometrial ablation, and nothing matched the scar tissue in Mylee's body."

"Perhaps the doctors in Thailand have a different playbook?" Jawara asked.

"Anatomy is still anatomy. It doesn't really matter if a procedure is performed in the East or in the West," the Medical Examiner explained it to them, simply, like children. "Doctors still have to follow the basic rules of anatomy. They're not likely to perform a penectomy when they've been asked to remove a person's tonsils unless they're blind or they totally flunked out of Basic Anatomy 101."

The conference room, which was mostly full of men, became suddenly silent. Several of the detectives shifted uncomfortably in their chairs, while the rest of the Homicide Bureau tried unsuccessfully to purge that image from their psyche. No one was prepared to discuss castration in the same breath as a tonsillectomy.

"Okay, I'd say you got our full attention now, Doc," Kate said, with a slight smile. "What does the scar tissue mean?"

Brogan nodded his head. "I think that's exactly what Doctor Romano may have asked herself right before she died," he suggested, clicking through several more slides. "Based on the evidence at hand, we can approximate Rosa's final actions with a high degree of certainty. We know, for instance, that she used a scalpel as a probe, and began by tracing a straight line from the sternum to the vagina with it. As she probed just below the epidermis, Romano must have struck a foreign object that was buried under the skin, and somehow broke its seal. It expelled the gas right in her face, and she was dead within a matter of seconds from cyanide poisoning."

"Christ Almighty!" Dawson exclaimed.

"This is the device that killed Rosa Romano," Doctor Brogan said, holding up a small, rectangular box, which was about the size of a small remote. It was wrapped securely in a plastic bag that was tagged and numbered. He handed it off to Clark who, in turn, passed it around the room for examination. "It's made out of a polymer-resin plastic that would not show up on an airport screen or trigger a metal detector."

"You've got to be shitting me?" Jawara reacted.

"Madre de Dios," Ramirez said, crossing himself.

"But what was it doing there?" Kate demanded, leaning forward in her chair to intercept the device as it was making the rounds. She took it into her hands, and examined it carefully, turning it around, trying to make some sense of it all.

"I can't say for certain, but my best guess is that it was deliberately implanted in Mylee's body as a kind of booby-trap," the Medical Examiner replied. There was a moment, a long, painful moment of silence, as he stared at Kate and the other men without expression. The word "booby-trap" seemed to hang right out there, but no one was brave enough or foolhardy enough to say anything about it. "There's evidence to suggest that Mylee was beaten up pretty badly by her handlers. Kicks to the lower abdomen may have been enough to break the canister's seal prematurely, or it's possible the cyanide gas simply leaked out of the polymer-resin shell. Either way, Mylee died without knowing what was happening to her. A terrible and tragic way to go."

Kate's eyes never left the Medical Examiner. "So, you don't think she knew anything about the surgical procedure?"

"No, I don't," he said, all business. "Both she and the other girls were probably told that the medical examination was strictly routine. Their handlers may have even said the exam was required to obtain their visas. Little did they realize, while they were deep under a general anesthesia, they were being prepped to deliver a lethal dose of chemical weapons to a particular target in the United States."

"Like the G-20 Summit?" Roberts interjected.

"Can you think of a better target?" Brogan asked him. "A blow to the world's twenty major economies could spell economic chaos in the West for decades to come, and the emergence of a new world order from the East."

"But who's behind all of this? And why?" Ramirez asked.

Clark sat forward in his chair, and said, "My money's on Russia. They've been itching for a fight even since the break-up of the old Soviet Union."

"You idiot, Russia is a member of the G-20," Balardi reminded him, "and so is China. You've got to think bigger than that. Like on a global scale. Who benefits the most from economic chaos in the West?"

"North Korea," Morris said, with authority.

Balardi nodded at the Justice agent. "That's right. North Korea."

"North Korea," Clark repeated. "You can't be serious."

"They're the only ones who would benefit from a global economic meltdown of all the nations in the G-20," Morris commented.

"Not one of our enemies in the Middle East?" Clark fired back.

"No. Even though they hate us and would like nothing more than to see us wiped from the face of the planet, they still rely on the West and our European allies for a stable economy to trade goods," the Justice agent said. "That's why sanctions generally work. Nations like Saudi Arabia, Lebanon, Iraq still need our vast food stocks and durable goods to survive."

Jawara raised an objection. "I'm having a hard time believing these five teenaged girls would go along with such an outlandish plot. I've got two teens of my own, and the only things they're interested in are boys and hanging out at the mall."

"These are not American teenagers, Mikhail. They are young women who have been trained as slaves since they were very young," the Medical Examiner replied, determined to make himself clear. "In addition to being trained and now weaponized, these girls were likely brainwashed or behaviorally-conditioned to carry out their mission, even if one or more of them were caught or killed. They don't have a will of their own. They are strictly following a set of commands that have been programmed into them."

Kate nodded to herself, as if Brogan had confirmed something she half expected to be true. She thought about it for another minute. "These women—this whole operation is a Trojan horse."

Roberts and Clark looked sharply at her. Dawson caught their glance, but before she could say anything to them, everyone in the room had stopped talking.

Concerned, she looked from face-to-face, as members of the Homicide Bureau sat quietly in their seats, considering the implications of her classical reference to the raid on Troy. They seemed to be lost deep in thought for a moment longer, then the Medical Examiner leaned forward to turn off the audio-visual program, and broke the spell.

"Yeah, that's right," Brogan said finally. "But instead of a great, big wooden horse that hid an elite force of the Greek soldiers in its belly, we have five beautiful women who carry a chemical weapon in their bodies capable of killing thousands."

"But we don't know where they are? They could be anywhere in the city," Dawson revealed, sharing a part of her investigation.

"Or, if they made it out of the city," Clark added, "they could be anywhere in the country by now. Los Angeles? New York? Washington D.C.?"

"We can't afford to think that way, Clark," she cautioned him.

"But we've got to consider what to do, if he's right," Matt Balardi said, and then decided not to press the issue. He retreated hastily.

Ramirez shifted uncomfortably in his seat.

"So, when the G-20 Summit opens on Thursday, we'll screen everyone going through the door," Lieutenant Roberts said resolutely. "We had already planned on checking everyone's credentials, so we'll just add one more layer of security. We'll have stop every woman of Asian descent, and conduct a thorough screening."

"That's racial profiling, Lieutenant."

"You got a better idea, Balardi?"

Dawson shook her head. "And how do you plan on screening them? Doctor Brogan's already told us the device they carry is made of a polymer-resin plastic that is invisible to normal screening methods."

"We'll figure something out," he replied.

"Suppose they enter as Moscone Center employees? Delegates?" Kate pressed.

"I'll tell you what you should do, Lieutenant," Jawara said, with his tongue firmly planted in his cheek.

"Make every Asian woman entering the Moscone Center drop her drawers, and have Brogan pretend to do a pap smear while he's looking around down there for the telltale scar. I happen to know a thing or two about female anatomy, and I'd be more than happy to help the good doctor out."

Clark glared at his partner. "After three marriages, Mikhail, I would have expected you to know more than a thing or two about women."

"Knock it off, you two," Roberts demanded. He took out a handkerchief and mopped his brow. The windows were sealed shut, and it was warm in the conference room. "I said we'll figure something out, and I mean it."

"What if they've targeted something other than the G-20 Summit?" Dawson asked, forever the voice of reason. "Or have a secondary target in mind, if they're not able to get close enough to the primary? They could still kill thousands at the San Francisco Stock Exchange, the Airport, AT&T Park, Fisherman's Wharf . . ."

"We'll just have to find those girls," the Lieutenant babbled on, without a real plan, distracted, lost.

Dawson turned to the Medical Examiner. "Is there a way to trace a particular strain of cyanide? Maybe back to its original source?"

"I've analyzed a trace sample of what was left in the device," Brogan replied, retrieving the device from one of the detectives. "It consisted of hydrogen cyanide (or prussic acid), a warning eye irritant, and an adsorbent known as diatomaceous earth. Then, when I looked at tissue samples taken from around Romano's eyes, I realized that I had seen this compound before in a cyanide-based pesticide invented in Germany in the early 1920s. The product was manufactured by Degussa in sealed canisters under the name Zyklon for delousing clothing and disinfecting ships, warehouses, and trains of pesky insects. But it's better known as Zyklon-B, a poisonous gas that was used by Nazi Germany to murder over a million people in gas chambers installed at Auschwitz-Birkenau and other death camps."

"Zyklon-B?" Dawson asked, repeating the unfamiliar word.

"It's hard to imagine now, some seventy-five years later, but the Nazis had no idea how effective a pesticide would be in killing large numbers of people," Doctor Brogan explained, familiar with the toxin. "But then, they had never run any real tests. Zyklon-B was first tested on Russian POWs in 1941 by *SS-Hauptsturmführer* Karl Fritzsch, a subordinate of Rudolf Höss, the commandant of Auschwitz. His experiments were shocking, to say the least, but proved quite effective for mass killings. By the middle of 1942, as large numbers of Jews from all over Europe began pouring into Auschwitz, Hitler's final solution called for mass exterminations. Those who were not selected for work crews were immediately gassed. Most were children, women with children, the elderly, and the infirmed. The victims were told they were going to be deloused and given a shower. They were then stripped of their belongings, and herded into the gas chamber. A special branch of the SS dropped the Zyklon-B pellets through vents in the roof or holes in the side of the chamber. Since hydrogen cyanide interferes with cellular respiration, most victims were dead within twenty minutes. The victims' bodies were then loaded into large crematoriums for disposal."

"Thanks for the history lesson, Doc, but you can't be serious," Jawara said. "No country in its right mind would dare launch an attack like that against the United States and its allies with a simple pesticide."

"Jawara's right," Clark added. "They'd be opening themselves up to condemnation and ridicule, the likes of which we haven't seen since World War II."

Balardi got in on the act. He leaned forward in his chair and smiled affably. "Guys, have you forgotten that the world's terrorists organizations don't give a rat's ass about what we think of them and their methods?"

"They can go fuck themselves!" Jawara remarked.

"Think about it. They're probably using Zyklon-B because it's cheap to manufacture," Matt Balardi said matter-of-factly. "Besides they could also be using it to send the rest of the world a message that they consider Western nations, like the United States, to be pests that need to be exterminated."

"Great!" Clark exclaimed. "Not only do we provide them with the right WMD, but we also come up with a good reason for them to use it on us."

Dawson did her best to hide the smirk on her face. She directed her next question to the Medical Examiner.

"Doctor Brogan, you said Zyklon-B was manufactured by a company in Germany during the war."

"Yes, Degussa," he replied, with a cool demeanor.

"While Degesch, the parent company, owned the rights to the brand name Zyklon and the patent on the packaging system, the chemical formula was owned by Degussa."

"Who manufactures Zyklon-B today?" Kate asked.

"Degesch resumed production of Zyklon-B after the war as a pesticide. The product was renamed Cyanosil in 1974, and is still produced under that name," Brogan reported. "Several other companies in Eastern Europe also produce it, but under the trade name Uragan D2, which means "cyclone" in English. Because Zyklon-B has a shelf life of only three months, it is continually under production."

Dawson nodded her head. "Then we should be able to trace it right back to its source, and find out who bought this current batch."

"That's excellent thinking," Brogan said. "I'll get right on it."

"We don't have a whole lot of time," she told him, glancing at her watch. "The G-20 Summit starts in less than seventy-two hours."

"Then the less time we spend talking about it—"

Dawson met his eyes. "Thanks, Edgar."

"What are we going to do about the girls?" Clark asked, taking out his notebook.

"I've got a notion," Kate said, looking at her boss who was still babbling on in a state of shock, "to get the media working for us, for a change."

"It's risky, and could backfire on us," Clark replied. "Do you remember what happened the last time they got wind of one of our investigations? Every caped vigilante in town was out chasing down Latino men."

"Have you got a better idea?"

"No."

"Then I want you and Jawara to contact our people in the media," Dawson explained, thinking fast on her feet. "We're going to leak a story to the press that we're looking for five young women who may have been exposed to a rare strain of the Asian flu on a commercial flight from Hong Kong. Emphasis on the word 'may.' We don't want to cause a panic, but at the same time, we do want people to take it seriously."

William Clark jotted down a few notes. "We might get better mileage out of the story if we used 'Ebola' in place of the 'flu.'"

"Yeah, maybe," Kate considered, weighing her options. "But let's think about this for a moment. Imagine that I'm John Q. Public, and I hear that police officials are looking for a person who may have been exposed to Ebola on a recent flight from Asia. I'd be concerned, but I would figure they had everything in hand. However, if this same member of the public hears that five people may have been exposed to Ebola on a recent flight, that sounds more to me like an outbreak, and I'm going to lock myself away at home until the danger passes. We want citizens who are going to help us find them, not run away scared."

"I see your point, Dawson," Clark said, with a nod. "We'll stick with the flu."

"Flu? Are you sick now, too?" Jawara asked, holding a hand over his mouth.

"No, you idiot. It's our cover story," he replied, closing his notebook. "And no one's really sick. They're just using that as an excuse to call out every day."

"I knew that. I really did. I just don't understand why we need a cover story."

Clark shrugged. "C'mon, Jawara. I'll fill you in on the way."

"Okay. Where are we going?" he asked, following his partner out of the room.

Jorge Ramirez slid over into the seat next to his former partner, and said, "Kate, what can I do to help out?"

"Now, I've left the most important task for you," she said, with an encouraging smile. "We need to mobilize all of our remaining resources. That's where you and Balardi come in. I need the two of you to round up every meter-maid, crossing guard and file specialist—really anyone who carries a badge—and get them out on the street, knocking on doors. Someone saw those girls and wants to talk to us about it. Use the composite drawings we got from witnesses, and start canvassing within a ten-mile radius of the hotel."

"Understood," Ramirez said.

"We'll get right on it," Balardi assured her.

As the last two detectives left the conference room, Gregory Morris shot Dawson a sideways glance.

"Rough morning?"

She shook her head. "Not really."

"Fun?"

"In a way."

"I'll bet," he replied, with admiration. "I watched how you

stepped up, and started making decisions when your boss sort of checked out. That was a real ballsy move, Dawson. Particularly in a department that's mostly men."

Kate looked at him for a fleeting moment, engaging his eyes, then looked away. "If I hadn't done it, I'm sure that Clark or one of the other guys would have taken over. We're a pretty competitive team."

"No, that's not what I see."

"Really?"

Morris nodded. "They respect you. They see you as a natural leader, and they'd follow you as the next head of the Homicide Bureau."

"That'll be the day," Dawson laughed. "A woman as the head of the Homicide Bureau. You'll have to order me a pair of those rose-colored glasses."

Morris shook off her objection. "I know what I'm talking about, Kate. I work with a lot of strong women at the Department of Justice. All Harvard or Yale graduates. Most of them wouldn't be able to hold a candle next to you."

"Ah, shucks, Morris," she said playfully. "You got a crush on me."

"Trust me. I know what I'm talking about."

"And what makes you such an expert all of a sudden?" Kate asked. "You're a field agent. What would you know about office politics? You probably haven't spent more than a day on the inside, kissing someone's ass to get ahead."

"I know people," he said defensively.

Dawson got the feeling that, right then and there, Morris was lying to her. "I hope you're not just buttering me up, so I give you a plum assignment," she responded, looking at him again, closely. "I hate subordinates that kiss ass."

"As a matter of fact, I was hoping that you had something for me to do," he replied, suddenly changing his tune.

"I want another crack at Wang Chi."

"That won't be easy, Kate," Morris said, with a frown. "The guy's got diplomatic immunity. He's not going to come waltzing back in here to give you another chance to humiliate him in front of his attorney."

"I mean to interrogate him, not just let him talk."

"I'm telling you he's not going to let that happen."

Kate smiled thinly at him. "Then I need you to pull some strings at Justice. Get his diplomatic immunity rescinded, or scare him enough to make him think that he's safer talking to me than his own handlers." She looked at Morris as she spoke. "As a field agent, I'm sure that you've had more than you fair share of skullduggery."

"Sure," he said.

"Alright, I need to get to Wang Chi, and you're my only hope."

"Okay, I'll see what I can do," he replied, walking quietly to the door.

Dawson watched him go. She then stood up at the table, yawned and stretched, flexing like she was ready to go another couple of rounds. She pitched what was left of her stale coffee at the wastebasket. She then picked up the materials from the table, and headed out. Just as she reached the center of the table, Roberts was still babbling on, "Of course, if it had been up to me—" He broke off hastily, and looked around at the empty chairs in the conference room. The look of utter surprise flashed across his face.

"Sir, the meeting's over," she reported, as a matter of fact.

"Dawson," said Roberts curtly. "See that trouble doesn't happen. Anywhere. You got that, Inspector?"

"I think so, sir," she replied, trying to head out.

At the door to the conference room, the Lieutenant staggered to his feet. He reached out, and took Dawson's arm to steady himself. "Kate, this is a really bad one," Roberts said, confused but coming out of it. "If we don't find those girls, this thing could blow up on us, and a lot of people are going to die. We've got to put our differences aside, for the sake of the department, and work together if we plan to stop them before that happens."

"Agreed," Dawson said.

"I was thinking about having Ramirez work with—"

"Your people all have their assignments, Lieutenant," she told him. "I wouldn't start to secondguess any of those assignments now. You have an excellent team, and they'll all do whatever is necessary to make you proud."

"What about you, Dawson?"

"I'd like the chance at interrogating Wang Chi," she replied. "You know, beat the grass and see what crawls out."

"You can't be serious?"

"I am."

"Well, for Christ sake, be careful," Roberts cautioned her. "The last thing we need is you triggering an international incident."

"It won't be me, Lieutenant," Kate said. "I can guarantee you that."

The Japanese Tea Garden in Golden Gate Park may have seemed like an odd place for Wang Chi to schedule a meeting with his North Korean handler, but he had his reasons for meeting outdoors in such a conspicuous location, not the least of which was his fear that General Chang may have wanted him dead.

Originally built for the World's Fair of 1894, the Japanese Tea Garden was the oldest one of its kind in the United States; its many paths, which were spread out over five acres of the park, featured different kinds of native Japanese and Chinese plants and flowers. The ponds and water gardens were stocked with "koi," a species of fish that were kept for decorative or ornamental purposes. Of course, the centerpiece of the garden was a real teahouse, with its six-story-high, Pagoda-styled roof. Wang Chi reasoned that he'd have plenty of places to hide out, and possibly get away, if he had any notion that the hit was on. In fact, Chi stood in the shadows just to the left of the decorative "moon bridge," watching the grounds through his binoculars for anything unusual.

A lone rider on horseback galloped along one the park's paths, beating down on the freshly-cut grass and firm ground. A tour group was departing the Recreation Center for a walking tour of the grounds. Two young lovers sat in the Garden's alfresco dining area, drinking tea and sharing fortune cookies with each other, while the maid of a wealthy Pacific Heights couple watched their children climbing like monkeys on the great, bronze statue of Buddha. Nearby the lake, a woman was adjusting the canvas on her easel prior to picking up her paintbrush and resuming her latest masterpiece. It seemed like another perfect day in San Francisco with a light breeze from the Bay, bringing freshness to the morning despite the sun's glare.

Wang Chi had finished his third sweep of the park, and was about to put the binoculars down when he heard the distinctive "thump-thump" sound of a helicopter, specifically the Bell UH-1 Iroquois or "Huey," as it approached the park from the southwest. He raised the binoculars back to his face, and followed the helicopter across the sky to the open field in Golden Gate Park where it finally landed after its own routine sweep of the grounds. Instinctively, Chi crouched down on one knee, and blended back into the shadows. As he spied on the general's men, he watched them jump from the helicopter in their civilian wear, and take up flanking positions in the field, deployed just like North Korean army regulars. He then adjusted the binoculars' field of vision, and focused on General Chang.

He recognized his handler as punctual and blunt as ever. No sooner had the general climbed out of the Huey and his boots hit the ground, he was once again issuing orders to his men. The first order of business, he heard the general shout, was to locate and detain Chi.

He looked down at his watch, and figured that Chang and his men would likely overrun his position in the next fifteen minutes, or so. But rather than run, Wang Chi stood fast. He wasn't about to turn himself in, but at the same time, the radio and television personality had had his fill of running. He surrendered to the first soldiers that approached his position, and waited patiently for the general to arrive. He figured that they wouldn't kill him right away, and therein lay his greatest advantage.

"Good morning, Comrade Chi," General Ri Kyu-Chang said, his voice husky and monotone with a thick North Korean accent, as he rounded the path near the moon bridge. Dressed in casual civilian wear instead of his five-star military uniform, he still commanded the respect of the men who flanked him on either side.

Wang Chi sensed the general's presence long before he actually saw him, but he refused to give Chang any sense of surprise or dread. Instead he treated the military man with complete indifference. He turned in his direction, but didn't meet his gaze, "General Chang. This meeting is ill-advised."

"A calculated risk, but necessary as you refuse to answer your control," he replied. Even though General Chang was in his early eighties, he was still a formidable man.

He looked healthy and fit, and had the strength and stamina of men more than half of his age. His chiseled features had been worn down by the years of intense politics and continuous hard work, but his olive skin gave him a sun-kissed look. He wore thin spectacles on the end of his nose, like an accountant who had been balancing ledgers for his entire life. A hardliner from the old days, before the War, he was first appointed by the Korean Workers Party as director of the Machine-Building Industry Department, and had proved to be a valuable asset promotion. He owed favors to no one, and had indeed climbed the ladder of success the old-fashioned way, through hard work, grit and determination.

In his rise to power, he had been the head of North Korea's nuclear and missile programs, and then later was named to the Central Military Commission of the Workers' Party of Korea in 2010. He proved time and again that he was a man to be feared and respected.

"Come to the point, General," Wang Chi demanded. His disapproval for being lectured to was evident, appearing bored with his arrogant tone of voice.

"You disregarded procedure," General Chang snapped. He put his foot up on the wooden bench and leaned into Chi, his eyes boring into him. "Your impulsive actions have jeopardized the entire mission!"

"I had no choice. The Americans were onto us, and I had to improvise in order to stay one step ahead of them."

The North Korean general studied his face for a long, silent moment, then looked away in disgust. "You had one task, and one task only. To get the girls into the United States without detection. We provided your cover identity. We arranged for all of the permits, the payoffs, the marketing and publicity, and the venue. All you had to do is produce an event like you had done dozens of times before. What happened?"

"The thirteen-year-old girl, Mylee," he replied, with some trepidation, "she stopped being cooperative. I had to discipline her in front of the others in order to keep one problem from becoming five others."

"You know nothing of true power and discipline."

"I knew enough to discipline one little girl."

"You were warned specifically not to harm any of the girls!" the general reminded him, the look of incredulity all over his face.

"I did not treat her that roughly," Chi defended himself. "She should not have collapsed on stage from a few slaps and whacks."

"Obviously, you were wrong."

"My people did try several times to recover Mylee's body from the authorities, but they were not successful," Chi reported. "Apparently, the coroner gets to keep the body for the first seventy-two hours in order to conduct an autopsy. But I would not be all that concerned, the Americans are notoriously sloppy when it comes to forensics work."

"You had better hope their skills have not improved."

"They've not, General. Trust me. Like typical Americans, they blunder around in the dark, looking for answers that are right in front of them."

General Chang grinned, all sharks' teeth. "And what about this police woman? What does she know?"

"Inspector Kate Dawson, SFPD," he replied, with a frown, "She is cleverer than most, but she's also in way over her head. She doesn't know it yet, but things are about to take a deadly turn for her."

"See to it personally, Comrade. There should be no one to stop us, this time."

"I've already taken care of it, Comrade General."

"Where are the assets now?" General Chang asked him.

Wang Chi shrugged. "I don't know. We were separated when the police arrived, and I have not yet recovered them. But it is only a matter of time."

The North Korean general looked at Chi as if he wanted to

kill him then and there. "This is completely unacceptable! You were supposed to have looked after them, cared for them, and then delivered them to the target arena. I simply cannot believe how your reckless actions have jeopardized this mission."

General Chang walked away from his man, starting toward a path that lead back down the side of the hill where the Japanese teahouse lay nestled in the gardens to the open field below. Chi hurried after him.

"Tell me, Comrade," he called over his shoulder.

"Would you have sought out my counsel if I had not reached out to you first?"

Chi stopped on the path, and was immediately flanked by the general's men. "No. Their basic programming is sound. They have been conditioned by the best behavioral scientists in the East. I have a high degree of confidence the girls will be in the Moscone Center when the G-20 conference opens, as planned."

"That's not the point!" Chang exclaimed, on the verge of blowing his top. "There are so many things that could still go wrong between now and then. Regardless of how you may see them, those girls are living and breathing time bombs. Your job was to watch them, keep them safe. They are useless to us if they blow up prematurely. Reprisals from the West might well jeopardize all future operations!"

"You have jeopardized mine!" Wang Chi shouted back. He took a moment to regain his calm, toying with his binoculars. "I had a very lucrative business, selling women to the highest bidder. Over a billion dollars in net profits each year."

"That is regrettable, but I warned you not to take part in this venture unless you were fully committed to its political agenda. Economic chaos in the West has always been one of the goals of the Democratic People's Republic of Korea," General Chang said seriously. He started down the path, towards the field again.

Chi followed. "You did not give me much choice in the matter. You held a gun to my head, and demanded my obedience in exchange for my life."

"Precisely," the general remarked, as he stopped and turned back to Chi. "That is the essence of true power and discipline, Comrade Chi. You have to be ready to pull that trigger if you expect others to fear your power."

"The issue is irrelevant, Comrade General," Wang Chi dismissed, with a wave of his hand. All at once, the general and his North Korean army regulars were outflanked by Tongs who had been hiding in plain sight. The lone rider on horseback, members of the tour group, the two young lovers, the female painter, the maid, and even the two children held their ground with automatic weapons trained on the soldiers.

"So, you've aligned yourself with the Tongs?"

"General, let's just say I've made new associations," Chi said, with a smirk. "I no longer consider myself an agent of North Korea."

One of the general's bodyguards, a stern-faced man with a mop of black hair, stepped forward. "Comrade Chi, we trained you. We financed you. We gave you purpose for your life. What would you be without us?"

"A very wealthy man," he replied.

The bodyguard spit on him, and said, "You're nothing but a man without honor."

"Now, what exactly did you say about power, Chang?" he asked, with a wicked laugh. Wang Chi then reached inside his jacket for his gun with a silencer, and shot the bodyguard three times, once in the head. "Oh, yes, now I remember. 'You have to be ready to pull that trigger if you expect others to fear your power.'"

Those words of his had stung, but Chi's impulsive act of

murdering the bodyguard in cold blood had stung even worse. In a matter of seconds, the level of tension increased tenfold as those combatants on either side maneuvered themselves into combat positions. Several of the North Korean army regulars produced sidearms, while an equal number of Tongs released their safeties and cocked their weapons. A beefy, army sergeant who had wrestled in the Olympics for North Korea grabbed hold of one of the Tongs, and lifted him over his head, like a children's toy. General Chang stepped back as his remaining bodyguard pulled out his sidearm and aimed it at the lone rider. Behind Wang Chi, two of the Tongs with Soviet-made AK-47s pushed through the ranks, and knelt beside him on opposite sides, with their automatic rifles primed and ready to shoot. It was a stand-off, with the wrestler holding the frightened Tong in the middle and the rest of the other combatants a heartbeat away from total war.

"Enough of this," the general shouted, waving his hands at both parties. "We're in a public park. If anyone should see us and report this altercation, we'll be answering to the local authorities."

"Why do you think I chose the Japanese Tea Garden for our meeting, Comrade? It's the most isolated part of the Golden Gate Park, and no one ever comes out this far on a weekday. We're safe here," Chi commented.

"I will not stand by, and watch this turn into a blood bath."

"Very wise, General," Wang Chi remarked, smiling. "I would suggest you withdraw your men, and depart immediately. We wouldn't want your helicopter to draw any unwarranted attention."

General Ri Kyu-Chang nodded at his sergeant-atarms who, in turn, dropped the Tong on one of the wooden benches. The man fell hard, crashing down against the iron bars that formed the bench's arm rest, breaking several ribs. "Payback," the sergeant told him, "for the one who had been shot and killed." As for the rest of his men, Chang barked out several orders, and most of the North Korean army regulars fell into their ranks and started back down the path, toward the field below. The two that lingered behind picked up the body of their fallen comrade, and carried him honorably between them.

"Further conflict between us is quite unnecessary," Chi said, stating the obvious.

As the general scrambled to keep pace with his men along the path, Chang turned to face Wang Chi, his eyes flashing. "Comrade, you will come back to us one day. No one ever leaves the State Security Service."

"We'll just see about that, General, won't we?" he laughed shortly.

As the Huey transformed into a spec on the horizon, Chi and his men melted back into their surroundings and were nothing but ghosts as several squad cars from the SFPD converged on the serene locale, but they found nothing. No helicopter and no armed men, as had been reported by several visitors to the park—nothing but a pool of blood in the grass.

CHAPTER FIVE

Barron Brown had been flying helicopters for Aventura Air for more than twenty years. The majority of his missions were short ones. They called for picking up rich, corporate clients at their hotels in the downtown area, and getting them out to San Francisco International Airport on time for their flights home. Tuesday's flight was no different. He had been contracted to pick up a group of Asian models and their handler at the Fairmont, and deliver them to the airport so they could catch their 7:55 pm Korean Air flight back home. He thought that it was rather unusual for models to be booked at the Fairmont. Perched high atop Nob Hill, the venerable Fairmont was the hotel where Tony Bennett first crooned, "I left my heart in San Francisco," and the rich and the famous enjoyed gilded opulence unlike any other hotel in the city. Presidents, kings, and other heads of state stayed at the Fairmont, while fashion models typically stayed at the Hilton or the Hyatt or the Marriott. Even more unusual was the fact that they were staying in the presidential Suite. Built in 1926, the Fairmont had San Francisco's most fabulous presidential suite, complete with an outdoor terrace and a movable bookcase in the library that concealed a secret staircase to the rooftop helipad. There was something odd about the whole set-up.

So, when he heard on the news at noon the police were looking for five Asian women who may have come into contact with a unique strain of the flu, Brown put two and two together, and called 911.

At the Hall of Justice, Dawson ran down the corridor, and stuck her head in the cubicle Morris had been assigned, "We may have gotten our first break!"

"You're kidding?" he asked, looking up from his desk.

"No," she replied, breathing hard. "A pilot who runs a shuttle service between the airport and the downtown area hotels confirmed that he has a scheduled pick-up this afternoon for several Asian women and their handler."

"Where?" he returned.

"The Fairmont," she added, with a smile. "It has a helipad that's accessible only through a hidden stairway in the Presidential Suite. It's just the sort of thing I would have imagined them hiding in. It's about two blocks from Chinatown, and rumor has it there are a series of tunnels that connect the two."

"We've got to make sure they don't get into those tunnels."

Dawson nodded. "Our staging area is Huntington park, which is two blocks west, in the opposite direction from Chinatown."

"So, what are we waiting for?" Morris asked.

"Get suited up. We're going in full body armor," Kate told him, more of an order than a command, as she headed to the motor pool for deployment.

Fifty-five minutes later, Kate Dawson walked the perimeter of Huntington Park, observing the frenzy of activity as the might of the San Francisco Police Department had descended on the quiet little park just northwest of the downtown area. First, uniformed police officers in patrol cars had cordoned off a three-block radius around the Fairmont Hotel, and had begun re-routing traffic and other passersby to alternate routes around California and Mason streets, which was considered ground zero. Next, unarmed predator drones began crisscrossing the air space above the Fairmont, maintaining an eye-in-the-sky presence for all those on the ground. Then, members of the elite SWAT unit were deployed to respond to and manage the high risk and potentially volatile situation with their military-style weapons and specialized tactics. Snipers were posted on the roof of the Fairmont's vintage-1961 tower and near the helipad, so they wouldn't be able to fly the girls out at the last moment. A handful of other SWAT team members were sequestered on the roof near the presidential Suite, with gas masks at the ready. And finally, plain-clothed detectives infiltrated the lobby, corridors and restaurant of the hotel. They were about as ready as they could be. They were just waiting for the Chief of Police, the highest ranking member of the SFPD, to supervise the operations.

As intel continued to pour into her location, Dawson went over the last of the reports, nervously consulting her watch. They had to move no later than 4:05 pm, if they planned on catching the group before they boarded the helicopter. Once they were on the move, the possibility of losing them or incurring hostages loomed as very real factors. Intelligence reports from the Fairmont Hotel concluded that there were five Asian women and one Asian man holed-up in the Presidential Suite. They had checked into the hotel over the weekend, and had maintained a very low profile, keeping largely to themselves and making few appearances in the hotel itself or the surrounding neighborhood in the last forty-eight hours. Room service and the hotel's excellent housekeeping staff had already confirmed that all six of the Asians were all there which was very good news. With any luck—Kate crossed her fingers—they'd swoop right down and catch the lot of them.

"This had better be good, Dawson," snapped the Chief of Police, as he stepped out of the back of his Lincoln Town Car. Nelson Gates was a stocky man in his early fifties with salt-and-pepper hair. He was dressed in full body armor, and at that particular moment in time reminded Dawson of Teddy Roosevelt, the gung-ho leader who was ready to lead his men on a charge into hell itself, if it was necessary. "I passed on a very important meeting with the City Council members over the "sick-out" in order to be out here with the men. You damn well better not disappoint me."

Lieutenant Roberts followed him out of the car.

He had heard what the Chief said, and felt it necessary to add, "Inspector Dawson has been on top of this case right from the beginning, Chief."

"Okay, so what's the situation?"

"The five women and their handler are in the presidential Suite on the sixth floor," she explained, handing the Chief of Police a pair of binoculars and pointing at the Fairmont Hotel a couple of blocks away.

"When I give the word, they're going to shut off power to the elevators, and cut all power going into the suite. The forward command will then lead an elite team of SWAT members into the room, and seize all six hostiles. They're equipped with gas masks just in case the hostiles somehow manage to trigger the cyanide gas. I also have men posted on the roof and the nearby tower just in case they try to make a run for it."

"How good is your intelligence, Dawson?" he asked, surveying the front of the hotel from his vantage point with the binoculars.

Kate swallowed down hard. "We've confirmed there are six Asians in the room, five women and one man. They've been holed-up in the Presidential Suite since Sunday, but no one has seen them other than housekeeping. Honestly, I cannot confirm or deny this is the group we're looking for."

"What's your gut telling you, Dawson?"

"I don't know, sir," she replied, after a moment's hesitation. "I'd like permission to have a look for myself, Chief. I could get into the suite disguised as a member of the housekeeping staff, dropping off towels."

The Chief of Police shook his head. "Negative. I'm not going to hand them over a potential hostage. Besides from what Roberts tells me, their 'handler' got a pretty good look at you in his office."

"What do you think we should do, sir?"

"Well, in about five minutes, they're going to have the might of the SFPD descend upon them!" he exclaimed, ready to kick some ass. "We'll let God sort it out once the firefight is over."

With binoculars held to his face, the Chief of Police surveyed the Fairmont from a safe distance, like a general looking over the battlefield before the first volley of cannon fire. Plain-clothed officers lurked in the doors, the lobby, and corridors of the beautiful hotel, while members of the SWAT team were deployed on the roof and helipad, their black suits and body armor a stark contrast against the elegant marble and stone that had once defined the world of luxury from a bygone era. A handful of others had flattened themselves on the tower with their sniper rifles and high-powered scopes. Their weapons drawn, uniformed policemen crouched down behind their squad cars that formed the make-shift cordon around California and Mason streets. They watched and waited for the signal to converge on the hotel. Other cops scrambled along the edges and in shadows of the area.

The air was filled with thick tension that could almost be cut with a knife as members of the SFPD readied for the attack.

"Sometimes, Dawson, you got to make the tough decisions, if you want to be a leader," he said, lecturing her about command. "It's not for everyone. Only the best of the best are called upon to lead."

"I'd like to join my partner and the others in the forward command, sir," Kate asked, humbly, but not one to kiss ass.

The Chief shot a glance over his shoulder at Dawson. "I do hope you've alerted the local media. I'd like them to see my boys in action, and then maybe we could silent those bleeding-heart liberals on the left."

Dawson nodded. "Yes, sir. It's all been taken care of."

"Outstanding," he remarked, pushing through the cordon and moving brusquely past the police officers who were stationed around the perimeter of the hotel. He took large, broad steps, and walking quickly, he crossed the divide in no time at all and ambled into the lobby of the Fairmont, with Kate and Lieutenant Roberts close at hand.

"Poor devils. I actually feel sorry for them. But then, they knew the risks of going up against a superior force, like the SFPD. By the time they figure out what hit 'em, they'll all be in body bags."

"Don't you think we should give them a chance to surrender?" Kate asked, with a panicked look on her face.

The Chief shook his head. "No, the last thing we want to do is give them time to think. If we do, they'll trigger the cyanide gas."

"But what if they're not the hostiles we're seeking?"

"Let me deal with that, Inspector," he replied, growing fatigued of her questions. "Command decisions are better left to commanders."

"Chief, we're just about ready," said one of the SWAT unit commanders, as he stepped forward and saluted.

"I'm coming," the Chief replied, stomping up to the fourth floor.

Another unit commander with a walkie-talkie stopped him. "I've got Spencer on the radio, Chief. He's in the forward command."

"Spencer," the Chief spoke into the radio.

"Yo," was the only response he gave.

"Get ready to kick some ass!" he ordered, then handed the walkie-talkie back to the unit commander.

"Sir, I really think this is a bad idea," Dawson pleaded.

The Chief of Police ignored her, as he took a second walkie-talkie in hand. "Have you noticed any movement at all in the Presidential Suite?" he asked one of his two top snipers, positioned in the tower.

"None whatsoever, Chief," the first sniper replied.

"Sir, everything looks quiet over there," the second sniper added. "They're just sitting around, waiting for the 'copter to arrive."

"Okay, time to get this show on the road," the Chief said. He looked down at his watch, counted down ten seconds, and then shouted, "Go!"

Dawson looked terrified, as the Chief's men took off running. "I hope you know what you're doing, Chief."

"Anytime you want to go home, Dawson" he said, turning away from her in disgust, "consider yourself dismissed."

She and the Chief of Police exchanged glances, like the crossing of swords. "No, sir. You couldn't drag me away."

Seconds later, the SWAT team stormed into the presidential Suite, like a group of Leathernecks taking a beachhead, and swarmed all over the suite, knocking over lamps and destroying rare antiques, carelessly, like the proverbial bull in a china shop. The two hotel room guests, who had been lounging comfortably on the furniture, were pushed to their knees by members of the SWAT team, and forced to lock their fingers behind their heads as a form of surrender. The one Asian woman was crying out in terror, while the solitary man who looked more like a gardener than a handler kept his face down on the floor, in total obedience. Older and a bit wiser, he knew that surrender was the only way to prevent things from escalating into a massacre. They dragged a second woman out of the bathroom by her hair, and made her sit on her knees, with her fingers interlocked behind her head. The look of fear flashed across her face, but she was smart enough to keep it to herself.

Two SWAT team members, armed with M-5 machine guns, then peeled away from the rest of the group, and began searching through the bedrooms on the first floor of the suite, one by one. They were perfectly coordinated in their actions. As one of them opened a door, the other looked inside from the hallway, and then the two moved on quickly to the next. They charged down the hallway very quickly, moving fast through each of the bedrooms. At the end of the corridor, they reached the fifth bedroom and threw open the door to reveal two of the Asian women in the throes of passionate lovemaking on the bed. The two SWAT guys smiled at each other, then entered the room. A moment later, the first woman, trying desperately to pull up her sweats, and the second woman, buttoning her blouse, were pushed out into the hall, and forced to join the others in the living room.

Within a matter of moments, the siege was over.

Five of the hotel room guests had been herded into the center of the living room where small tables and chairs had been pulled back to create a make-shift fort. Several of the girls were whimpering, while the Asian man kept his head down. The youngest of the girls kept looking around the room for someone. She was so intent on this that she didn't see the SWAT guy waving her forward into the circle. Exasperated, he simply shoved her forward, and she glared at him.

When Kate Dawson finally wandered into the suite, followed by Agent Morris, Lieutenant Roberts, and the Chief of Police, she was mortified. She knew immediately that they had made a terrible mistake, and holstered her Beretta handgun. The Asian women who had been bunched together were young and vibrant, but Just not young enough. She guessed that they were likely in their mid-twenties, and looked a lot like the young models from the Korean Air commercials that had been running regularly on the television. They were not the teenaged slaves from the Sunday evening slave auction.

Their handler was Chinese, but he didn't look a thing like Wang Chi, and was in fact little more than a chauffeur and baggage handler.

The Chief of Police stepped up on top of a desk, and looked over the group. He reached into his pocket for the court order that had given him permission for the raid, and began to unfold it slowly when a fifth Asian woman appeared.

"What is the meaning of this *intrusion*?" demanded the Chinese woman.

Dawson and the others turned. Standing at the top of the stairs was a beautiful brunette, her brown eyes almost black and set wide. Her cheekbones would have been the envy of any fashion model in the West, and her thin lips were bigger and brighter with red lip gloss. She wore a black and gold embroidered blouse, blue jeans, and black, high-heeled shoes with a splash of gold.

Lovely, thirty-eight-year-old Ziyi Zhang, the famous Chinese actress from *Crouching Tiger, Hidden Dragon* (2000) and *Memoirs of a Geisha* (2005), walked down the winding staircase from above. In spite of her diminutive size, she looked like the kind of woman who was used to getting her way.

"We're sorry to disturb you," said Dawson, as the backup lights came on, "we thought you were a group of—"

"Are you Immigration?" asked the Chinese woman coolly. If she was frightened of the police, then she was doing an excellent job of hiding her fears behind a calm exterior. "I assure you all of our paperwork is in order."

"Homicide," said Lieutenant Roberts.

Ziyi Zhang nodded to herself, processing the information slowly but efficiently through her brain.

"What do you want?"

Dawson hesitated a moment, then said, "I'm afraid, Madame Zhang, we've made a big mistake. Please accept my apology on behalf of the City of San Francisco—"

"I don't understand," Ziyi replied.

A half hour later, the Chief of Police walked out the front door of the Fairmont Hotel with a handful of his men, and pushed his way through the press that had gathered with their lights and television cameras and microphones. He didn't have anything to say to them, but a spokesperson for the SFPD was doing a fast repair job on the police department's image. The spokesperson stood with reporters from the big three networks, and discussed the hard work, training and dedication that it took to be a member of the police force. He then said that it was important for the department to run impromptu tests regularly to see if they were ready to handle a real emergency. He apologized as sorrowfully as he could for the snafu in communications that must have led them to believe it was an actual emergency. The spokesperson smiled a faraway smile, as he spoke with them, but kept the specific details of the operation and its outcome to the barest minimum.

"Roberts," the Chief of Police said curtly, "I've never been so humiliated in all of my life. Your 'man' should be taken off this assignment immediately. See if she can make coffee and file reports because, quite frankly, she's no good to me as a detective." He continued walking on to Huntington Park with his men. "I'll see you back at the Hall of Justice."

"I'll have to do what he says," the Lieutenant confessed, turning back to Dawson.

She smiled thinly at him. "I know."

When they reached Roberts' battered 1980 Cadillac Seville, parked along Mason Street, the three of them had walked nearly a block without saying a word.

He had a certain amount of trouble stuffing his large frame into the all-leather interior. Clearly, the man was a hundred pounds overweight, but he didn't seem to care and was not the least bit worried about his image. He revved the engine a couple of times, like a dragster, then roared off into the night. She and Morris continued walking another block, and found her car parked on the street in front of Huntington Park.

"I wouldn't want to be the civil servant picking up the tab on this one," Kate said, off-handedly to Morris. "I can just imagine the City of San Francisco is going to pay royally for all the damages."

"I'm more inclined to think about the litigious repercussions that are going to come out of the rough handling of Ziyi Zhang and her party. Some attorney is going to be making a fortune from their claim."

She shook her head. "Are you kidding me? Several fortunes. Zhang is going to hire the biggest and best law firm in Hollywood, and sue their asses off!"

"Grab some dinner?" Morris asked, as he climbed into the passenger side door.

"I can't," Kate replied, putting her key into the ignition and starting the car. "I've got a date tonight. But honestly, after today's events, what I should do is go home, and soak my head in a bucket of cold water."

"It wasn't your fault, Kate," Morris said, trying to comfort her. "We both saw, with our own eyes, how eager he was to get his men into combat."

"I should have known better."

"I don't see how."

They drove several blocks away from the Fairmont in silence. Gregory Morris seemed anxious to talk with her, and changed topics. "So, who's this week's lucky contestant?" he asked her.

"Jonathan Prinze," she said, with a twinkle.

Morris shook his head. "I'm sorry. What was his name?" he asked, shooting her a sideways glance. "I could have sworn you just said 'Jonathan Prinze.' But that can't be right. Isn't he the suspect on trial for snapping his girlfriend's neck, and then throwing her down a flight of stairs?"

"Yeah, that's him," she replied, pulling away from the curb.

"I don't think that's a very good idea, Dawson. I don't care whether you're attracted to him or his millions, but that is a serious conflict of interest. You know that you could get suspended just for looking at the guy the wrong way."

"Relax. I'm not that crazy," Kate said, with a forced chuckle. "I just wanted to see if I could get a rise out of you."

Morris glanced at her again. "You mean 'you're joking' with me."

"Yeah. My date's name is Charles Moran."

"Ha, ha. Very funny."

Dawson stared off, down the road. "You know, I've been trying to decide all day whether to go through with it or not. I was out last night on another blind date, and I keep thinking, if I had been home, maybe I could have done something that prevented Rosa's death. I know that doesn't make any sense."

"You've told me that Rosa Romano was your best friend," he reminded her. "The last thing she would have wanted was for you to stop living your life."

"Yeah, I know that," she replied. "It's just sort of funny, but the last time we talked, I told Rosa I had a date. She seemed happy for me."

"I'm sure she was," Morris said, as he checked the time on his watch. "What time were you supposed to meet your mystery date?"

"Six-*ish*."

"It's nearly five-forty," he reported.

"You see, I'll never make it," Dawson said, shaking her head. "I'd be better off just calling and canceling the date. So would he."

"No way, Kate. He's already there, waiting for you at the restaurant."

She shrugged. "How do you know, Morris?"

"Because if it was me, that's what I would do," he replied, looking out the window at the two names at the intersection. "Pull over at the next street. I'll walk over to Columbus, and pick up the cable car there."

"Are you sure about this?" she asked, growing nervous.

"Yes," he replied. "You never know. This guy might be the one."

"A stockbroker?"

Dawson pulled over at Lombard, and watched Morris cross the street, heading for the Powell-Mason cable car line that stopped on Columbus. She sat there, until he was way out of sight, and then banged her head against the steering wheel. After her last date, with the guy who wouldn't stop talking about his investments, she'd been hesitant to meet another blind date. In fact, she considered canceling the date several times, but the thought of Rosa Romano scolding her—from beyond the grave—was just too much for her to bear emotionally at that point. Kate did a complete U-turn, and headed towards Fisherman's Wharf. With some encouragement from Morris, she had decided she'd rather sit through an hour-long lecture about tax annuities than spend the rest of the week tossing and turning in bed.

Kate had a change of clothes in the trunk of the car. At Fisherman's Wharf, she went into one of the public restrooms, and threw on some makeup, then changed into a pair of slacks and her nice Versace blazer, but kept her comfort shoes. They had agreed to meet at the restaurant on Forbes Island, located in the world famous Sea Lion Harbor, between Piers 39 and 41. She was already running late when she validated her parking at the Pier 39 Parking Garage, and jumped onto the complimentary shuttle boat that provided the only access to the island. She couldn't seem to shake off her sense of nerves.

Forbes Island Restaurant was something a little different, a dining experience almost entirely underwater.

In fact, the novelty of the restaurant was that it was the only restaurant actually in San Francisco Bay. Inside, with portholes over each of the tables, casual diners could imagine they were on a submarine, like the Nautilus, taking a long sea voyage. The view through the underwater portholes, where the little fish swam by and the crabs played, was awe-inspiring, and so too was the décor, a catacomb of amazingly decorated rooms and antiques with a magical, nautical fantasy motif. Kate half-expected Captain Nemo to emerge from the underwater bar's wine cellar dressed in a Victorian diving suit and announce they had just completed their journey 20,000 leagues under the sea. Almost all the tables were full of guests enjoying a delicious gourmet meal. Large chandeliers provided the largest room with a warm glow and the atmosphere was one of utter contentment. Gentle piano music lulled the diners into a sense of relaxation and amour. Above them towered a forty-foot lighthouse, with amazing views of Alcatraz and the Bay, giant palm trees and white sand patios that completed the total island experience, nestled right in the heart of the bay.

As Dawson hurried into the larger dining hall, a stocky man with slicked back, thinning black hair and a moustache, stood up to receive his guest. The first thing that crossed Kate's mind was how different he looked from his profile photos; in which he looked fit and trim, and considerably younger. Even though he was supposed to be a wealthy stockbroker, he embodied the image of a jolly, French baker who had eaten too many of his own pastries to be healthy, fit and trim. The two shook hands and she gave him a polite peck on the cheek before they were seated. A young, fresh-faced maître d' brought the couple a bottle of champagne, took their meal order and left them a bowl of thick olive oil and complimentary dipping bread. She and her date raised glasses and toasted, then he took a generous mouthful of the champagne and it brought instant rosy-red color to his cheeks.

"Bollinger, '74. I see you are a connoisseur, Charles," she said, observing the bottle of champagne he had ordered.

"I like fine wines and champagnes, Kate," he replied, taking another gulp. "I would have preferred the Laffite Rothschild '69, but as their wine cellar was so poorly stocked, I had to settle for the Bollinger."

"Oh, it seems like such a lovely choice," she remarked.

Moran raised his glass again to Dawson.

"Cheers!"

"Cheers!" she replied, as she took another sip.

The champagne tasted dry yet sweet and was instantly better than anything else she had had. "It's good."

Charles Moran took out a gold Mont Blanc pen and a small notebook. "Do you have a favorite wine or champagne? I'd like to add it to my list."

"To be perfectly honest, I don't care much for wines or champagnes. The bubbles in champagne always tickle my nose. I prefer a full-bodied beer, often with a bourbon chaser," she confessed, revealing her common tastes. "You like beer, Chuck?"

"Not especially," he answered, with a distasteful frown. "And my name is Charles. Not Chuck, and certainly, not Charlie."

"Okay, fine. Charles," she repeated. "You can call me Kate or Katherine. Just don't call me 'late for dinner.'"

Moran didn't laugh at her joke. Instead, he started on the bread and oil, all the time keeping an eye her.

"Katherine, what kind of food do you like?"

"I love a good hot dog," Kate replied. "AT&T Park. September. Hot dogs have been boiling since the opening day in April. Now, that's a hot dog."

Moran raised an eyebrow. "But wouldn't you rather have a good steak? Filet mignon? Porterhouse?"

"I'm afraid that a filet mignon would be wasted on me, Charles. My pallet is not very sophisticated. It comes from years of stakeouts when we'd have to eat a lot of carry-out food, from hamburgers and French fries to kung-pow chicken."

"You're the cop," he said, with a surprised look.

Dawson looked modest as she was about to identify herself. She said, "I work as a detective in Homicide for the SFPD—"

"The SFPD! What a bunch of boneheads!" Moran exclaimed,

and then made fast work of apologizing to her when he realized the connection. "Sorry, Kate, I didn't mean to suggest that you were a bonehead. It's just that I watched the media coverage this afternoon on CNN, and I can't believe how stupid they were in assaulting that China doll and her entourage in the President's Suite at the Fairmont."

"I must have missed that broadcast," she said coyly.

"Well, take it from me, they seriously screwed the pooch on that one," he replied, as the house lights dimmed. Dawson noted a shadow moving upon the portal directly over them, but didn't make a big deal of it.

The audience clapped as the head maître d' walked onto the small stage, revealing a glamorous string quartet and solo guitarist. "Ladies and gentlemen, in honor of our tenth anniversary, it is my pleasure to present Dominique."

A beautiful woman in her early twenties, wearing nothing but a powder-blue gown, took to the stage. She picked up a guitar, and sat in a chair on stage as the restaurant went quiet in anticipation. The quartet began a soft piece by Mansini, while she strummed the guitar and sang the hauntingly tender beat. A lovely sight, thought Dawson, but basic entertainment done on the cheap. She turned to her date to say something, but she noticed that he was totally transfixed on the girl, his sly look turning from awe to infatuation with each note she sang. During the song, the waiter served their two starters, which included a rich tomato and herb soup for Moran and a small salmon soufflé for Dawson.

Her date still hadn't taken his eyes from the lovely guitarist, but did manage to say, "I've seen her perform every night for the last two weeks, and the more I listen to her sing, the deeper I grow in love with her."

Dawson tried simply to ignore the comment, and to bring

focus back on the meal, but it was difficult. The more she stared at Moran, the more she wondered why this connoisseur of food and drink had even bothered to contact her in the first place. They had nothing in common, and his comments about the SFPD were downright insulting. Kate wondered if she had gotten up at that moment, and left the restaurant, if Moran would have even noticed. He seemed to be so infatuated with the guitarist.

Out of character, she leaned over to check the cell phone in her purse for the time, and at that very instant, a blow dart struck Moran in the side of neck with a sickening pop as the guitar solo reached its coincidental climax. Dawson didn't have time to register the shock in Moran's face before he collapsed dead, face first into his soup, but realized that the blow dart had been meant for her. The guitarist screamed in terror as she saw the dead man fall, but soon the whole restaurant was on its feet in pandemonium, trying to get a look at what happened.

Kate Dawson reached inside her Versace jacket and withdrew her 9mm Beretta from the triple-draw shoulder holster she had on her left shoulder. She gripped the gun tightly in her right hand, and then reached over and checked Charles Moran's pulse but found none. Dawson noted the shadow upon one of the portholes had turned and fled out of the service exit door. Their waiter came running up with the look of sheer panic on his face.

"*Qu'est-ce qu'il y a*, Madame?" he screamed in French.

"Call 911, and don't touch anything," shouted Dawson, dashing through the crowd to the exit, following the assassin.

A single drop of blood ran down Moran's neck and dripped onto to the white tablecloth. At the carotid artery, a plastic dart with a poison-coated tip, was all that remained of the crime.

Bounding out the service door, the assassin knocked over a

couple of diners on their way out of the restaurant, and vaulted over a railing, leading up to the forty-foot lighthouse and its large, metal winding staircase. As this area was currently closed to the public, the assassin had free reign over the metal structure heading up the outer lattice of the tower.

Dawson blasted out of the exit, with her service weapon in hand, and following the shouts and pointing of the scattered tourists in the court, knew exactly where to go. She headed for the railing, once more shoulder-butting the confused diners out of the way, and jumped over, leaving them in a whirlwind of bewilderment. She tore off her jacket and cast it aside. She then raced for the lighthouse, and threw open the door, moments behind the figure in black robes as he continued racing up the stairs, carrying his blowgun. Dawson caught her breath, already finding the staircase tricky to navigate in bare feet, and traced her path to the assassin above. The only handrail was on the inside, against the wall, while there was nothing protecting her from falling down the center shaft to her death on the concrete floor below.

A billow of black caught her eye from above, and she fired two shots from her Beretta, impacting on a rung inches below the assassin with a metallic ring. The figure took the blowgun and threw it down the stairs at Dawson.

As she covered her face to shield it from any other toxic dart, the bamboo weapon struck her ankle, and she missed a step, falling hard on the metal stairs. Dawson had to grip the inside edge of the stairs, holding herself back from totally falling over the edge and to her death. As the blowgun was flung away in panic, the mystery figure continued to ascend the staircase. Losing valuable time, she had no choice but to stop and climb back safely onto the stairs and take hold of the outside handrail. She limped to her feet, and continued the dangerous climb.

The door to the lighthouse was looking smaller and more distant with each step.

She fired another two shots upwards with the hopes of hitting or injuring the assassin, but to no avail, as they echoed through the lattice impacting on the metal framework. In a change of tactic, the assassin cleared a set of stairs now a few levels from the top of the tower itself and climbed over the protective metal railings onto the outer beams with nothing to stop his fall. Expertly and nimbly, the figure climbed out the window towards the outer edge with no apparent way to go, except a fall down to the gardens below. Dawson's bare footsteps could be heard coming up the stairs. The figure saw her arrive on the stairs and wasted no time, jumping spread eagle off the tower beam. Dawson reached the railing, and simply watched the figure fall. She imagined that he was trying to take flight in order to reach the Bay just beyond the manmade island, but he never made it. The assassin's body hit the outdoor patio with a thud that she heard forty-feet away in the tower.

After she descended, Dawson walked out onto the patio and found that a crowd of onlookers had gathered around the body. The crowd was comprised mostly of a half dozen diners, all curious to get a look. They parted as Kate approached, as if she carried the plague. She crouched down, right next to the body, and carefully moved the assassin's neck from side to side to conclude that he had broken his neck in the fall. She holstered her sidearm, and then conducted a routine frisk, working her way up-and-down the body. She found nothing in the assassin's pockets, except lint. No identification. No money. No car keys or transit pass. Obviously, he had been traveling light in his mission to kill her. The only thing she could find as far as distinguishing features was a small tattoo on his left arm. It looked like three roses that were linked together by thorns. *A Tong sign*, she thought to herself, and swallowed hard.

Within twenty minutes, the usual crime-scene carnival had descended on Forbes Island, and taken over parts of Fisherman's Wharf and the ferry. Several police cars, their red lights flashing, were parked at strategic spots between Piers 39 and 41, along Beach Street and the Embarcadero, to discourage any curiosity seekers, but they still managed to gain access to the quaint, little island through the complimentary shuttle, which continued to run, ferrying police personnel back and forth. The turnout had been bigger than the previous crime scene, but not by much. Considering that there had been a police shooting, the numbers were pitifully low, with most officers choosing the 'faux flu.' Still, as Dawson looked around, there was a healthy police presence there, with uniformed officers directing people away from the actual crime scene and plain-clothed detectives taking statements from eyewitnesses who had seen the whole thing go down.

As she paced back and forth, Dawson watched a few of the crime-scene boys working the body, while Lieutenant Roberts, Clark and Jawara, and several uniformed officers stood around and observed. None of them looked very happy to see Kate, not after the fiasco from earlier that day, but she was none too keen to see any of them either. Everybody had been so eager to blame her for what had happened at the Fairmont that nobody had bothered to ask her side of the story. She didn't think it was very fair. As far as she was concerned, if anyone was to blame, it was her gung-ho Chief of Police. He had been so excited about scoring points with the press that he lost site of the big picture. She had warned the Chief—had begged him to let her confirm the identity of those in the Presidential Suite—but he just didn't care.

"Is there anything more that you'd like to add to your

statement?" asked Ramirez, taking down her account of the evening's events in a formal report.

"No," she said, flatly. "Let's just get this over with."

"Kate, I'm going to ask you to read this over carefully," Ramirez said, as he finalized the document for her, "and sign it for me."

But before Ramirez could turn the statement over to her, Roberts ripped the document out of his hands and waved it under her nose.

"This crock of shit is your statement? You're not actually going to sign your name to this garbage, are you? Ever heard the word 'perjury' before?"

"Why shouldn't I sign it?" Dawson asked. "It's all true."

Roberts slapped the statement with the back of his hand, as if hoping to punish the words themselves for being false. "Let me get this straight, Dawson. You're having dinner with a man you met on one of those dating sites, and all at once, some ninja assassin shows up and fires a poison dart at you. It conveniently misses you, but strikes your date. Dead. You take chase after the assassin, and when you have him cornered in the lighthouse, he leaps from the tower to his death. You really expect me to believe this fantasy?"

"Well, Lieutenant, that's how it happened," she replied.

"Bullshit! This is all bullshit!" Roberts repeated, crumpling up her statement in his fist, and tossing it aside.

"Ninja assassins? Poison darts?"

Clark butted in. "Lieutenant, it's been a long day for all of us. Why don't we just pick this up in the morning?"

The head of Homicide waved his top detective off.

"I'm tired of you fucking with me, Dawson," he said, raising his voice. "I don't need a reason to lock your ass up overnight. I've got plenty."

"What do you want from me, sir?"

"Your resignation."

"I'm not going to quit, sir," she insisted.

Roberts was on the verge of blowing his top.

"You're obviously dressed for a night out, Dawson. Did you stop along the way and have a drink, or two? And then maybe, have some wine with dinner, a couple of cocktails?"

Jawara interceded, walking in between the two of them. "You don't have to answer that, Kate. In fact, you don't have to answer any of his questions without a union representative being present. That is the correct action, *sir*."

"It's really up to her," the Lieutenant replied, looking at Jawara.

"I think I'm going to listen to Mikhail," she said like a deer in headlights.

Roberts nodded. "Did the crime scene boys already take your side arm for ballistics?"

"No, sir," Dawson replied.

"Give me your gun, Dawson," the head of Homicide demanded.

"Jesus Christ, Lieutenant," Clark said quietly, "Kate is one of ours. Couldn't you just go a bit easier on her?"

"No, we have to exercise due diligence on this one, or the press is going to have a field day. Just give me your gun, Dawson."

Dawson shrugged, slipped the weapon out of her shoulder holster, and handed it over. The head of Homicide took it by the barrel, and placed it safely into a large, plastic zip-lock bag. He passed the gun to one of the crime scene boys who, in turn, logged the weapon into the crime scene ledger and locked it away.

"Okay, so now what?" she asked.

"You're going on administrative leave, Dawson," Roberts replied, angry. He couldn't look her in the face, and instead turned away. He was going to stalk away into the night, but she stopped him before he got a few feet away.

"For how long?" Dawson asked.

The head of Homicide froze in his tracks, and turned slowly around. "Department policy mandates ten calendar days, but in no way is it punitive," he answered, somewhat mechanically. "I'll need to have you escorted from the scene."

Jawara stepped forward. "I'll do it."

"I'm fine," she said. "I can walk out of here on my own."

"This is mandatory procedure," Roberts reminded them.

Dawson looked from face to face. She said, "I guess I'll see you in ten days." She and Jawara headed back towards the restaurant.

Two morgue assistants were lifting the assassin's body from the outdoor patio onto a gurney, as they walked by. His dead, sightless eyes were open and staring right at Kate, and that image stayed with her the rest of the night.

A few minutes after 10 pm, Kate caught the water taxi back to Fisherman's Wharf, and reclaimed her car from the parking garage at Pier 39. She drove towards South Beach, taking the long route along the Embarcadero. A light rain was starting to fall when she pulled onto Delancey Street, and made the turn-off for Bayside Village Apartments. She rolled to a stop at the curb in front of her building, and killed the engine of her BMW 5.25i sedan. The only sound was the rain tapping lightly on the roof as she reached around the backseat of her car and grabbed her briefcase.

Dawson climbed the steps to the third floor, and walked down the length of the corridor. As she approached Lenny Provolone's apartment, she paused for a moment outside his door. The lights were on, and she could hear movement inside the apartment. She had not seen him since early Monday morning, the same night they argued about his participation in the slave auction.

For the last several months, Lenny had been so obsessed with her friend Rosa she found it hard to believe that he had stuffed his pants pockets with thousands of dollars in in order to buy himself a young, Asian sex slave. She knew him to be narcissistic, but never a callous man.

Kate had not bothered to stop by his apartment and talk about Rosa's death. So much had happened in twenty-four hours, she decided to knock on his front door.

"Lenny, this Kate," she said, after a couple of knocks.

"Are you okay? Is everything all right?"

"Who is it? What do you want?" he asked, sounding dazed and confused, as if he had been awakened from a sound sleep.

"This is Kate. Kate Dawson. Open the door, Lenny."

"What's wrong? What's the matter, Kate?" he replied, cracking the door and cautiously peeking out through the crack. "You're not here to borrow my car again, are you?"

"No, I don't need your car," Kate replied, with a smile, remembering that she had indeed borrowed his car a couple of times. "I haven't seen you since Monday, and I just wanted to know how you were holding up."

"Okay? Now's not a good time," he stammered, closing the door up tight.

"Have you got a girl in there?" she teased him, all in good fun.

"No," he said nervously, cracking the door partially open again. "What gives you that idea?"

She pointed down at a trail of clothes that started at the front door. "I can see women's clothing on the floor."

"I just haven't picked up in a while," he lied, turning from the trail.

Dawson pushed the door wide open, and he stepped back and away, leaving a clear pathway into the front sitting room. She took a couple of steps, leaned over, and scooped up a woman's brassiere, an expensive one from a top designer, size 34-D. Kate held it out in front of Lenny, who was still wearing the same motheaten, dingy gray t-shirt and briefs from Fruit of the Loom that he always wore around the apartment, and said, "Since when did you start wearing women's underwear from Victoria Secret?"

Lenny snatched it out of her hands, and tucked it behind him, saying, annoyed, "What do you want, Kate?"

"I've got some bad news, Lenny," she said finally, the life gone completely out of her.

"Can't it wait until morning?"

"No, it can't wait," Kate insisted.

"Big boy, get your buns back in here. I'm horny, and I want you two or three more times before I have to go home," a woman's voice called from the bedroom.

"So, you do have a girl in there?" Dawson whispered, quickly retracing her steps back to the front door. Her face was flushed red with embarrassment.

"It's Rebecca," Lenny replied, with a lowered voice.

"Rebecca? Isn't she the one who filed the restraining order against you?"

He smiled and nodded, as if to himself. "Yeah, but after we had the chance to talk things through, we realized just how much we mean to each other."

"Lenny, that's crazy," she said, lowering her voice. "You know Rebecca's not very stable. She could snap at any moment, and then you'd be back in the slammer. You're just inviting trouble."

"I hate to be rude, Kate, but this is no concern of yours. I can handle her."

Dawson looked at him sharply. "She's a little girl, Lenny, half your age with emotional problems! I'm telling you she's going to be nothing but trouble."

"That's for me to decide, *not* you," he said. "So, what's this bad news?"

"Rosa Romano was—"

"Shit," Lenny swore out loud, totally out of his character. "I forgot to call her tonight. We were going to make plans to go see a movie this weekend. I guess I'm going to have to level with her now about my relationship with Rebecca."

"I'm sure she already knows," Kate replied.

"Why would you say that?"

Dawson hesitated a moment. "She's dead, Lenny," Kate said at last. "Rosa Romano died a couple of nights ago while conducting an autopsy on a body that was contaminated with a very deadly poison, Mylee."

"You're lying to me," he said, tears forming in his eyes.

"I wouldn't lie to you, Lenny. Not about Rosa."

He never took his eyes off her. "You've somehow made a mistake. She can't possibly be dead. Not Rosa. She was so full of life, and we'd made so many plans together. You've got her mixed up with someone else."

"I'm sorry, Lenny," Kate said softly. "She died on Tuesday night. In the line of duty."

"I don't believe you!" he shouted, slamming his door on her, crazed thoughts running through his head.

Kate lingered outside his apartment for a moment or two in silence. She was really worried about him, but had been unable to reach that part of him that needed reaching. Feeling very uneasy, she walked down the corridor to her apartment, and a night of troubled sleep.

CHAPTER SIX

Early on Wednesday morning, the sixth day of the "sick-out," Kate rode the Powell-Hyde cable car line north towards the Marina, across the Municipal Railway, and into the famous San Francisco Port. She felt a chill in the air, even as the last clouds of the evening shadowing the sunrise were beginning to dissipate in the earliest hours of the morning. Shadows from the tall buildings began playing their familiar game of hide and seek as the first rays of sunlight crept over the hills to the east, lengthening them at first and then, with each passing hour, reducing them back down to size. One of the most famous ports in all of America, the Port of San Francisco was simply *massive*. An enormous scale of large shipping and industrial imports and exports spanning nearly one hundred years was a magnificent sight. Smaller boats and ships belonging to fishermen, miners and other trades populated the ports and provided a rich and prosperous culture for the city. One of the best places in the city for fresh and local produce was at the ports themselves and a number of fresh fish stalls were set up along the jetties enticing the passers-by with that rich, salty, mouth-watering sea smells.

Dawson waited until her cable car had stopped at the port.

She then released the strap-handle and hopped onto the curb. She pulled her casual leather jacket tight around her as she walked along one of the docks towards Fisherman's Wharf. The cry of seagulls above was mixed with the shouts and busy conversation from traders and fisherman along the board-walk. The sun continued fighting its battle to break through the patches of cloud and low mist, but it was a losing battle, and it seemed like the day was going to be far cooler than she had earlier anticipated. Kate kept walking as the boardwalk became busier and busier thanks to the popular stalls selling fresh fish to patrons. The breeze whipped through her long, blonde hair and she inhaled the fresh air, making her feel refreshed and truly alive.

She continued walking by the stalls, taking in the sights and smells. Eventually, she came across a Chinese fishing stall which was bustling with people, buying up bizarre yet tasty foods fresh from the waters of the Bay.

The Chinese family behind the stall was very busy helping each customer in turn. Dawson stood to one side for a moment, waiting to catch the eye of the middle-aged Chinese man packing crates behind the counter. After a few moments, the man noticed that he was being watched by her. He packed yet another crate, and then stood up with a friendly smile.

"Looking for something special?" he asked.

"Yes," Dawson said, "soft-shell crabs."

A sly smirk crossed the man's face, and he replied, "Might have some in the back, ma'am. $32 per pound?"

"Fine," she replied.

Chinese man took off his gloves, and opened the side door to the stall. "I'll be a few minutes," he called back to one of his family members, and then took a brown envelope from under the counter with him.

Dawson met him at the side of the stall, and together they began to walk across the jetty. The man pulled a card from under his blood-stained apron, and handed it to Dawson. "Michael Lee, Pinkerton Detective Agency. It's a pleasure to be working with the SFPD, even in these trying times."

She let the comment go, like water off a duck's back. "Thanks, now what have you got on that tattoo I sent you?"

Lee nodded and opened the envelope, pulling out a photo-copy of an illustration of three roses that are intertwined by their thorns. When he showed her the illustration, Dawson nodded her head. He said, "The Morag Tong is an ancient guild of assassins that date back thousands of years to the very First Xia Dynasty. In fact, it has long been rumored that the guild served the first Emperor of China in his quest for the throne, eliminating all of his rivals. Typically, Tong assassins are hired by the Emperor or nobles from one of the Great Houses to target a particular individual in order to accomplish a political goal. It would be difficult for us to determine which great noble was responsible for contracting the writ of the Tong. Morag assassins are sworn to utmost secrecy, and are required to give themselves up immediately rather than reveal the person who contracted for the job."

"I have a pretty good idea," Kate said, with a grin.

"Inspector, once you are targeted by the Morag Tong, they will not stop until you are dead," Lee revealed.

He was in his mid-thirties and quite athletic with receding black hair and an American accent like he had been raised by popular culture. He was smaller than Dawson but had a very friendly face, round and cheery.

"Great!" she exclaimed, shaking her head from side to side. "So, then I can expect more blow-guns and poison darts?"

Lee shrugged his shoulders. "Every Morag Tong assassin is

different. This one used a blow-gun and poison darts, while the next one may employ a garrote. You never know until you have sprung their trap."

Dawson chewed over the information. "Were you able to get a line on Wang Chi? The five Asian women?"

Michael Lee chuckled to himself, sidestepping a box of crabs on the jetty in order to avoid stepping on it.

"Ah. You got a real winner there. He has been one of the most popular entertainers in Southeast Asia for the last ten years. He's won nearly every award that can be won, and five different countries, including China and Thailand, have offered him a home in their capitol. He's like the fuckin' Bob Hope of the East."

"Tell me something I don't know," she insisted.

"He is also a silent partner in one of the biggest sex cartels in Thailand," Lee reported. "Those five Asian women are his girls, and he stands to profit hundreds of thousands of dollars from their sale in the Asian sex trade."

"Any line on the girls?"

Lee nodded. "We tracked them back to a cargo ship, the MSC Fabiola, which tied up in Oakland to unload its cargo ten days ago. Apparently, they were shipped in one of those large, cargo containers, then smuggled into Oakland by their handlers."

"Anything more recent?"

"No, they seemed to have vanished into thin air."

"I still think they're hiding out somewhere in Chinatown," she surmised. "But in terms of cash for the girls, it's my guess they've already been sold, and for top dollar."

"To whom?"

"I don't no. Maybe North Korea?" Kate said, with a raised eyebrow.

"Sure. That would explain it," Lee said, pulling out several photographs and handling them all to Dawson.

The first was a typical passport photo of a burly man in uniform. The next was the first in a series of black-n-white snapshots taken at the Japanese tea garden, featuring Wang Chi's meeting with the North Korean general. The last one was a photograph of a dead body, actually one of the Korean soldiers. "This is General Ri Kyu-Chang. He's a hardliner from the Cold War days who used to run North Korea's nuclear arms program. Today, he is still highly respected among the party leadership, and is rumored to be Kim Jong-un's successor, if Kim ever steps down. He didn't seem to be getting along very well with Wang Chi yesterday. They seemed to talk, then they argued with one another, and finally Chi took out a pistol and killed one of Chang's northern army regulars."

Dawson stopped walking, and took her time to look through Lee's pictures. "So, he actually killed one of Chang's men?"

"That's right," he said. "Shot him point blank, right through the heart."

"Where did this exchange take place?"

"In Golden Gate Park," Lee replied, pointing to a couple of familiar markings in the photos. "By the japanese tea garden."

"I'm surprised you found Wang Chi so far outside the safety and comfort of Chinatown," she remarked, with a frown on her face.

Lee puffed his chest out. "You want me to pick him up for you?"

"No, not yet," Dawson replied, "but make sure you keep a good tail on him."

"Whatever you want, Inspector. The Pinkerton Detective Agency has a one hundred-seventy-five-year-old reputation to protect."

Dawson looked closely at one photo. "And who are all these people?"

169

"We figure the ones in the black fatigues are the north Korean army regulars," Lee said, providing commentary for several of the photographs. "They were choppered into the park by a Huey Bell UH-1 Iroquois. Once they'd landed, General Chang ordered his men to find and detain Chi. Given the fact that these others just suddenly appeared, we have concluded they infiltrated the park in disguise as ordinary visitors, and were ready to assist Wang Chi when necessary. They are, of course, local Tong. They probably belong to the Hip Sing Tong, but ultimately owe their allegiance to Lo Pan, the local mob boss."

"Yeah, I've had a run-in with him before."

"Lo Pan is a very influential man," Lee added.

"He's considered the Chinese Godfather for uniting all of the Tong in the States."

"So, it would appear that Wang Chi has changed bosses in midstream. He's blown off his North Korean handlers, and formed a new alliance with the local Tong," Kate said, trying to talk it through, piece it altogether. She had a puzzled look on her face. "But how does he profit by making an enemy of North Korea?"

Michael Lee shook his head. "The Chinese Tong are clearly a force to be reckoned with, most assuredly in a city like San Francisco, but they're small potatoes when you compare them with a nuclear power, like North Korea."

"Maybe he's planning on double-crossing the Tong as well?" Dawson suggested.

The look on the Pinkerton man's face was one of confusion. "Inspector, you don't suppose that whole scene at Golden Gate Park was staged, do you? You know, for the benefit of the home audience?"

Kate shrugged her shoulders. "If it was staged, then it was a stroke of genius. Right on down to the dead Korean." She thought about this for a moment, and then added, with a rather

disappointed look on her face, "Maybe, I've been underesti-
mating Wang Chi all along? Maybe he needs the cooperation of
the Tong in his latest scheme, and worked it out with Chang to
stage a betrayal that only the Tong would believe?"

"Well, you're not going to like this any better," Lee said, spot-
ting someone he knew. "Just play along with me, and I'll explain
it to you later."

"No problem."

Lee looked out over the port where a number of boats were
moored, unloading their catch. He leaned forward and cupped
his mouth, "Mister O'Rourke!"

One of the sailors stood up from tending to his catch, and
waved. "Aye!"

"Can you spare a minute?"

"Sure thing!" O'Rourke shouted.

Lee turned to Dawson, "O'Rourke is a crab fisherman.
Every day this week, he's gone out, and experienced some real
problems with his catch. I thought you might be interested to
know firsthand."

"You've got me intrigued," she replied, eyes as wide as
saucers. "But what has this got to do with Wang Chi and the
North Koreans?"

"You tell me," Lee replied, with a note of mystery.

Moments later, Robert O'Rourke stepped over the wall
from the steel ladder fixed on the jetty with rusty bolts. "Good
morning!" his voice boomed. He was a mountain of a man,
about six-foot-five, with a sea-worn face, thick stubble, and
a mustache. He wore a thick green woolly hat and light blue
jumper, which contrasted with his rosy red face. He stunk of
whiskey and day-old crabs.

The Pinkerton man pointed to Dawson, "Here's that reporter
I told you about, O'Rourke. Tell her what you told me."

Kate took his hand, which was as big as a polar bear's paw, and shook it with a warm smile, "Mr. O'Rourke, I understand you've had a problem."

"I've been fishing these waters for more than thirty-five years, Dawson," the fisherman spoke at the top of his husky voice. "Started as a boy, working for my father, and now, have my own boat and crew."

She listened intently to the fisherman's story, only glancing occasionally at Lee who was standing there, listening, right next to her. She just couldn't imagine how O'Rourke figured into the much larger mystery at hand.

"I'm no different than most. I work my sixty hours a week. I pay my taxes, and I go to church on Sunday," he continued, talking loudly, too loudly, and slurring his words. It was obvious to both of them that he had been drinking his breakfast that morning, and not some Instant Carnation. Whiskey, and plenty of it. He was one, possibly two drinks away from total inebriation. "Seen a lot of strange things out there, some things that still keep me up late at night with fear. I can't honestly say that I believe in sea monsters, but something strange is down there right now. '*It*' showed up a couple of times on radar, but that damnable beast just as quickly disappeared off the radar screen, right before my very eyes. It's totally ruined one of the best crab patches in the Bay. You want to find it, then you're going to have to hire yourself a boat and a sea captain brave enough to go after it. But '*it's*' out there. About a nautical mile or so, just northeast of the Lighthouse at Angel Island."

"Simmer down, Mister O'Rourke," she said, trying to pacify him. "No need to get so worked up about it. Just tell me your story."

"Bullshit!" he shouted, and everyone within a mile heard him. "Goddammit, don't you dare try to patronize me. I know what I saw. When I try to tell you there's something out there, there really is something out there. Big, about the size of a blue whale!"

"That's pretty big," she repeated.

"You damn straight it is," he agreed with her.

"You say, it scared them all away?" Kate asked him a direct question.

O'Rourke snickered, "They didn't go nowhere. They just disappeared."

"A crab patch just doesn't disappear," Lee interjected.

"Alright, college boy, you tell me what happened. I've been out crabbing every day this week, and ain't found a single crab. I'm telling you it was one of the best crab patches in the Bay, and you can ask anyone. I don't lie."

Dawson looked at Lee, "Well, I'd like to have a look at that point off Angel Island."

"That'll be tough. It's very heavily guarded," O'Rourke sighed, "by a sea monster." He reached in his jumper, and pulled out a flask. He took a long pull on his Whiskey, and stared hard at Dawson and the Pinkerton man, looking as if he was trying to unravel a knotty problem and his drink-addled brain was not cooperating.

Finally, he said, "Goddamn reporters, what the fuck good are you anyway?"

He staggered away down the jetty, back to his catch.

"So, what do you think?" Lee asked, staring at Dawson, as the bright, morning sun began shortening the length of their shadows.

"I think you put O'Rourke up to that," said Kate quietly. "I have to admit that it was a helluva performance, but sea monsters, missing crab, and a light house? C'mon, that's the stuff of B-movies that we used to watch as kids on Saturday afternoon. What was the name of that one movie called? You know the one where the dinosaur is thawed out by the atomic blast far north in the arctic circle, and then terrorizes the lighthouse?"

"*It Came from Beneath the Sea*?"

"No, that's not right," she insisted, puzzling over the title. "*It Came from Beneath the Sea* was the one where the giant octopus attacks the Golden Gate Bridge, and must be destroyed by the Navy's new atomic torpedo."

"You know your monster films," Lee commented, with a slight smile.

"No, not really," Kate said, thinking momentarily of her friend Lenny. "I've got a sci-fi buff for a neighbor who keeps insisting on showing me all these really old, corny black-n-white films on home video."

"*The Beast from 20,000 Fathoms*? A real classic from that guy, you know, the special effects guy—Ray Harryhausen."

She shrugged. "It doesn't really matter. The point that I was trying to make is that none of this is real. It's all make-believe."

"What if I told you it was real?"

Dawson shook her head slowly. "I don't know. I'd have to wonder if you'd been out too long in the sun, with your buddy there."

"It is *real*."

"You're teasing me again."

Michael Lee leaned in close, and whispered, "Suppose the blip that O'Rourke saw on his radar screen was a typhoon-class, nuclear submarine, with stealth capability, and not an actual sea monster? He'd still mistake it as a sea monster, considering it's about the size of a blue whale, but for a second-generation crab fisherman, in these waters, he'd never really know the truth about it."

"And the disappearance of the crab patch?"

Dawson put a cigarette in her mouth and lit it, waving out the match.

"Venting of waste from the boat's nuclear-powered engines," he answered.

"Shut up," Kate whispered, the look of incredulity all over her face.

Lee gave her a reassuring nod. "According to my contact at the NSA, there's a North Korean submarine anchored just off shore."

"Now, that's what I call a helluva 'fish story,'" she replied.

"Coincidence?"

"Do you mean if it's coincidence that we've got a North Korean general meeting with our top suspect in a murder case at the same time that a North Korean U-boat decides to pay us a hush-hush visit?"

"That's exactly what I mean," he said.

Kate smiled. "Let's just say that I liked your story about the sea monster better."

When they reached the end of the jetty, Dawson and Michael turned around, and started back towards his stall at the port.

"You do know for decades people have been reporting sightings of a creature said to resemble the Loch Ness monster in the San Francisco Bay," Lee reported, reading from a Wikipedia entry on his cell phone. "Many believe that these sightings point to some kind of aquatic dinosaur, resembling that of a Plesiosaurus, which still inhabits the Bay. They call it the San Francisco sea monster."

"You don't expect me to believe that, do you?"

"Sure, why not?" he replied. "There have been hundreds of sightings."

"Michael, have you've forgotten that I was born here?" Kate asked, reminding him that she had lived in the City by the Bay her whole life. "I've been hearing those same stories about the 'sea monster' since I was a kid."

"Then you don't believe that eyewitness account by Brother Bill and Bob Clark from 1985?" Lee challenged her with more information from his iPhone.

"They claimed to have seen the creature attempt to capture a sea lion. According to their report, the creature suddenly raised its head and body out of the water and lunged toward the mammal."

"No, not without a polygraph."

"You're such a cynic," he told her.

Dawson shot her cigarette butt into the sand. "I'm afraid that it goes with the job. If I can't prove it, then it doesn't exist."

An hour later, Kate Dawson walked into the Hall of Justice, carrying an empty cardboard box.

Roberts frowned at her from his glass-enclosed office when Dawson entered the Homicide Bureau. The glare on the Lieutenant's face said it all, *What the fuck are you doing here?*

"Just came in to pick up a few things," she replied.

"You've got five minutes, Dawson," Roberts ordered, standing at his door, "and then I don't want to see you again for the next two weeks!"

"I don't want to be here any longer than I have to."

"Five minutes," her boss repeated to himself.

With her head down low, Dawson hoped she looked like the image of a repentant sinner so that everyone would feel sorry for her. But she knew the remorseful look would only get her so far. She understood there was little point in asking forgiveness. Every cop in the Hall of Justice knew that it was always better to take action first, and then seek forgiveness, rather than ask permission and be denied. She had already crossed that line. Now Kate needed to appeal to her colleague's better nature.

She walked down the row of desks, and found William Clark sitting at his desk, typing a report, trying to make some sense of the notes he had scribbled in his notebook which was sitting next to the keyboard.

"Hey, how you doing, Clark?"

Clark looked at Dawson with overstated suspicion.

"How am I doing? I'm doing fine, Kate. What about you? Scuttlebutt is that you got two week's suspension without pay for that big fiasco at the Fairmont. Everybody knows it wasn't your fault, but somebody had to take the fall for it in the press."

"Yeah, I guess my name was just next up on the list. But to set the record straight, I'm going out on administrative leave for ten days for an officer-involved shooting," she said, putting her box down in such a way that the Lieutenant couldn't see who she was talking to.

Dawson glanced up at Roberts' office, then lowered her voice. "Listen, Clark, do you think I could get a look at this morning's security threat briefing?"

"You're on leave, Kate," whispered Clark, looking around. "I could get into trouble just talking to you."

Dawson grinned. "Yeah, yeah, yeah, I know all that. I was just hoping you'd bend the rules a bit. You know, for old time's sake."

Clark shot a glance at Roberts, then picked up a file from his inbox. He read through the report. "What am I looking for?"

"Anything to do with San Francisco Bay."

William Clark shrugged. "Not really. The U.S. Coast Guard is going forward with its plans to hold a series of maneuvers out at Angel Island, including some simulated war games over the weekend. And fishermen are being warned away from Point Blunt where higher levels of mercury contamination have been discovered in the local crab population, including patches nearest the lighthouse."

"Anything about a North Korean nuclear submarine?"

Clark shook his head. "No, nothing," he replied.

"You want me to call, and get an update from Homeland Security?"

"No, thanks. But I appreciate it, Clark," she said.

Kate had the look of disappointment written all over her face. "Dawson!"

"I was just on my way out, Lieutenant," she shouted, seeing Roberts glaring at her from across the room.

"Get in here before you go, Kate."

"Sure thing," Dawson replied affably, hiding her real emotions. She walked into the Lieutenant's office, and closed the door. She stared at the man behind the desk like he was a stranger to her. "What did you want, sir?"

"I don't buy the Kate-Dawson-Nice-Guy act that you're trying to sell," Roberts said, looking down his nose through a pair of horn-rimmed glasses that were balanced on the tip. "I know you. You're up to something."

"Well, why don't you tell me exactly what it is, Lieutenant," Kate challenged him, "and then, we'll both know."

"I don't like your attitude, Dawson," her boss stated, for the record. "I never have. You seem to think that your actions are above the rules and regulations of this department, but I'm here to remind you that they are not. The rules and regulations are in place to preserve the integrity of the crime scene as well as safeguard those officers in the field. You simply can't run around, shooting at a suspect, while there are innocent bystanders in the way. Thank God, we're only talking about a few scrapes and bruises. You could have actually killed someone last night, and then, where would you be?"

Dawson stood up straight. "Sir, the assassin came after me. What was I supposed to do? Let him get away?"

"You were supposed to follow procedure," Roberts insisted. "If you had, your suspect might be alive today, answering questions in interrogation about who put him up to that, instead of lying flat on a slab in the morgue."

"I know who hired him," she replied. "Lo Pan, the Chinese—"

The Lieutenant didn't look at her. "You've been dismissed from that case, Dawson. Period. End of story."

"I thought you'd reinstate me after you heard what I have to say."

"No way. You're not going to put my ass in a sling," Roberts replied, with a cold chill. He was silent for a moment, then added, "You heard what the Chief of Police said, and I'm not about to overturn his decision."

"I need you to think outside the box, for once, Lieutenant," Dawson argued.

The head of Homicide shook his head. "I know you don't think very highly of my methods. Conventional as they are, they've never disserted me in the course of an investigation. I know you consider me—what was that word you used?—a 'pragmatist.' Well, I've not risen through the ranks to become head of this department by being anything but pragmatic. You don't get ahead by bucking the system. There's a reason why we do things by a clear set of procedures, and I'm not about to throw that rule book out just because one of my detectives thinks that I may be old-fashioned."

Dawson folded her arms across her chest. "Rules are guidelines, sir. Nothing more. You can't possibly use the same measure in every circumstance. You have to be able to think outside the box, reason, and then make up your mind."

"You're wrong," he fired back. "As officers of the court, we are required to apply the law equally to every case. We can't afford to think or reason. The moment that we do, then we open ourselves up to anarchy."

"I disagree."

"I'm not surprised," Roberts remarked, looking down at a report on his desk. He picked it up with his right hand, and examined it more closely. "I did some checking on that 'friend' of yours from Justice."

"He's *not* my friend," she replied, with a frown.

"Apparently, they never heard of him," he continued, reading from his report. "The real Gregory Morris disappeared in Cambodia three years ago. They believe Morris was captured by the Khmer Rouge, tortured, and eventually killed. The Department of Justice received a severed hand with his college ring and some other personal effects in a FedEx box post-marked from Cambodia several months after he went missing. DNA taken from the hand matches medical records left behind by Morris."

Dawson reached across the desk, and snatched the report right out of Roberts' hands. He let her have it, without a fuss, and pushed a much larger folder on Morris across his des. As she scanned through the summary report very quickly, Kate couldn't believe her eyes, but there it was, all in black and white. The real Gregory Morris was missing, presumed dead. The man that she knew as "Gregory Morris" was nothing but a fraud. How could she have been so stupid to let a complete stranger into her life without knowing anything about him? Her involuntary reflexes folded the summary page in half, and put it in her pocket, but the Lieutenant took back the much larger folder from her.

She was aghast. "I sensed there was something 'off' about him."

"Women's intuition?"

"No," Dawson said, still shaking her head in disbelief. "The way he talked. The things he said. He didn't sound like a field agent."

"Well," Roberts replied, "he seems to have taken you and every member of your team in with his fancy talk. Right from the very beginning, I didn't trust him. It seems that I was the only one who saw right through his bullshit, but then, I didn't act fast enough either. I should have run a check on him with the DOJ much sooner."

"So, he'd been lying to you all along, too."

The Lieutenant hesitated a second. "That's exactly why we've got rules and procedures, Dawson. To prevent shit like this from happening. But don't worry your pretty little head about it. We'll find out who and what he is. I've issued an APB for his arrest. The boys will bring him in, and we'll sort this all out."

"Just in the nick of time," she commented, sourly.

"At least I did something about it," he returned.

She looked at him for a fleeting moment, then looked away. "Sir, I've got some intelligence to report from one of my sources."

"You've been dismissed from the case, Inspector."

"It's important, Lieutenant," she said.

"Everything is always important with you, Dawson," he sighed wearily. "Haven't you ever noticed that?"

Kate ignored his question. "Sir, our chief suspect Wang Chi met with a high-ranking North Korean general, named Chang, yesterday out in Golden Gate Park—"

"At the Japanese tea garden, no less?"

"—and there's a North Korean nuclear submarine with stealth capabilities sitting out in San Francisco Bay."

Roberts suddenly lost his temper. "Do you know how crazy

you sound? Get out of here before I have you locked up for your own good."

She picked up her cardboard box, and walked out of the Homicide Bureau without a backward glance.

CHAPTER SEVEN

Dawson's BMW 5.25i was parked at the curb in front of the Hall of Justice. She walked out the entrance, and placed her cardboard box in the trunk. She then climbed into the driver's seat. She gunned the car into traffic and took off fast down Bryant Avenue. A couple of minutes later, she was out in the mid-day rush of traffic.

The warmth from the afternoon sun made her drive through the city steady and relaxed. But as Kate rolled down her driver's side window and let the breeze lap her hair, she felt a sense of unease. The bull's-eye was still on her back. The Tong had already tried once to kill her, and they weren't likely to stop after one attempt. They would be back, and in greater numbers. She couldn't afford to be complacent. She continued fidgeting with the channels on her radio, but stayed keenly aware of her surroundings, as drove down the street. A few cars behind her was a black Toyota Tacoma 4x4, keeping a steady distance, but still tailing her.

She reached for the police-band radio in her glove compartment, and pulled out her earpiece. "Dispatch, this is 10-William-40. I'm 901 in the area, and I am requesting an 11-54 on a late model black Toyota Tacoma 4x4, California Plate 3-1-5 November-Delta-Golf."

"10-4, Inspector," the radio dispatch replied, and then a moment later added, "Vehicle is registered to Sandra Salazar, 12717 Sunrise, Pacific Heights. No wants. No warrants, at this time."

"10-4," Dawson signed out, with a deep sigh of relief. Looking up in her review mirror, she watched as the Toyota Tacoma 4x4 fell back in traffic, and then turned right.

It took Dawson only around ten minutes to reach the heart of San Francisco's hip, trendy South Beach by the Bay Bridge, and to the small, studio apartment she rented a few steps from the water's edge. Leaving the city well-behind, Kate turned down the street that led to Bayside Village Apartments, and drove between the lush greenery and down the one-way street that led to the large parking lot in her complex. She had noticed several vehicles in her rearview mirror following closely behind her, but each one turned off, including another black 4x4.

In fact, she hadn't assigned any significance to the Toyota Tacoma until she saw it again following her down the one-way street to home. Purposely, she may a wide turn into the parking lot near her building, and circled around the outer edges, driving her car ever so slowly, as if she was looking for a particular parking spot. The black 4x4 continued to follow her. After she had passed up several good spots, which presumably the other vehicle should have taken, Dawson realized that she was being followed.

She continued around to the one-way street exit on the far side, and pulled back out into traffic. Her tail followed.

Driving back down Bryant Street, towards the Hall of Justice, Dawson wondered just how long it would take before the 4x4 was upon her. She knew the Tong would never let her get back to the safety of police headquarters.

Somewhere in the next few blocks, Kate reasoned, they'd force her off the road—most likely into a collision with another car—and then try to grab her forcibly from the driver's side door, or simply kill her where she sat. If she wanted to live, she was going to have to stay out in front of them, but that wasn't going to be easy. The Toyota Tacoma had an intercooled, super-charger engine that was superior to her BMW's humble six-cylinder engine.

Faster, right off the line, the 4x4 was decidedly a better vehicle than hers. She'd never outrace them, so she'd have to be clever enough to outthink them. She pulled the belt tight around her waist, as tight as she could manage.

Carefully, she watched them in the rearview mirror, and when it looked like they were beginning to pick up speed, Kate steered her BMW down a side street and out onto a main road, heading away from the Hall of Justice and the crowded streets where pedestrians might become targets for the Tong. A couple of cars squealed to a stop as she made the unexpected turn without slowing down to signal her intentions. The 4x4 collided with the rear fender of a slow-moving vehicle. Cursing, the Tong driver pulled away in reverse, and then, in order to get back on track, spun his wheel hard and took chase. Two other cars sped past, swerving to avoid the traffic now held up and stationary; total pandemonium in the intersection. Inside Kate's BMW, she leaned forward, reached under the dash, and flipped the siren switch. The loud wail came on, blaring out with the flashing red lights installed in the grill of her car pulsating, already clearing others for the speeding car. Dawson smiled, a bemused look on her face, but she was brought back instantly to the realization of the chase when she glimpsed the 4x4 on her left, through the side mirror, trying to box her in.

Tapping the brakes slightly, Dawson turned the steering

wheel left and then right, swerving her car across the road, forcing the 4x4 to take evasive action in order to avoid being hit or crashing into cars parked along the street. She gripped the emergency brake and pulled liberally on the handle, as she took the next left turn, knocking over a group of mail boxes on the sidewalk and pulling down a small streetlight, showering the cars around it with sparks. With the road ahead nice and straight, Kate floored her BMW, racing down the main street alongside the district towards Market Street, leading them back to the SOMA area. She figured the area would be busier with afternoon traffic, and there would be plenty of banks, drive-ins and shopping centers on either side.

Perhaps she could pull through and loose them behind a bus. Of course, on any other week day, she might have been able to enlist a meter maid or traffic cop to help her get away, but with the "sick-out," Kate knew she was all alone; she'd have to call for back-up. Dawson checked her rearview mirror, and saw that the 4x4 was right behind her again, within the range of a small handgun.

Just then, an Asian woman leaned out of the passenger's side door window, and fired two shots.

Dawson gasped as the two bullets seemingly whizzed right by her head. She quickly rolled up the driver's side window, and tried to hit 'call' on the radio.

Oncoming cars sounded their horns as she drifted left into their lanes, but she was quick to pull back into her lane.

The 4x4 rammed her, and out of sheer desperation, she slammed on her brakes, and then stepped on the accelerator, flying through the next intersection.

With a half-block lead on the 4x4, Dawson tried again to call for back-up.

"Dispatch, this is 10-William-40!" she screamed into the microphone. "Being pursued by murder suspect in black

Toyota Tacoma 4x4. He is armed and very dangerous; already had two shots fired at me. Just crossed Market and Freemont. West bound."

"10-4, Inspector," the radio dispatch replied. And then, a moment later, an announcement was broadcast: "To all units, officer needs assistance. Shots have been fired. Murder suspect, in black Toyota Tacoma 4x4, in pursuit. Market and Freemont. West bound. Beware: suspect is armed, and considered to be very dangerous."

Dawson glanced up at the moon-roof, and said, *Thank you*, silently.

Just around the next turn, two officers were sitting inside their parked squad car, drinking coffee and eating donuts when the bulletin came in over the radio. They exchanged glances at the message, then turned on their ignition as the BMW flew by with the Toyota on its ass.

They revved the engine, activated their siren and pulled out to join the pursuit. At exactly the same instant, another patrol car which was turning left onto the same street took the turn wide, their tires screaming as the brakes kicked in. Both police cars crashed into each other's sides, their vehicles colliding and spewing small fragments of glass and metal. The force of the impact propelled them forward right after the BMW and the Toyota 4x4, but they were stuck together, locked by the chewed metal of the fenders, one's side hanging off in a crumpled mess.

She witnessed the collision in her rearview mirror.

"Pull away you idiots!" Dawson shouted into the microphone, as she settled back into the driver's seat, but then she had no way of knowing her message would be conveyed.

"We can't! The fenders are locked!" one of the patrolmen shouted back, fighting to keep on a parallel course, while still avoiding distressed drivers.

The pursuit took a steep gradient up another hill.

Dawson looked up at her rearview mirror, and saw the two police cars locked in a strange coupled dance across the street, their flashing lights creating a dizzying state.

Taking a moment to watch them struggle to get free from their dilemma, Kate lost track of the 4x4 for only an instant. The Tong reminded her they were still there by ramming her again. Dawson bucked back and forth, and plunged her foot down on the accelerator.

"I told you, the fenders are locked," the irate officer repeated, struggling to pull his squad car away from the other car, as they took the hill down, gaining speed.

Sparks began to fly from the fender and the bodywork as the two cars started to grind against each other, going down the hill. Up ahead of the street where the road split into two, a metal sign post was erected guiding traffic to either side. It seemed like it would provide the perfect opportunity to break the two cars apart, and both drivers headed directly towards the center, hoping that was the answer.

Dawson glanced in her rearview mirror. She had seen the sign post up ahead, and didn't know which way to move, left or right, until she reached it. Now she wondered what the two squad cars would do. She made the turn, just in time, but the speeding cars missed the mark, and drove directly into the pole. Kate had been following their progress, but she had to turn away at the last instant. "Fuck!" She had seen enough accidents in her career to know no one was walking away from that one.

The nightmare image replayed over and over again in her mind. "Oh, my god!"

As the traffic light turned from yellow to red, Kate Dawson stepped on the gas, and raced through the intersection with the 4x4 right on her tail. The flash of red from the traffic light focused Kate's attention back to the road, and she swerved to avoid hitting a late model sedan pulling out into the street. The black, Toyota Tacoma 4x4 wasn't as fortunate, and smashed right through the left side of the vehicle, spinning it like a top, before it crashlanded right behind her. Dawson watched, her panic causing the BMW to veer left and right all over the road.

She picked out another street to use and turned a corner onto another stretch of road, this time starting down one of the many hills of San Francisco. The Tong driver climbed out of his vehicle, dazed and confused. He was young and wiry, with a mop of black hair that made him look like an Animae character. He shrugged off his concussion, and walked around to the passenger's side.

The woman's neck was broken, probably the airbag.

Getting his bearings, he focused on the traffic around him, looking for another ride.

At that very moment, a Good Samaritan, driving a brand new Dodge Challenger, pulled to a stop at the curb. He rolled his window down, leaned out, and asked how he could help, but the Tong quickly shoved a gun in his face, and yanked him forcibly from the car. He then jumped behind the driver's seat and raced after Dawson, clocking zero to sixty miles-per-hour in less than twelve seconds.

Recklessly, Kate took the next curve too wide, and flew up over the curb, clipping the wires of a large pink and yellow neon sign on the edge of the sidewalk belonging to her mechanic. Men in the garage ran out of the service bay, and watched as the sign buckled like paper from the impact of her car's back end. As the wires ripped away from their connection in the wall, a shower of sparks sprinkled down like fairy dust, and sent everyone running for cover. Moments later, the sign fell inwards onto the road, landing on a parked car, causing two others to brake hard and swerve into each other in order to avoid any real damage. The Tong driver blasted right through the intersection, his pedal all the way to the floor. Within moments, he was right behind her again, tapping on Dawson's bumper.

Kate Dawson clung tight to the steering wheel, and cursed herself, "Holy fucking shit! He didn't die!" *He must have jacked another car*. She quickly assessed the situation. He had the advantage. She knew if she had any hope of beating him, she'd have to be the better driver. In a flat-out drag race, she was lost. But if she accelerated through the turns and used a degree of unpredictability in her driving, she might just get away. Kate spotted the traffic sign for Coit Tower and Telegraph Hill, and then realized there was still one trick left in her playbook.

Instinctively, Dawson turned left at the next intersection, down-shifted to first, turning right onto Filbert Street and started down a large set of stone steps—four hundred to be exact—the Filbert Steps. They connected Kearney Street on the West side to Filbert on the East side. Kate figured the Dodge Challenger would be too low to the ground for the steps, and would bottom out, going down the first step. She reasoned the Tong's only choice was to circle around Pioneer Park to pick her up on the other side. That maneuver might just give her the time she needed to get away from them, once and for all. The car bounced down each flight of stairs, and spun an impressive three hundred and sixty degree turn on the steps as it entered Pioneer Park. The people on the stairs screamed in shock, running and pushing each other into the sides of the steps' wall to avoid being hit. Knowing full-well the car's undercarriage was toast, she pressed on, able to straighten out the car for the final descent off the lower ledge and across the pavement, weaving into the traffic already in full motion on the road. Dawson shifted the car into second and hammered the gas, driving toward the Embarcadero. A few blocks away, she spotted the Challenger coming off Lombard Street, and cursed aloud. She hadn't been as fast as she had hoped she'd be. She hung a left at the next street and cut over to the Embarcadero, purposely traveling the wrong way on the one-way highway.

Numerous cars sounded their horns in alarm as she sped past, expertly weaving between open-topped convertibles and family-sized SUVs all heading across the city. The horns kept blaring, and were followed by a mixture of flashing lights and angry cursing, as Dawson realized she had misjudged the street she was on. Driving slightly faster due to early afternoon rush hour, she moved steadily down the road. Just past Pier 17, she saw the crossover for Green Street rapidly approaching, and worked her way into the furthest lane to exit. The timing was perfect and the crowds along the sidewalks were staring in amazement at the wide U-turn that she made.

She fought to control the car amongst the traffic she had Just joined, noting that it was sometimes easier to travel against traffic than it was to maneuver for a spot in traffic all heading the same way. Unfortunately, the delays in fighting against the traffic flow had given the Tong enough time to catch up to her on the Embarcadero, and they continued racing down the street, heading to the Lefty O'Doul drawbridge.

Traffic was steady over the drawbridge crossing 3rd Street over the lazy San Francisco Bay water at the China Basin, the lower side of South Beach. The bridge operator was an elderly man who sat in his comfy slacks, shirt and jacket and lucky Giants baseball cap, reading the local paper when he received a phone call from the office that monitored traffic conditions all throughout the Bay area. The busy voice on the other line didn't give him a chance to speak, let alone comprehend what he was being asked to do, but he listened with respect. Nodding his head and standing up on his feet, the operator sucked in his chest, and saluted as if responding proudly to Old Glory being carried by veterans in a parade.

"Yes, sir," he replied, his voice raised above a shout as he placed the phone back on the receiver.

Driving down 3rd Street towards the drawbridge, Dawson looked ahead to see the red brake lights of the traffic slowing down. The barrier was coming down across the road and the bridge was starting to rise steadily.

There was no doubt in her mind that someone from the traffic office must have called ahead to have the bridge raised and block them off. If she could trust that her fellow officers would be there to take the Tong driver into custody, Kate reasoned that it would make sense to end the chase right there. But she couldn't take that chance.

She accelerated, crossing over into the opposite lane to avoid cars that were stopped, and hit the end of the bridge going fast enough to clear the bridge, coming down in a shower of sparks as her car bottomed-out on the pavement and bounced down the other side of the drawbridge.

Undaunted, the Tong driver was behind her; a shower of sparks erupting as the Challenger slammed into the pavement.

Kate Dawson made a hard left, just beyond the drawbridge, accelerating through the sharp turn, and continued to push her battered car down the narrow straightaway, following the little access road to the end of China Basin Park. AT&T Park and Oakland-Bay Bridge were on her left side, and Pier 48 was on her right. All at once, she realized that she was running out of road. She glanced over her shoulder at her pursuer, less than a car-length away, and then ahead at the make-shift barrier of a dozen cement baseballs, each the size of compact car.

Kate reached down and pulled her seatbelt tighter, as tight as she could bear, then ramming her foot down on the accelerator, she grabbed the emergency brake. She had to time her stop for the very last second if she hoped to be rid of the Tong driver once and for all. Even though their two vehicles weighed about the same, Kate knew she had better brakes.

Dawson pushed herself down in her seat, screaming, closing her eyes just as she pulled up on the emergency brake, screeching to a stop, mere inches away from the barrier. The Tong never had a chance. Hitting the barrier, the car was propelled over the cement balls, and smashed into a patch of grass before it plunged into the Bay. The last thing Kate saw was the vehicle hitting the water, and the airbag exploding in the Tong's face.

Kate Dawson clicked her seat-belt and tumbled from her once-beautiful car, scrambling on wobbly legs to the waterfront. She wasn't about to be cheated out of her chance to watch him drown. When she reached the shoreline, she collapsed down on one knee, exhausted from her ordeal, gasping for air. Watching intently, she smiled with satisfaction as the Tong driver struggled to get free, at first with the airbag, and then his seatbelt.

With no power to lower the window, he banged on it in vain. Most of the others on shore who had seen the accident gawked at a safe distance with curious abandon.

Not one person seemed eager, or ready to cast aside his or her shoes, to leap into the cold waters of the Bay to affect a rescue. Behind them, a caravan of squad cars with their sirens blaring and their bright lights flashing came racing down the little access road and pulled up next to Kate.

After the jacked car hit the water, it bobbed up and down

for a moment, like a cork, as the currents and eddies gently carried it away from the shoreline. Then, like pasta shells in boiling water, the automobile's chassis began tumbling forward, water bubbling all around it, shrugging-off its last air pockets. Eventually, the weight of the car and the pull of the water sucked it down deeper and further out into San Francisco Bay. In a matter of minutes, the Challenger was submerged in its shallow, watery grave—presumably the Tong driver with it.

"That was incredible, man," one of the bystanders said, in fact, the first one to reach her. He was panting hard, and could hardly contain his enthusiasm. He leaned over, nearly suffocating Kate, and clicked off a "selfie" with his iPhone. "I'm gonna remember this day for the rest of my life! You're one helluva driver!"

The second bystander raced up, and dropped down on his knees in front of her. He looked like he was going to cry. "I've never seen anything like that," he shouted.

"What a spectacular finish! You are truly awesome!"

A young couple, holding hands, ran up, and joined the others. "We can't believe you're still alive!" they said, in chorus. "That was some driving!"

With her eyes wide open, Kate Dawson scanned the Bay, looking past the groupies who had witnessed her ordeal without lifting a finger, and spotted several of the one-person watercraft of the marine patrol and a small Coast Guard vessel approaching. She climbed unsteadily to her feet, and headed to the outcrop of thin, wavy long grass which led from the beach to the main road into the city. She limped back to her car, and waved at several officers she knew as they stepped out of their squad cars.

"Nice of you guys to join the party," Kate said, with a hint of sarcasm.

"You okay, Dawson," one of the cops shouted.

"What the hell happened?" another one barked.

She swallowed down a deep breath, and smiled.

"Well, let me tell you . . ."

Late in the afternoon, Kate Dawson sat alone at a back table in McGinty's Public House, nursing a tall draft beer with a Wild Turkey chaser, while smoking one of her favorite brand of cigarettes. McGinty's was a bar that was located a few blocks from the Hall of Justice. Favored by members of the San Francisco Police Department for its hospitality and friendliness, Dawson felt perfectly comfortable there, and after the day that she had had, she needed the down time. She relaxed in the shadows an hour or so before the older, more conservative, law-andorder crowd came in to drink. Of course, these days, with the "sick-out," the Irish pub saw considerably less business. With fewer officers reporting to work, there was far less drinking and unwinding after work. Kate imagined that she'd be able to sit and drink and smoke without being disturbed, but she was wrong.

"They told me I'd find you here," 'Gregory Morris' said, walking up to her table with a draft of beer.

"The place is nearly deserted, but they said you'd be sitting at the back table, drinking a beer with a Wild Turkey chaser."

"Well, well, well. Look what the cat dragged in," Dawson said, a bit tipsy but not entirely drunk. "I wouldn't get too comfortable. There's an APB out for your arrest, and hiding out in a bar that caters to cops is never a good idea."

He sat down opposite her, and put his drink down on the table. "I wasn't planning on staying."

"Good," she replied, looking at him with disgust, "because I don't remember giving you permission to sit down."

Morris ignored her comment, chalking up her impolite behavior to the booze. "I heard about what happened to you today."

"Huh? Who hasn't heard?" Kate said, carelessly flicking her cigarette in the general direction of an ashtray. The butt missed the tray by nearly a foot.

Morris reached over, picked up her cigarette butt off the table, and put it out in the ashtray. "Are you okay, Kate?"

"What do you care?"

"I do care," he replied. "I care about you."

Dawson swallowed down the bourbon before slugging back half of the beer in one, big gulp.

"Ahhhhhhhhhh," she exhaled in satisfaction. She then reached up with the sleeve of her Versace jacket, and wiped away the foam on her lips. Even though it still tasted mighty good to her, it had lost some of its luster.

"I'm kind of surprised you'd show your face around here, Morris," she said finally, shooting him a puzzled look when she paused to say his name. "Just who the hell are you anyway?"

Morris paled. "He told you, didn't he?"

"Roberts didn't have to tell me anything. I've sensed there was something 'off' about you from the very beginning," Kate replied, shaking her head. "You're no field agent and don't think for one moment I bought that story about you just quitting smoking. You're soft, out of shape, like you've been sitting behind a desk most of your life. You'd never even qualify to take the field exam."

"Hey, that's not very nice."

Dawson's words were clear and clipped, and steeltipped with hostility. "You lied to me."

"I didn't tell you the truth because I was afraid you wouldn't believe me," Morris confessed, with genuine feeling.

"Why is it that everyone who gets caught in a lie always cops to the same plea? 'I didn't tell you the truth because I knew you wouldn't believe me,'" she asked her question rhetorically.

"Why didn't you just leave that up to me? Or, are you simply that cynical about people?"

"I never thought I was cynical," he reflected.

Kate reached for her purse, and took out a small sheet of paper which she unfolded into a larger document.

She passed it across the table to him. "According to the Department of Justice, the real Gregory Morris disappeared in Cambodia in 2014. That was three years ago. They believe Morris was captured, and then later killed, by the Khmer Rouge," she reported dully.

"Sometime after he was reported missing, the DOJ received a severed hand with his college ring and some other personal effects that clearly identified the missing agent as Gregory Morris."

"This report only tells half of the story," he replied, holding the paperwork up to her at eye-level for additional review. "I know that because Gregory Morris was my brother."

"Your brother?" Kate replied, with a raised eyebrow.

"My name is Philip. Philip Morris," he added, with complete honesty. "You see, I also work for the Department of Justice, but I'm the Morris that's been buried in the basement in Research and Analysis for the last ten years."

"Of course. That explains the reason why you always had the facts and figures right at hand," Dawson said, nodding her head. "A field agent deals in generalities, while a good analyst must always have the latest numbers available in short-term memory if the Attorney General needs to make an informed decision, but it doesn't explain the reason for the masquerade. Philip, why did you find that it was necessary to assume the identity of your dead brother?"

Morris sighed. "When you work for an agency like the DOJ, you quickly discover there's a clear pecking order. Field agents almost always have the 'juice' to get things done, while the rest of our requests are placed on a long list, with analysts' requests being at the very bottom," he explained, detailing the inner workings of a typical bureaucratic agency within the federal government. "I soon realized that, if I wanted to get something fast-tracked, I'd have to take it to my brother, convincing him to integrate it into the field work that he was already doing."

"Sort of a quid pro quo?" she asked, sobering up.

"I want something, and you want something. You give me what I want, and I'll give you what you want. But what did your brother get out of this arrangement?"

"He not only got the latest and most up-to-date intel," Morris said proudly, "but soon he was breaking cases that the Attorney General, in his wildest imagination, could never have imagined. For instance, do you remember that case from a few years ago that involved a police officer in Ferguson, Missouri, shooting and killing an unarmed black man after a physical altercation? It was front-page news for weeks, and all of the major networks carried the case, including the decision by the grand jury not to convict the officer and the looting and violence that followed. Well, I researched and analyzed the case for the Department of Justice, and my brother took my one hundred and two-page report to Attorney General Eric Holder and turned everything around. While my report still found Darren Wilson blameless in the shooting death of Michael Brown, I was able to substantiate a pattern of civil rights abuses by Ferguson's police department and courts against people of color that went back over five years."

"That was pretty big news," Kate replied, remembering back to the events in 2014 that had precipitated the violence in that small Missouri town. "I seem to recall the findings from your report caused residents in small communities all throughout

the U.S. to re-examine how their mostly-white police departments governed minorities in small-town America. That led
to landmark legislation as well."

"Yeah, I'd have to say that it was our finest hour," Morris
concluded. "The work that Greg and I did with the Attorney
General represented some of our best work at the Department
of Justice."

Dawson smiled thinly at him. "So, when did you first start
masquerading as your brother?"

Morris leaned across the table, his eyes freely engaging hers.
"You make it sound like it was a conscious decision on my part,"
he said, without expression. "Like I woke up one fine morning,
and suddenly started calling myself Greg. It really wasn't like
that at all."

"Okay, then, why don't you tell me what happened?"

"With the election of the new President, there was also a
shake-up in the upper echelons of the DOJ. Eric Holder was
out as the Attorney General, and the names of several replace-
ments were being thrown around, including Donald Verrilli,
Kamala Harris, Kathryn Ruemmler, Massachusetts Governor
Deval Patrick, and preet Bharara. Ultimately, David Jackson,
the former Homeland Security secretary, was approved by
Congress to be the next Attorney General," he said, after a
moment of long silence. "The shake-up not only affected
personnel changes, but also a change in direction for the DOJ.
Since the President had run on a platform of cleaning up the
whole problem of human trafficking, she had made it one of the
priorities for her first term."

"So, then, I guess you shifted away from battling civil rights
in Middle America to dealing with human rights on a global
scale?" she asked.

Morris nodded his head. "With the President knee-deep in

a nuclear showdown with Iran, she wanted the United States to project an image of solidarity. We were all supposed to be part of one, big, happy family with the Harrisons as the Mom and Dad. You can't exactly do that, if you're investigating civil rights violations in Ferguson, Missouri, or Anytown, USA."

"No, you can't," she said, agreeing with him.

"So, just after the new Attorney General was sworn into office, he scheduled a meeting with several of the key players at the Department of Justice, including Greg, and told them that we were going to close down the Asian Sex Trade," Morris briefed her, all business. In fact, Dawson could hear the determination and passion in his voice to set the record straight. "Attorney General Jackson even contacted me about drafting the plan of action. Apparently, he had read my doctoral dissertation on the Asian Sex Trade, and charged me with delivering a report that was equal to, if not better than, the 102-page report I had given Eric Holder on civil rights in Middle America."

"Sounds like you were the 'go-to' guy at Justice," Kate commented, smiling brightly. "Perhaps even 'fun'?"

Morris's eyes never left her face. "It may have been 'fun' in the beginning. You know, as an analyst, you work mostly in anonymity, locked away in the basement of the Department of Justice for months on end. Your work rarely sees the light of day, unless it's needed for a big case. I liked writing that report, drafting the plans that were going to bring down those sex cartels," he admitted.

"But it stopped being fun the moment Greg was reported missing in Cambodia. For every day that he was missing, I imagined the worst. It's not fun, imagining someone you love getting tortured and then beaten to death by the Khmer Rouge."

"I can imagine," she said, her smile turned upside down.

"Then, put yourself in my shoes, the day the FedEx package

arrived with Greg's severed hand and college ring," Morris spoke softly. "I was a basket case the minute it arrived in the office."

Kate shook her head slowly.

"Up until that point, he was still alive in my mind, and I could visualize Greg putting up the good fight against those communist bastards," he continued, with tears forming in the corners of his eyes. "But when I saw what they had done to his hand, I knew that he was probably dead."

"How did you feel when they told you he was dead?"

"I felt as if someone had reached into my soul, and stripped away the very best part of me," he replied.

Morris twisted the sheet of paperwork in his hands, and as he spoke, he started ripping it into individual pieces. "I was filled with such rage that I just wanted to beat the living daylights out of every slant-eyed bastard I could get my hands on, and then tear 'em to shreds."

"So, if I were a betting woman, I'd guess you were suspended from the DOJ for a few months, and recommended for a psychiatric discharge?" she asked.

He nodded curtly. "Three months, to be exact."

"What happened?"

"What do you think happened?" Morris replied with a question that simply hung out there between the two of them. "I cracked up. I marched straight into the Attorney General's office, without an appointment, and I started making demands, not the least of which was bringing my brother's body back for a proper burial. I must have sounded like a real crazy person because the next thing that I remembered was being wrestled to the ground by agents and handcuffed behind my back."

Dawson didn't look all that surprised. "I'm sorry."

Morris was blasé, brushing off her show of sympathy. "One moment, I'm a genius for writing this report that leads to landmark legislation, and the next, I'm a mental case who should be locked up for grieving for his brother. Fundamentally, I was still the same person, but no one could see that, except me."

"And that's when you became Gregory Morris?"

Kate finally asked the question that she had wanted answered.

"Yeah," he replied sourly. "I figured that my career at Justice was over anyway, what with a psychiatric discharge pending. The only thing that really mattered to me was bringing those that had killed my brother to justice. I grew a goatee and shaved my head, so that I would match my brother's DOJ badge, grabbed a box of his business cards, his service pistol, and set out after his killers."

There was a moment, a long moment of silence.

Dawson stared at him without any kind of expression.

"That's quite a story, Morris," she said, at last.

He nodded. "I swear to you it's all true."

"Don't worry. I believe you," she replied, with a smirk. "I just don't know who else is going to believe you."

Morris smiled brightly at Dawson. "We could take it to your Lieutenant. He already knows most of it. But my guess is that, when I fill him in on the blanks, he's likely to be sympathetic to my cause."

"Jim Roberts is the last person I would take anything to," Kate said, with an unctuous smile. "He's the pragmatic bureaucrat who's sworn out the APB for your arrest, and he means to see it enforced. I'd be very cautious around him. He has a ruthless streak a mile wide, and likes to play 'gotcha' games with you in order to show off his 'superiority.'"

"Then, what are we going to do?" he demanded, in a panic. "The G-20 Summit starts tomorrow, and we've got to figure out a way to get inside the Moscone Center and stop those girls from triggering World War III."

"I don't know," she confessed, with a shrug. "I've been

thinking about it all day long, and I just don't know how we're going to be able to penetrate that security without giving ourselves away to the SFPD."

Morris thought about it for a moment. "Why don't you just go to the Lieutenant, and tell him what you know?"

"Morris, haven't you heard a single word I've said? Roberts isn't someone that we can trust," Kate replied. "Besides, I've already tried talking to him about it. He doesn't believe me. In fact, he called me crazy, and threatened to have me locked up, if I didn't get out of his office."

Philip Morris shook his head from side to side, and muttered, "Seems like what we really need is some criminal element to get us inside."

Dawson sat upright in her chair. "What did you just say?"

"I was mostly just thinkin' out loud," he said casually. "I said what we really needed was a criminal to help us break in."

"Prinze," she whispered under her breath.

"Prinze?" he asked, but she remained silent.

"Hey, Kate," asked the bartender, from across the room, "you want me to get you another double? A glass of beer?"

"No thanks, Johnnie," she replied, half-heartedly.

"Better make it black coffee, and lots of it!"

"Prinze?" Morris repeated the word as a question, but she ignored him, glancing through the numbers in her cell phone.

A few minutes later, Johnnie O'Flynn, the bartender, placed a generous beaker of coffee on the table in front of Dawson, and lined up a spoon, a couple of packets of raw sugar, and some cream with a large coffee cup.

"Thanks, Johnnie. Be a pal and run me a tab, would ya?"

"Sure thing, Kate."

There was silence for another couple of minutes, while Dawson continued looking through the "incoming" numbers that had been recorded in her iPhone. She paused on one number, and then nodded her head as she dialed it.

"Jack, this is Kate. I've got a favor to ask you, but I was hoping that we could meet for dinner tonight so that I could ask you in person. Wonderful! The Waterbar? Down on the Embarcadero. Yes, I know where it is. I'll see you around 7 pm. Bye."

Morris looked at her with raised eyebrows. "I know how seriously you take your dating," he said, as delicately as he could manage, "but don't you think this is one night that you could have begged off?"

"That was Jonathan Prinze," she replied.

"Prinze," he repeated sourly. "We're not talking about the guy that snapped his girlfriend's neck and threw her down a flight of stairs."

"Yeah, that's him," she responded.

"You're not actually going out on a date with him, are you?"

"Yes, I am."

"I don't think that's a very good idea, Dawson," Morris cautioned her. "Let's forget about that fact that he's worth millions of dollars, for a moment, and concentrate on the man. This guy is a first-class sociopath who showed no remorse for killing his girlfriend and their unborn child."

"It's because he's rich that I called him," Kate said, with a shit-eating grin. "He'll have a place at the table when the G-20 Summit opens tomorrow, and he'll be able to get us in as his associates."

Morris frowned. "I certainly hope it doesn't cost you too much."

"Me neither. I've heard the Waterbar is a really fancy place, and I don't have a thing to wear."

"That isn't what I meant," he said, with a long, sour puss.

Dawson nodded. "I know, but right now I need you to focus

on Wang Chi. You told me that you had a line on him. I think it's time we brought him in and had a serious conversation with him."

"I agree," he said, with a nod of his head. "And I've also got the right location picked out for his 'come to Jesus' meeting as well."

"Good. I'll touch base with you later."

Kate Dawson steadily climbed the stairs to the third floor. As she reached her apartment and unlocked the door, Lenny stepped out of his apartment, took a couple of steps towards her, then stood silently in the shadows with a pained look on his face. From the tear stains on his cheeks, she could tell that he had been crying. She smiled slightly and nodded her head at him.

Kate then opened the door, and welcomed him into her small, studio apartment. With his head held low, he marched right into the front room, and sat down on her moth-eaten couch. She hung her dry-cleaning on the handle of the door to the bathroom, and then pulled a bottle of water out of the refrigerator. Dawson opened it with a single twist, and swallowed down a mouthful.

"Can I offer you a soda or bottled water?" she asked, hovering near the entrance to her small kitchenette.

"No thanks," he replied, and then added, "I really can't stay very long."

Dawson glanced down at her watch. "Okay. I'm actually working under a bit of a deadline of my own."

"I wanted to apologize to you for my recent behavior," he said, very formally, as if addressing a member of the royal family. "It was totally inexcusable, and I would be very grateful if you accept my word that it will never happen again."

"Sure, Lenny, whatever you want," she said with a shrug, knowing exactly which transgressions he committed.

"Rosa Romano meant a great deal to me. More than you'll ever know," Provolone said, sniffling back some tears. "She was the one woman, other than my mother, who loved me for who I was, and not for what I could do for her. I'm ashamed to admit that I was actually fucking another woman when I heard the news of Rosa's death. That was a wretched thing to do to her. She clearly deserved better."

Kate smiled sympathetically. "I'm certain that she's forgiven your infidelity, Lenny. Rosa Romano was not a woman who held grudges against people. She was a very loving and compassionate woman."

"Perhaps too forgiving," he replied, and then started weeping.

"I know how you feel, Lenny. She came to me once, in a time of great need, and I turned her away because I didn't understand," Dawson confessed, recalling the one time that Rosa had approached her with bisexual feelings. She put her arms around him, and placed his head on her shoulder. "Now, we can either stand around here and feel bad for ourselves, or we can make up our minds to do something about it."

Lenny pulled his head away from her shoulder, and looked into her eyes. "What exactly do you have in mind, Kate?"

"I'm putting together a team to go after the people who were responsible for Rosa's death," she replied, with a very determined look. "It's not entirely legal, and we could be looking at jail time, if we're caught. But I could really use someone with your technical know-how and his very own 'eye-in-the-sky' to help out."

"Count me in, Kate," he said, turning his thumb upward. "I'll do whatever you need me to do."

"Thanks, Lenny."

"I still feel bad for the way that I treated Rosa."

He then sat up, looking directly into her eyes.

Dawson nodded. "I know you do. In time, those feelings will lessen, but they will always be with you."

Provolone swallowed hard, feeling a different kind of pain. "The funny thing is that I knew I had found something very special with Rosa," he said, all choked up, "and I guess a part of me felt I didn't deserve it. The only women who are ever interested in me are the mentally insane. The normal ones take one look, and then go running off, screaming into the night. Rosa was different, and I just didn't learn it in time."

"You'll find love again, my friend," she reassured him. Kate put out her hand to touch him, to offer him some sign of encouragement. "Use this time to grieve, and to think about all that she taught you about love. And then, in time, you'll realize that love isn't about finding a twenty-three-year-old girl with a hard-body, but meeting a mature woman with wrinkles and graying-hair who shares your values and interests, and loves you for the person who you are."

"Thanks, Kate," he said, holding her in his arms for another second.

Eventually, Dawson broke their embrace. She rested her arms on Lenny's shoulders, and looked him in the eye to make a point. "I've got to get dressed now for a meeting, and you should go home and get some rest."

"I'll be ready when you need me," he replied, shoulders back. Lenny marched right out of her apartment, and start gathering his equipment together.

CHAPTER EIGHT

Located in the shadow of the Bay Bridge, on the South end of Rincon Point, the Waterbar was not only San Francisco's foremost seafood restaurant but was also situated in a prime location on the waterfront, offering breathtaking views of the City's iconic skyline. Guests enjoying the restaurant's famous Oysters or Dungeness crab often sat outside under the stars, and enjoyed such notable sites as San Francisco Bay, the Embarcadero, "Cupid's Span," the Bay Bridge, Treasure, Yerba Buena Islands, and the Berkeley hills just beyond. The Waterbar's amazing food was supported by an outstanding service staff that offered the best dining experience available in the Bay area.

So, when Kate arrived for her dinner date with Jonathan Prinze, she was escorted to the best table in all of San Francisco and served the best champagne. She sat down in a short, black cocktail dress that was handbeaded, and sipped the glass of Moet's 2004 Brut Dom Perignon. It was the first champagne that she liked. When she sniffed the bubbly drink, Kate could make out hints of apricot, pear and grapefruit. The fruity taste was what made it especially appealing to her.

Jonathan Prinze arrived a few minutes later, wearing a black

Armani suit with an off-white silk shirt and tie. As he was escorted to the table by the maitre d', Prinze spotted Kate across the outdoor seating area, and refused to take his eyes off her. "You look absolutely gorgeous. You truly belong here among the stars of the night," he said finally, taking both her hands and leaning over to kiss her cheek. Prinze then sat down, opposite her, with the help of the maitre d'.

"Thank you," she said coolly, playing her cards very close to the vest.

After Jonathan Prinze had settled into his seat and pulled the table napkin across his lap, he looked up, and his eyes met hers again. He smiled, and said, "I'm surprised you came."

"I told you that I had a favor to ask," Dawson replied.

"You could have asked that favor over the phone," Prinze insisted, staring directly at her. "So what's the real reason?"

She hesitated a moment. There was an undeniable chemistry between the two of them, whether Kate wanted to admit it to herself or not. He was a very handsome man, and the darker, rougher edges of his personality appealed to her. Had he not been under indictment for murder, she might have taken a more direct route to get to know him, but she didn't want him to know that. Instead she smiled, and slipped away from the question like a fighter dodging a couple of jabs in the ring.

"I suppose I could say that I'm surprised you came, too," she said, coyly, raising her heavily mascaraed eyelashes.

"I have to apologize for the way I acted," Prinze said honestly. He sat in silence for a moment, as if collecting his thoughts, and added, "I should have been a lot more sensitive to your needs that night. After all, your friend had just died—"

Kate stopped him. "The less said about that night the better."

"Okay," he agreed.

"So . . ."

"Can I offer you some more champagne?"

"Thanks, Jack."

Prinze reached across the table, and took the bottle of Dom Perignon in hand, topping off her flute, filling his glass, then returning the Dom to its ice-filled bucket.

Finally, he raised his glass to her and they clinked glasses.

"Cheers!" he said to her.

"Cheers to you!" she said back to him.

Without taking her eyes from his face, Kate took another sip from her drink, smiling like the Cheshire Cat.

Normally, she didn't care for champagne since the bubbles tickled her nose, but there was something special about this vintage. She smelled an aroma of almonds and powdered cocoa, yet tasted a fruity-fruit. She had decided to remember the brand the next time a man offered her champagne.

Prinze put his glass down, and looked out at the Bay. "I love this City. It's like a diamond that's been freshly cut, beautiful from so many, different angles. Especially, the way San Francisco Bay lurks at the end of every street. I was hoping that you'd like this spot as much as I do."

"It's beautiful, Jack."

"Not as beautiful as you, I'm afraid," he said softly, turning on the charm. "Not even close."

Dawson smiled, and took a generous mouthful of the champagne, which brought an instant rosy-red color to her cheeks.

Their waiter approached the table, took their meal order, and left a small assortment of breads on a platter.

Dawson ordered the seared sea scallops for her first course, and the Dungeness crab with a side of parmesan French fries for her main course, while Prinze requested the shellfish bisque for his first course, with the restaurant's famous Oysters with fried Brussels sprouts as his main meal. As they waited for the first part of their meal to be brought to the table, sharing the bread and continuing to drink champagne while making small talk.

"Life is really strange, isn't it?" Prinze asked rhetorically. "If I hadn't been arrested as a suspect in my girlfriend's murder, I might never have met you. We travel in such different circles."

"The strange parts are what make it interesting," she replied, with a part of the story that trumped his.

"Originally, Matt Balardi and I weren't supposed to be assigned to your case. We were going off duty, but Clark and Jawara were late in reporting in due to some domestic dispute in the neighborhood. We got the call, and put in an additional six hours overtime that day."

Prinze shot her a look of surprise. "I'm glad you turned out to be the officer of record. You've been very fair with me."

"I'd rather not talk shop, Jack," Kate said, shaking her head, "if that's okay with you?"

Jonathan Prinze shrugged. "It's funny. You know so much about me. I don't know anything about you."

"Hilarious!"

"I should have said 'peculiar,' not 'funny,' shouldn't I have?"

She sipped her drink, and watched him over the top of her glass. Prinze seemed like he was genuine, serious about getting to know her. She even found it endearing how, when he used the wrong words, he asked politely what he should have said instead. He wasn't at all the man that she initially thought he would be. Kate replied, "What do you want to know?"

"Where did you grow up?" he asked, sitting forward in his chair.

"Right here, in the City," Dawson responded, with renewed energy. "My parents were hippies who met during the Summer of Love. They actually lived in Haight-Ashbury in 1967. In fact, that's where I was born. I can remember growing up to all that great music, and dressing in those funky clothes. My mother always made sure that I wore flowers in my hair, you know, just like the song."

He nodded. "So, then you never left?"

"No."

"What do your parents do?"

Kate hesitated a moment. "They're both dead now. But when they were alive, my mother worked in a bank, and my father was a painter."

"A painter," Jack repeated, his eyebrows raised in interest. "Like Peter Max? Or that guy, Wyland, who paints all those marine art murals?"

"My dad painted houses," she confessed, slightly embarrassed. "He was very much a free spirit, and didn't have an occupation, per se. When my parents needed money, he'd work long hours painting houses, office buildings, apartments, really anything for a couple of bucks. Then he'd stop working and just hang out. You know, smoke some pot, listen to music, and hang with friends."

While Dawson was talking, the waiter served their two starters, which included a small baby beet salad for Prinze and an onion soup for Dawson. They chowed down on the first course, and seemed to lose themselves in small talk about the tasty food and the large portions they enjoyed. One course followed another course, and by the time they had reached desert, which included coconut layer cake and homemade sorbet, Kate had worked up the courage to ask her favor.

She looked across the table at Jonathan Prinze as he spooned another bite of the sorbet, and said, "I need your help, Jack."

"I assumed that was the reason why you called," he said, wiping his mouth with the large table napkin.

"I need to get into the G-20 Summit when it opens tomorrow morning," Kate said, putting it all out there.

Prinze looked at her sideways. "I already assumed that you were going to be there tomorrow with the SFPD," he replied, with a confused look on his face.

"Why don't you just go in with the police?"

"It's complicated," she answered.

"Complicated?"

"Goddammit, Prinze, why are you making this so difficult for me?"

"You asked me for the favor," Prinze answered.

"Remember?"

"Okay, fine then," Dawson said, at last. "I'm serving a two-week suspension for having used my service pistol during a recent homicide."

"Now that wasn't too hard was it," he said softly.

"Why don't you tell me what happened?"

"I was on a dinner date at Forbes Restaurant, with a stock-broker that I met online, and a Tong assassin came after me," Kate explained. "He killed my date, trying to get to me. I chased him up to the top of the lighthouse, and rather than surrender to me, the Tong assassin jumped to his death."

Jonathan Prinze smiled, enjoying her predicament.

"So, you kinda got sucked into it then? Did you like it?"

"No one ever likes it. No one in their right mind, that is."

"And you? Were you in your right mind? How many drinks had you had? Tell me about the coke, Dawson. How much coke did you do that day?"

"I don't know what the hell you're talking about," she declared. "I don't take drugs. I never have. And drinks, OK, maybe I had one or two. But not enough to impair my judgment."

"Kate, when did you first find out?" he whispered in her ear.

"What?" she heard herself ask the question aloud.

"When did you first realize that you had the capacity to kill? To take a human life?" he asked her again, his voice just a whisper.

"What did you just say?" Kate asked.

Jonathan Prinze took her hand gently, and stroked it. "You haven't heard a word I've said to you, have you?"

"No, that's not true. I heard everything, including some things that someone else may have said to me."

"Someone else? What are you talking about?"

"I'm sorry, Jack," she apologized, with a yawn.

"It's been a really long day, and while I've enjoyed our dinner together, I've got to get up early in the morning to make arrangements to get into the Moscone Center on my own now."

Prinze was scratching his head. "I don't understand," he said, confused. "I thought we'd agreed that you'd be joining my team in the morning. We have only a limited amount of time to get into the Moscone Center before the first workshops are opened to G-20 members."

"I must have blacked out, or maybe the champagne has gone to my head, but I don't remember that part of the conversation."

He reached for his cell phone. "I'm calling you a cab, unless you want me to come back with you to your place?"

"No, I can't," she replied, sobering up. "Not tonight, and I drove myself."

"Okay, then. We'll make it another night," Prinze concluded, walking her to the front entrance. "This has been a really memorable evening, Kate. I do hope to see you again, very soon."

"You will," Dawson acknowledged, leaning over and giving him a kiss on the cheek. "I'll see you first thing in the morning."

On her way home to change clothes, Kate's phone buzzed. "Did you find him? Is he there?" Dawson asked, speaking into her iPhone, cautiously optimistic.

"Yes," Morris replied, keeping the detail simple and to the point. "We picked him up outside a convenience store in the Tenderloin. He tried to run, but they stopped him. Cold. Colonel Shears is with him now."

"I'll be right over," she stated, and hung up.

Fifteen minutes later, Philip Morris greeted her at the door to the late model Victorian home in Pacific Heights. She had traded her black beaded dress for a pair of jeans, a button-down blouse, and windbreaker. "Nice outfit," he joked, thinking he might catch her in a black cocktail dress. "Hope he enjoyed the sneak preview."

She looked at Morris in mild disgust, then followed him through the house to the basement door in the kitchen. They went through the door, and started down the steps to the base-ment. As the two of them continued walking down the narrow stairway, into the darkness that lay below, Kate couldn't help but feel a flash of déjà vu. The neighborhood, the house, the base-ment, all reminded her of the "Angel of Death" serial murders and the first time that she had seen a fullyfunctional dungeon.

"Kate, I really don't think you want to be a part of this," Morris said, reluctantly leading her down to the basement. "These men are all trained ex-military, and they will do whatever is neces-sary to extract the intel that we need."

"This is still my show, Morris," she replied, hellbent on getting to the bottom of the stairs of the DOJ's safe-house.

When Dawson reached the last rung, she stepped out onto the concrete floor, and immediately found herself in a shadow realm where waterboarding and enhanced interrogation techniques had replaced diplomacy. She took a breath, and was overcome by the stench in the room. It was an unwelcome concoction of vomit, feces, and urine. She put a perfumed handkerchief over her nose, but that barely cloaked the smell. She looked around at the sound-proofed walls and the puddles of water on the floor, and knew immediately she was in an interrogation room, but not at all like the one at police headquarters. This was the kind of CIA black site that she had read about in reports from the Middle East.

She pushed her way through several, very large men, and found Wang Chi's severely beaten body hanging from shackles in the center of the room over a pool of blood and vomit. Three men wearing ski masks to hide their identity stood around the body in a circle, taking turns, using Chi as a punching bag, while a fourth man who was at least a foot taller than the others stood beside him, shouting in his right ear. He stopped long enough to flash Dawson a big, toothy grin that let her know that he was in charge, and then went right back to work. Kate was visibly shaken by what she had seen, but didn't say anything. She waited for the leader to take a break.

"This is not at all what I wanted," she said finally.

"You know, you really shouldn't be here, ma'am," the leader replied sarcastically, pulling off his ski mask and walking back to the stairs, out of Chi's sight. He pulled out a cigarette, and using a Zippo lighter with a four-leaf clover, ran the flint along the leg of his camouflaged fatigues to cleverly light his smoke. He took a couple of puffs, and added, "You'll sleep better at night not knowing what we have to do here to break a suspect."

"I've been interrogating suspects my entire life, Colonel, and not once have I ever had to beat a confession out of one," Kate said proudly.

"It's Shears, ma'am," the big man corrected her.

"We hardly ever use our rank down here. And with all due respect to the SFPD, interrogation only works if the suspect knows that he might die. We break 'em down, take 'em right to the edge, and then give 'em the chance to sing."

"He'll talk to me," she said with assurance.

Colonel Shears laughed out loud. "He isn't talking shit to anyone. Just so you know, it's going to take a while to break him down. He hasn't learned yet how helpless he really is."

"Let me talk to him," Dawson pleaded.

"All right," said Shears, yielding to her request.

"You want to talk to him, talk to him. Convince him to tell us what he knows, or else you're going to let us do whatever is necessary."

With extreme caution, Dawson approached the bruised and beaten body of her adversary, Wang Chi. She leaned over and whispered in his ear, "Wang Chi, I know you remember who I am."

He grunted his acknowledgement, spitting blood.

"The men in this room are professional interrogators," she explained to him. "They will continue to beat you and torture you until you tell them what they want. Tell me now what you know, and I'll make certain they don't raise another hand to you. You may not have another chance."

"I have diplomatic immunity," Wang Chi replied, through gritted teeth.

"Diplomatic immunity, my ass," Shears snickered.

"Shears!" Dawson said, in an effort to shut him up.

The Asian captive struggled to stand tall, and said, "I demand to see the Consulate-General."

"Wang Chi, you must understand that the normal channels do not exist down here in this basement," she tried to explain it to him. "There are no diplomats. Only the living and the dead."

"I demand immunity from prosecution—" Chi continued, but was cut off in mid-sentence.

"We're wasting valuable time here," Shears commented.

"Sir, don't make me remind you again," she said, looking him squarely in the face.

"Carry-on," Shears yielded, once again.

Dawson leaned in, and said, "Wang Chi, you've got only two choices here. You can tell me where you've sequestered those five girls, or I will turn you back over to Shears and his men to extract it from you. Make your choice right now, or I'll be forced to make it for you."

Wang Chi remained defiant in his silence.

"I told you that he wasn't ready yet," Shears said, glaring at Kate.

Colonel Shears calmly turned around to his men, and nodded. All at once, he forced Wang Chi to the floor, and two of his men pinned the Asian's limbs to the cold concrete at an acute angle. The third masked man smothered Wang Chi's face with a towel as he struggled to get free. Shears glanced across the room at Dawson, and then shouted, "Grab that pitcher." She followed his gesture to the corner of the basement where she found an ice chest filled with water and a plastic pitcher. She picked up the pitcher, not knowing what to do.

"What the fuck are you waiting for?" he howled at Kate, like she was a green recruit. "Put some water in it, and bring it over here."

Dawson dipped the pitcher into the water, her hands shaking uncontrollably.

"C'mon, c'mon, let's move it!" Shears screamed.

Anxiety was written all over Dawson's face as she brought the pitcher back to the Colonel, dripping water as she scrambled back. Shears refused to take it from her, and instead grabbed her hand. With her hand still holding the pitcher, Shears started pouring the ice water on Wan Chi's face, which was now covered by a towel. Wang Chi thrashed with the rising panic of being waterboarded, struggling to get free. Two of the masked men held him tightly in place.

"You brought six women into this country to sell as sex slaves," Shears shouted into his right ear. "One died. I want to know the names of the other five, and I want to know their whereabouts at this moment."

Wang Chi gasped for breath beneath the saturated towel. "I . . . don't . . . know, you"—cough, gag—"asshole."

"Wrong answer, dickhead!" the Colonel said, enraged. He grabbed Dawson's hand on the pitcher of water, and poured nearly the rest of the water on the towel covering Wang Chi's face. The coldness of the water shocked him, making him inhale sharply. It went up his nose and down his windpipe, gagging, asphyxiating him, creating the sensation that he was drowning in only a few inches of water. "Now, I'm going to ask you again. Only this time, I want the right answer." He removed the towel to hear the answer.

"Why are you doing this to me?" Wang Chi cried out, like a baby, in between gasps and sputters.

Shears laughed. "You're a fuckin' terrorist, pal. Don't be so stupid! You threaten my country with terrorism, and you have the nerve to lie to me and pretend like you don't know why this is happening."

"Fuck you!" Chi screamed, spitting water in Spears' face.

"No, fuck you, pal," the Colonel replied, covering his face again, forcing Dawson to pour the last of the water over the towel directly into Wang Chi's nose.

The man formally known as "the auctioneer" thrashed up-and-down in the arms of the Colonel's men, struggling to breathe.

Angered and enraged, Shears grabbed the stainless steel pitcher out of Dawson's hand, and threw it across the room. He then ripped the rag off Wang Chi's mouth, and water spurted out. Wang Chi was nearly gone. As he gasped and sputtered for air, on all fours on the cold concrete floor, and vomited what was still left in his stomach.

"Get him up," Shears ordered his men.

Two of his guards forced Wang Chi to his feet, while the third tied his arms off to the shackles above his head behind his back. He hung there over the pool of vomit and blood, a mere shell of a man.

"You've got a temporary reprieve, Wang," the Colonel said softly, the tenor of a therapist, "while I go out and have a cup of coffee and a smoke. But I'll be back with more questions. Any time you want to stop this, let me know, and I'll see that you get a cup of J and a smoke, too."

Shears walked back to the stairs, and picked up his pack of cigarettes. Dawson followed him.

"Are you planning on doing this all night?" she asked, watching him light his cigarette.

He inhaled a deep, lung-full of smoke, and let it out between gritted teeth. "Yeah, as long as it takes." His steely stare and buzzed cut, as well as his size was most intimidating.

Kate stared at him for a moment. "Shears, I think you actually enjoy torturing him, watching them squirm."

"It's a job, lady," he replied, without any emotion, "and it's what is going to get you those names and that location."

"But at what cost, Colonel? Every time you 'interrogate' a prisoner to obtain critical intelligence data, ten more terrorists, just like him, come forward to take his place. Terrorist recruiters really don't have to do much to recruit new jihadists. We seem to do it all for them. And forget about taking the moral high ground when our own citizens, who deplore these techniques, lose faith in their own country's moral standing."

"Officers who represent the executive branch have a solemn

obligation to protect the American people. It is our highest responsibility," Shears said, casting aside his cigarette butt. "We're not good Samaritans, and we're not good neighbor Sam either. If there is a serious threat of a mass-murder attack against the United States or its people, we are obligated to take all reasonable steps to stop it. And what is 'reasonable' depends on the circumstance and the exigency. I'd waterboard a hundred suspects if that meant I could protect the life of one American."

"And what about Wang Chi? He's a Chinese national, with a diplomatic passport. What about his rights?"

Colonel shook his head. "He's expendable," Shears said simply. "As far as I'm concerned, he gave up his rights the moment he started plotting against the United States and its people."

Dawson shrugged. "A diplomatic passport means nothing to you?"

"No. It's nothing but a fancy 'Get out of Jail Free' card that diplomats use when they get into trouble."

She took a couple of steps back, and said, "I'm beginning to wonder who's scarier, you or the terrorists?"

"You'd better hope it's me, if we expect to make any headway tonight with Wang," Shears replied, with a big, toothy grin. "Listen, why don't you just go upstairs, find a bed, and get some sleep. It is likely to be another couple of hours before the man cracks. We'll wake you when we've got something."

Dawson glanced at her watch. "The G-20 Summit starts at 8:30 tomorrow morning. That's less than ten hours away."

"Then I think you should get the fuck out of my way," he demanded, pushing her towards the stairs, "so that I can get my job done."

She went upstairs to find adequate accommodations.

Shaking off her loafers, she lay on the made-up bed. Unable to sleep, she stared at the ceiling.

Several hours later, Dawson was thrashing from a nightmare when Morris came to wake her with the news that they had broken Wang Chi. She had been dreaming about waterboarding, and remembered spending most of the night, imagining she had a towel wrapped around her face, while Shears poured endless amounts of water into the towel, laughing a sadistic laugh. Kate struggled to move, to rouse herself from drowning, but her body was pinned down by his soldiers, looking to break her spirit.

She knew, in the back of her mind, that it was time to wake up, and once again, sound the alarm and save the day. She jolted to consciousness as Morris shook her awake.

"They've broken Wang Chi," Morris said, almost a whisper. "We've got an address for the girls. Somewhere in the Tenderloin."

"Christ, why didn't you wake me?" Kate demanded.

Morris looked deeply offended. "I'm waking you now."

She rubbed her eyes. "I only wanted to sleep a couple of hours."

"Are you always this cranky when you get up?"

"Cranky?" Dawson sat up in bed, and looked around. It was still dark outside. "Feels like it's the middle of the fuckin' night."

"It is," Morris replied, hovering near the bed.

"The boys worked on Wang Chi all last night and into the early morning."

"So, what happens to him?" she asked, swinging her legs over the edge of the bed.

"Shears wanted to put a bullet in his head," Morris answered, "but I managed to convince them to seal him in a body bag and drop him at the Chinese embassy. They'll think the Tongs beat him up."

Kate shook her head. "I hate to admit it, but Colonel Shears is right. The only way to deal with vermin, like Wang, is to kill it."

"My-my, aren't we just cheery this morning," Morris joked.

"I haven't had my morning coffee," Dawson said, with a shrug. She glanced around the room, and sighed.

"Did I miss Shears and his men?"

Morris nodded. "Yeah, they bugged out ten minutes ago."

"Too bad," she remarked, with a hint of regret. "I was going to ask him if I could borrow a gun with a bit more firepower than my old service model. I guess it will just have to do."

"You normally carry a 9mm Beretta. Right?" the justice agent asked, as he walked into the kitchen of the safe house. He unlocked the pantry cabinet to reveal a hidden armory. He pulled down a Beretta and box of shells, and handed them to her. "Consider it a loaner from Uncle Sam."

"Thanks, Morris. I guess we'd better get this show on the road." She stood, smoothed out her blazer, slipped on her loafers, and accepted the semi-automatic.

It was a little after 3 am on Thursday morning, the seventh day of the "sick-out," when Kate Dawson and Philip Morris made the left at Hyde and O'Farrell, and turned into the Tenderloin. All around them, the city lights of San Francisco were twinkling majestically, and the Golden Gate Bridge could be seen in the distance across the Bay, a pleasant, welcome sight to most in the early morning hours. But in the Tenderloin, the only lights on the street were the darkened theater marquees and street lamps above the old, abandoned railway line.

Morris' late-model Ford Escape rambled slowly down

O'Farrell Street with the traffic, past the hookers, pimps, and the street people hanging out in front of the bars and all-night movie theaters. The Regal-Majestic Hotel was halfway down the street on the right, and they slowed as they drove past. Just beyond the hotel, Morris pulled into the alley, and drove over the abandoned tracks. There were alleys and freight bays on either side.

Morris stopped, threw it into reverse, and trained his headlights on the outer wall of the hotel as he backed it into place. Everything seemed to be very quiet, as they climbed out.

"Once we get inside the hotel and locate the girls, we'll bring them through the back door and load them out here," Dawson said, pointing to the rear exit of the hotel.

"We're less likely to be hassled by the locals, including panhandlers, if we can keep everything out here, away from the street."

Morris nodded. "That makes sense," he replied, looking up at the eight-story structure and its oldfashioned fire escape.

"If either of us gets separated—for whatever reason—this will be the rally point," she added.

"Whichever one of us makes it back here first will wait for five minutes, blow the horn twice, and then get the hell out of here."

"Alright now, let's not get all sentimental, Dawson," he said, smiling.

"This should be a simple snatch-and-grab, Morris," Kate reminded him. "No one knows we're coming, so we've got the element of surprise on our side. I'm guessing they'll be two, maybe three, guards, and most likely, they'll be asleep or passed out. Five minutes in-and-out. And if anyone gets in our way, shoot 'em, and we'll worry about their Miranda rights later."

"That's easy for you to say," Morris quipped.

"You have no idea how much paperwork the DOJ requires

for every agent-initiated shooting. I could be filling out forms for the next ten years."

Dawson stared at Morris for a long moment, and then shook her head, as a slight smile creased her lips.

"Whoops, I almost forgot," Dawson said, as she reached into her pocket and produced two tiny earpieces. She handed one to her partner, and placed the other into her right ear. "This wireless earpiece is used in much the same way that you'd use any other hands-free or Bluetooth device. The difference is that you don't need to connect it to your cell phone. It receives signals from a powerful receiver-transmitter that's located in Lenny's truck several blocks away."

You mean you'll be able to hear everything I say and hear?" he asked, inserting the device into his ear.

"Testing-1-2-3 . . ."

"Yes, and you'll be able to hear me," Kate replied.

"Got it."

Lenny is going to be tracking our movements on a very powerful, 'eye-in-the-sky' satellite that he developed at Northrop-Grumman with a grant from FEMA," she revealed to him for the first time. "At the first sign of trouble, we're pulling the plug on this operation, and getting the hell out of there."

Morris shrugged his shoulders. "I wish we'd been able to include the boys in this operation," he remarked.

"They've handled dozens of snatch-and-grabs just like this one. Mostly on foreign soil."

"Sorry," Dawson said, shaking his head. "We're already way out on a limb on this one. If it blows up on us—and it still might—we're gonna have plenty to answer for. The criminal justice system doesn't take too kindly to armed civilians taking the law into their own hands, and right now, that's what we are—armed civilians. You have no status with the DOJ, and technically, I'm on suspension from the SFPD. Can you imagine the hue and cry from the American public if they learned 'Captain America' and his 'howling commandoes' were on a black ops mission on American soil? They'd crucify us, and bury them in shallow graves. I'm sure they're good guys, but we're better off keeping this operation small, rather than risking turning this whole thing into a big shoot-out, like on the streets of Beirut."

"I know you're right, but it still gives me a moment for pause."

"Just stick to the plan," Kate reassured him, with a nod, pulling her long blonde hair back into a ponytail with a scrunchie. "Everything's going to work out just fine."

She and Morris worked their way around the back of the building, and walked down the alleyway to the street. They then inched their way along the sidewalk, and approached the hotel with great deal of caution. The Regal-Majestic was an old and tired, weathered building that had not aged well crammed up against a set of rusting railway tracks that had been abandoned in the thirties. A neon sign swung over the entrance: TRANSIENTS WELCOME.

Back in its day, the 1908-vintage, wood-framed hotel with seventy-eight rooms had been a tourist class hotel property that served a wide variety of visitors from all around the world. But now, with the exception of a handful of rooms set aside for poor and formerly homeless people, the management mostly rented rooms by the hour. The rundown hotel had been targeted for demolition several times by the nonprofit Tenderloin Neighborhood Development Corporation, but advocates for the homeless had managed to save it time and again for their constituents. No one seemed to care that its roof leaked, or the power went out regularly, or its solitary elevator creaked, or its dingy holes teemed with drug dealers and reeking trash.

Morris opened the wire-framed glass door to the lobby, and allowed Dawson through to the front desk. The only elevator was dormant, and the whole place was eerily quiet, except for an ancient cat in heat mewing loudly. The floor and bottom half of the walls were made of small black and white mosaic tiles, badly chipped and stained with urine. Dawson walked up to a floor-to-ceiling cage made of three-inch-thick Plexiglas armor with a small porthole in the center, and knocked. Inside an old man named Lloyd sat still, watching wrestling on a small black-n-white television. He spoke with a raw hoarseness that hinted at a lifetime of smoking cheap cigars and drinking cheap whiskey, "Yeah? What do you want?"

Dawson flashed her badge. "I'm looking for five, young Asian women. They're all under age, and considered runaways. I got a reliable tip they're here, and I just want to get them back to their parents."

"I don't want no trouble," he growled.

Dawson looked at Morris, and then turned back.

"You just tell us where they are, and there'll be no trouble."

"Room 605," Lloyd reported, passing a key to her through the small porthole. "Make sure you bring that back."

"Is there a connecting door to 607?" Dawson asked.

"Why, yes, there is."

"Give me that key, also."

Lloyd shrugged. "Why? There's no one in 607."

"Good," she replied, reaching for the other key.

"Just give it to me."

"You know if there's a reward for any of these runaways?" he asked, holding up the second key.

"You'll get what's coming to you," Kate promised. It was an empty promise but Lloyd didn't have to know that.

Morris moved to the elevator call button and pressed it,

bringing the elevator car down from the third floor. She collected the room keys from Lloyd, and strolled across the lobby to the elevator. Morris was already inside the lift, holding the door as she joined him inside. The ride up to the sixth floor was silent as Dawson reached under her Versace blazer and pulled out her new 9mm Beretta. She kept her head to the door, and listened, as each floor passed. Morris held onto the rail that encircled the interior of the elevator car, his gun to his chest, and watched the led display of numbers counting towards the floor: 3, 4, 5, 6. The door chimed open into the dark hallway, quiet and desolate. Dawson walked out, with her gun held out in front of her, followed by Morris who carefully kept a keen eye for anything unusual. Only the sounds of their footsteps walking softly on the marble floor could be heard as they tip-toed the rest of the way, ominously moving in the shadowy hall. They both noticed there was a light coming from under the door to Room 605, which meant the girls were probably still there.

Dawson indicated to another door further down, adjacent to 605.

Dawson unlocked the door to 607, and crept inside; the room black with only the light from a lamppost outside spilling in through folded blinds. Morris walked past her, and when he switched on the light to the bathroom, a nest of cockroaches went scrambling for cover. He fought back the urge to scream in terror, by biting down on his fist, but Dawson pulled him back from edge by switching off the bathroom light and leading him to the bed.

"I'm sorry," he whispered, sitting down on the saggy mattress. "I'm terrified of cockroaches and any other creepy-crawly bugs."

"A helluva time to tell me," she replied softly.

His bald head was covered in sweat. "I'll be all right, Kate."

"Good," she whispered to him. "Just sit here and relax for

a moment, and I'm going to check on the girls. If they are in 605, I should be able to see them through the keyhole of the connecting door."

Morris nodded, and sat on the bed to collect himself, while Dawson knelt on the floor next to the connecting door. She peaked through the keyhole, and counted three of the girls with their armed guards. Two of them were dressed and a third was being fitted for a uniform which looked vaguely familiar to her. Kate had seen the egg-shell blue blazer teamed with a cream skirt and a white neck scarf before, but she didn't remember where she had seen it. The two guards didn't look like guards either. They were dressed in black fatigues with body armor, and carried semi-automatic, military-grade pistols. They looked more like North Korean army regulars, but before she could react, the door flew open behind them. The lights came on, causing Morris and Dawson to squint briefly and adjust to the figures in the door way.

"Alive and well I see," a badly-beaten Wang Chi said, his distinctive announcer's voice booming, almost gleefully, "and still blundering around in the dark." He stood in the door, bandaged from head to foot, aiming a small Walther PP-S at the two of them. General Chang was next to him, along with a handful of soldiers who were fully armed with automatic weapons.

"And this is the resourceful, Inspector Dawson?"

Chang asked, stepping out and away from the group. His admiration for her was clear, as was the contempt that he had for his own man.

"I told you she would be here," Chi stammered.

"Yes, but I suspect due more to your complete negligence in handling this affair than to her innumerable skills as detective," he replied, annoyed.

Wang Chi shrugged. "How was I supposed to know their intelligence unit was going to grab me? At least, I made them waste valuable time interrogating me. Time that you used to land your men ashore."

"I would not have had to land my men ashore had you not endangered the safety of our assets with your incompetence," the North Korean general barked. "I regret that I must now take over operational control."

"There's no need to do that, Comrade General," Wang Chi assured him. "I still have everything under control."

"I don't share your optimism."

He pointed his semi-automatic pistol at the two Americans. "Once Dawson and her partner are dead, no one else will know where we've hidden our assets. We can then strike from here without anyone suspecting."

While Wang Chi spoke rather grandly about his plans, Chang secretly unbuttoned the cover to the holster on his belt, and slowly withdrew the Russian-made Makarov PM. He pulled a silencer from his pocket, and screwed it to the barrel of the Makarox. He listened patiently for another moment or two, and then fired the gun point-blank at Chi, who crumpled to the floor. Dead.

Chang then walked over to the body, and put two more bullets in the head, before he holstered his weapon.

"Oh, my God!" Morris cried out.

"What the fuck?!" Kate screamed.

"You have to be ready to pull the trigger yourself, once in a while, if you want others to fear you," the North Korean general said, repeating the words that he had once used with Chi.

Wang Chi's body lay on the floor, bleeding out into the moth-eaten carpet. The famous television personality from the East had hosted his last auction, and had delivered his last monologue. Several of the girls sequestered in 605 heard the shots, and had feared the worst about their owner. They were already crying for the man who had enslaved them and turned them into weapons of mass destruction.

Chang motioned to two of his men, then pointed at the two Americans. "Search them," he ordered in Korean.

"They're probably armed, and make sure you get whatever cell phones or pagers they may have."

Two, very large North Korean army regulars stepped out of the muster of his elite troops, walked over Dawson and Morris, and started frisking them for weapons and other contraband. One took the Smith-and-Wesson .38 caliber from Morris and tucked it in his belt, while the other soldier quickly relieved Dawson of her Beretta. In fact, he held the Beretta on both of them, as his partner ran his hands over Dawson, finding no cell phone or pager. Morris chose not to test the soldier's gun-toting temper, and quickly surrendered his iPhone. They also made them surrender their ear-pieces as they were both clearly visible to the naked eye. They then forced the two Americans at gunpoint over to the hotel room door and out into the hallway.

"What's going to happen to us, General?" Dawson demanded, as she was pushed face-forward into the wall.

Chang lifted the cap off his head, and scratched his full head of hair. "You have been a worthy adversary, Inspector. I truly regret that we did not meet under different circumstances. Not all Asian men are like Chi."

"Prove that to me, General," Kate insisted, as if she was already three steps ahead of everyone else in the hall. "Show me that you are a man of honor. End this now before anyone else has to die."

"I cannot do that. Regrettably," he replied, as a matter of fact, "the West is weak and corrupt, and must learn a valuable lesson in humility. Economic chaos in the West is the only way that we can possibly succeed in teaching the United States and the rest of the world about true suffering, disease, and famine. After tomorrow, a new power will emerge in the East, and North Korea will take its rightful place as the supreme leader of all the great nations of the world."

"I'm begging you, General, put an end to this," she pleaded with him. "I'm sure once the great powers learn what you and your men have done to stop the madness of Wang Chi, they will welcome you with open arms."

General Chang shook his head. "You are indeed a worthy adversary, Inspector, and I look forward to that time, many lifetimes from now, when our paths will once again, cross."

Lloyd, the old, front desk manager, pushed his way through the soldiers, and looked tentatively at Dawson. "I heard shots," he said, sourly. "I warned you that I didn't want no trouble."

"Call the police, Mister Lloyd," Chang said, handing him Morris' cell phone.

"What's going on?" Lloyd asked, no one's fool.

"Tell them there's been a shooting," Chang added, formulating a plausible story in the back of his mind, "and ask them to get here as soon as possible."

Morris looked straight at the front desk manager, stone faced. "You're being used Mister Lloyd." The last couple of words tumbled out of his mouth as he was struck on the back of the head by the butt of a rifle, and collapsed to the floor. The North Korean soldier who had struck him shouldered the rifle, and then kicked Morris in the stomach for good measure.

Lloyd looked down at Morris as he doubled over in pain, and then to Chang for some answers, but the north Korean general remained detached, enigmatic. He simply replied, "Do it." Confused, the front desk manager fiddled with the operation of the cell phone, but finally managed to dial 9-1-1 for emergency services.

Meanwhile, the soldier pulled Morris to his feet, and shoved him up against the wall. The back of his head was bleeding, and he was shaking. Dawson looked at the DOJ analyst, watched him helplessly at gunpoint, as her guard tightened his grip on the Beretta. Behind them and down the corridor, several soldiers with gasoline cans were tossing the flammable liquid on doors and walls and carpets.

"Hello," Lloyd said, finally talking to a 911 operator, "we've had a shooting down here. Regal-Majestic Hotel. Sixth floor. Come at once."

Chang took the cell phone from the old man, and ended the call. "Thank you, Mister Lloyd. Unfortunately, your services will no longer be required," he said coldly, and then shot him twice in the head with Morris' service revolver.

"Brilliant!" Dawson exclaimed, her voice cold, tinged with disgust, "I suppose that's the fate that awaits the rest of us. A bullet to the head?"

Walking down the nearly empty hallway, General Chang pressed the elevator call button, and waited for the elevator car to arrive. Kate surveyed the corridor, looking for something that would inspire her to attempt an escape, as she was certain she knew what was to follow. She saw that several wires to the elevator's call button had been pulled out of the casing, stripped and ready to be reconnected. The soldier stood with Dawson's weapon aimed at them as the elevator chimed gently and opened its doors.

"Please," Chang motioned to the door with his Makarov.

Dawson led her injured partner slowly into the elevator, the soft light illuminating them both in the mirrored confine of the glossy aluminum paneling and in the single aluminum-metal rail that encircled the middle of the car like a belt. Chang kept his gun aimed high, as he first reached into the elevator and pushed the button for the first floor, then backed away, letting the door close, trapping them in the elevator for its journey down. The elevator did start moving, but midway between the fifth and sixth floors, it stopped. *The wires pulled from the elevator call button,* Kate reasoned. *Chang or one of his men stopped the elevator between floors.*

A dozen of the North Korean army regulars emptied the remaining gasoline cans in the corridors on the fourth, fifth, and seventh floors, while several others gathered Wang Chi's girls together and escorted them down the stairs to a waiting van. General Chang had pulled open the elevator door with the help of his two aids. The shaft was in darkness; the elevator car with Dawson and Morris stationary only a few yards below. The General's demolition expert had made three Molotov cocktails, prepared from ready bottles of liquor and waste paper. He handed one to Chang and the second to Chang's first officer. He then took a lighter from his fatigue pocket and lit the paper fuse on the third. It fanned out to a large flame, as he quickly dropped it down the elevator shaft.

Inexplicably, it hit the roof of the elevator car below, but shattered on a nearby girder, and immediately burst into flames, spitting out liquor and dousing the cables and walls of the elevator shaft, crackling and burning freely.

They moved away from the shaft, and let the elevator doors gradually close.

The demolition expert lit the second one, and Chang's first officer threw the deadly mix into Room 605, where once more the Molotov cocktail erupted into a wild fire, catching onto everything in its path. Whatever evidence that had been left in the room, identifying the five girls, was quickly incinerated.

The remainder of Chang's men retreated down the hall, and followed the stairs down to the lobby. With one final cocktail, Chang used it on the hall, hurling it to the floor, smashing and setting the marble and carpet ablaze blocking off the elevator, the rooms, and the stairways up to the eighth floor. From the ornamental plants to the cheap pictures decorating the walls, across to the doors of the hotel rooms, occupied or not, rugs, incidental furniture, like desks and chairs, the flames illuminated the sixth floor with a devilish orange glow as it roared away.

"Come on, move. Get out!" General Chang shouted as he followed his officers down the six flights of stairs, keeping them moving as the fire behind them started to spread and smoke began to fan out. They quickly reached the last floor, and exited to the street through the hotel lobby. A handful of residents who had heard the explosions or smelled the smoke trickled out the door behind them. They were the lucky ones. The remainder of the hotel's guests were most likely consumed by the fire.

The heat from the fire baked the isolated elevator, like a warm tomb. Morris was crouching low to avoid the heat and the wisps of smoke seeping through the air vent.

He was still a bit shaky on his feet, but the bleeding from the injury to his head had stopped. He'd need stitches, but that was the least of his concerns at the moment. The single emergency light which continued to illuminate the elevator helped him and Dawson to see the escape hatch above their heads. Because she was closer, Dawson reached up to give the hatch a push, but the scalding heat from above burnt her fingertips when she dared to touch it. The pain shot into her hand like a barrage of needles, and she pulled back instantly, cursing herself for rushing ahead. The fingers on her hand started to throb and sting.

The metallic groan and whine from the elevator cables under

the immense strain of the car trapped between floors started to become louder, more menacing as the fire ate away at them above. Morris let out a sharp gasp every time there was a slight movement from the elevator itself or a noise from outside. Not knowing how to escape a fiery furnace or how long they had before they dropped nearly six floors in seconds wasn't something he wanted to think about. Dawson ripped the sleeve from her jacket and wrapped it around her tender hand to both sooth the burning and protect it from the heat.

Reaching up once more, this time more tentatively, Dawson used the back of her bandaged hand to pat the hatch; the heat now more bearable to the touch.

She pushed hard and the hatch opened, but the roar of the flames up the side of the shaft made them both duck down instinctively, as the intensity of fire was greater than they could imagine. The heat rushed in, and the sound of the crackling fire was much louder. Taking one more moment to compose her strength, Dawson pushed again on the hatch, and managed to open it, flipping it over on the roof.

The smoke started to pour into the elevator car, and the orange glow was now outshining the elevator's emergency light. They had more than enough light to assess their situation, and it was a grim one. The only way out of the car was through the hatch in the ceiling.

"Kate, be careful!" Morris shouted, fighting to be heard over the intense roar of the flames.

"The thought had occurred to me," she replied loudly.

Dawson tore the other sleeve off her jacket. Then, using the jacket sleeves and some good, old-fashioned elbow grease, Kate managed to hold onto the lip of the hatch and pull herself up, using the elevator's inner metal railing as a foothold. The flame from the fire was largely contained to the far back wall of the elevator shaft. Her greatest fear—that the car itself had been totally engulfed in fire—was not yet realized, but she wasn't about to wait for that to happen. The heat's intensity increased with each passing second. As she crouched on the roof of the elevator, the cable holding the car in place started to creak more. She could see the fire above her was eating away the steel fibers, causing them to buckle and twist under the strain. Eventually, they would give way, and the elevator would crash through the burning structure.

"Kate, don't leave me!" Once more from inside the elevator, Morris' cry filled the elevator shaft. "Don't leave me!"

Dawson had heard her partner's cry for help. She looked down, the smoke was starting to cloud her vision.

Coughing, frequently, with beads of sweat tickling her face, she knelt down over the hatch and extended her hand to Morris, his face full of desperation, still reeling from the head injury.

"Come on, Morris. Give me your hand," she shouted, as the cables above her creaked under the weight.

Morris crept forward in the elevator car, carefully shifting his weight as he moved. He'd torn the fabric pockets out of each side of his pants, and used them like gloves to protect his hands from the heat. Cautiously, he held out his arm, stretching as far as possible for Dawson.

"Come on!" Dawson shouted at the urgency of getting him out. For an instant, she glanced down at the cable holding the elevator car, and watched as its steel fibers were unwinding and buckling under the heat. It was seconds away from snapping with a loud clang of metal on metal. When the elevator shook again, she shouted, "We're out of time. You've got to do it now! Use the railing to climb up, just like I did."

Morris nodded his head, and with his left foot braced on the elevator's inner metal railing, he threw himself up to Dawson's waiting hand, clasping it tight, holding onto her for dear life.

Dawson pulled Morris up with all of her strength. Morris got up into a crouch, and held his gloved hand in front of his face.

"We've got to get to that door," she shouted, pointing to the fifth floor elevator door, giving him a small smile.

Morris nodded and tried to return the smile, but the smoke was too much and forced him to cough hard instead.

Out on the street against the night sky, the fire was now visible throughout the Tenderloin, licking out of the windows to the rooftop. It was a devastating yet somewhat mesmerizing sight to behold as the fire danced into the night sky and the roof started to give off a hellish glow. Bypassers below were crowded on the street and the sidewalk opposite the hotel, looking up helplessly, chatting and shouting in fear and despair. The sirens of the city police and fire department could be heard wailing as a wave of communal panic spread. No one seemed to notice General Chang, his North Korean army regulars, or the girls leaving the grounds, piling into their parked vans, ready for the perfect getaway amongst the commotion.

Within minutes, the fire blasted out of the sixth floor elevator door. Dawson covered her head and quickly glanced over the re-enforced shaft. She realized the elevator must have been installed in the hotel after it had opened for business. The steel structure—a collection of interconnected girders built around an elevator door on each floor—should have been strong enough to hold their weight. All they needed to do was to use the structure, like a ladder, and climb down to the next safe floor. She tested the girder for heat with her bandaged hand, and discovered that it was only warm, cool enough to get a grip on. She stretched out and lowered herself down the girders, using the joints as footholds and the girder lips as a grip for her fingers. She tried to resist inhaling, but the black smoke prevailed, making her gag and cough.

Letting herself down, nearly one rung at a time, Dawson managed to get to the fifth floor elevator door. She put her bandaged hand against the door; hot, very hot. The fire must have reached the fifth floor already.

Looking up the shaft, Dawson could see the figure of Morris watching her, the smoke lapping against him.

"We've got to climb down to the fourth floor," she shouted. "We dare not open this door."

"Understood!" he screamed back, his voice hoarse from a mixture of screaming and smoke inhalation.

Her body racked with searing muscle pain and sweltering heat, her lungs consumed with smoke, she climbed down the next rung of girders. When she reached the next doors, she was facing the elevator wall. Placing her foot on the lip of the door, she reached over with her hand to test it; warm, but not unbearably hot. Dawson grabbed the latch on the door, and pulled herself over, now clear of the shaft. Kate's arms shook as she pried the doors apart, made stiff by a lack of power, and only wide enough for her to squeeze through. She slipped her body between the slight gap, wedged her foot against the door and pushed it further open, stepping out unsteadily into the smoky hallway. The cries of her partner were the last things she heard as the door slammed shut behind her from the pressure of the hydraulic springs. Out in the hall, the flames could be heard echoing throughout the building.

Dawson grabbed the fire-axe from an old-fashioned fire emergency case in the hotel corridor, went back to the elevator door, the smoke trailing across the way. Using it to pry open the doors, she wedged the fire-axe between the gap.

"Help me!" Morris cried, becoming more and feebler with each passing moment as he worked his way down.

"I'll be right there!" Dawson shouted to him, letting Morris see her smoke-stained face, a reassuring sight in a hellish situation.

"I don't think I can make it," he replied hoarsely, coughing out loud. "Too many goddamned cigarettes."

Kate Dawson took hold of the girder that supported the fourth floor elevator door, and leaned out as far as she could reach. "C'mon, Morris, just take my hand," she shouted, coaxing him to reach out for her hand.

Morris slowly descended, holding onto the girder with one hand and steadily reaching out for Kate's hand with his other. "I can't reach you!" he cried out, each time as the agent stretched across the gulf between them. "I can't reach you!"

"C'mon, Morris, take my hand," Dawson shouted. She knew he could do it. He just needed the confidence to reach out and grab hold.

"I can't—I really can't!" he cried, his fingers tantalizingly close, but still just out of her reach.

"Goddammit, Morris! Will you just take my hand!"

When Morris felt the intense heat almost swallow him whole, he knew he had run out of time. Climbing down one more rung, he stretched out again for her—felt her fingers, then her palm, and finally her hand. He grabbed her hand, and pulled tight, nearly taking Dawson down with him. She was surprised by the sudden weight, but she had braced herself, pulling him in over the lip of the door into her arms. Kate cried out in victory, thankful to finally have him safe, as they crawled to the other side of the hall.

The metallic springing sound of the cable fibers snapping echoed in the shaft and out into the hallway as the flaming elevator car plummeted a good five stories down to the base-ment, a falling fireball that impacted on the ground with a dull thud, sounding louder in the confined space. They felt the thud, as did anyone left in the building that was still alive.

"Thanks, Kate," Morris said finally. "I couldn't have done it without you."

"Don't ever scare me like that again," she admonished him.

Morris nodded. "I'm definitely going on a diet after all of this. And if you ever see me take another smoke, you have my permission to break the fingers in both of my hands."

"Count on it," Kate replied, coughing uncontrollably.

"I've got a really stupid question," he said, after a moment's respite.

"What's that?" she asked, covering her mouth with her arm.

"If the fire is above us and below us," Morris asked, pointing up at the ceiling and slapping the floor, "how do we get out of here?"

"Bitch, bitch, bitch," Dawson replied, angry. "I got you out of there. Do you expect me to have answers for everything?"

The proud, red San Francisco fire engines had erected large ladders from two of the trucks reaching to the fourth floor fire escape. With oxygen tanks and protective masks, firemen climbed onto the rusted platform, and broke through the fire escape window. They found Dawson and Morris out in the corridor, both unconscious from smoke inhalation, but alive. Firemen carried them down to the street level where they were provided with oxygen and damp towels for their shoulders. Jets of cold water continued to spray out the affected areas of the Regal-Majestic Hotel as the sky was lit up by the fire pluming from the roof and windows, the smoke spiraling into the darkness.

By the dawn's early light of morning, the hotel was just a shell; the girders from the elevator shaft, the only structure still

JOHN L. FLYNN

holding it together. Less than twenty bodies were recovered from the fire—Wang Chi and Lloyd among them—and those bodies were lined up in body bags on the street for the coroner to identify and tag.

Those badly-burned victims, who were still alive but had suffered from smoke inhalation, rested in a triage area.

Dawson and Morris were there, lying together on the pavement.

"Morris, you're safe," Dawson said, sitting up, looking east towards the sunrise, as she held her partner's trembling hand softly.

For an instant, he pulled the oxygen mask away from his face, and said, "Thanks, Kate, I owe you my life. If it hadn't been for you, I'd be dead."

"I'd say we helped each other through," Kate replied, with a deep raspy cough, as she helped him put his oxygen mask back on.

Lenny Provolone scrambled by the police who were keeping the media and curious onlookers away from the injured, and looked up-and-down each row until he found Dawson. He said with relief, "Oh, my God! You're still alive. When I lost your signal, I feared the worst."

"They took away our earpieces, Lenny," she explained, still coughing. "We had no way of getting in touch with you."

He nodded. "I'm just glad you're safe."

Kate Dawson looked up at him. "We have no time for sorrows, my friend. The G-20 Summit is still going ahead as planned later this morning, and we have to stop those girls before they turn into WMD."

"What do you want me to do?" Lenny asked, after taking a deep breath.

"We're going ahead as planned," she said, quickly thinking

things through. "But without our earpieces, we'll have to rely on cell phones in order to stay in communication with each other."

"Cellular phones are less than optimal at the Moscone Center," he reported. "Far too many dead zones."

"We'll just have to make due, Lenny."

"What about Agent Morris?"

She reached over and examined her partner, who wasn't very responsive. "I think we're going to let him sleep it off."

"That's a lot of convention floor to cover," Lenny reminded her.

"I know," she sighed, tired and exhausted. "You'll just have to keep your 'eye' out for me, and let me do the rest."

A police siren wailed behind the crowd which was bustling along the sidewalk, people shouting and pointing at the shell of a building. The police car left its lights flashing, and the officers got out of their squad car with their black batons drawn in order to keep the crowd at bay. The police captain also got out, and fixed his hat square on his head, his leather jacket zipped up tight. He was a big man with a grey mop of visible hair under the hat and a short moustache that made his face appear larger than it was. He battled through the excited crowd, and approached Inspector Dawson and her two companions.

"I wanna talk to you," the captain said. "Dawson, is it?"

Dawson struggled to her feet. "Captain, if you can get to sixth floor, you'll find the building manager's body there, as well as the body of a Chinese national named Wang Chi. They were both shot to death by General Ri Kyu-Chang, a North Korean hardliner from the Cold War days, who is here with some of his men."

"We found both of them, and this gun," the captain replied, holding up a clear plastic bag with a badly burned 9mm Beretta. "This yours?"

"Yes, it's mine. I borrowed it so that I'd have more firepower," Kate said, reaching for the bag. Instead the captain handed the weapon over to a police officer behind him. "If you bothered to check, you'd find the 9mm Beretta hasn't even been fired once."

"Then you deny shooting those two men?" he asked.

Lenny heard the question, and decided that was the right time to make himself scarce.

Dawson was stunned by the accusation. "I didn't shoot anyone. General Chang shot both of those men. Your forensics will confirm that he used a Russian-made Makarov PM."

"What were you doing in that building?" the captain demanded.

"Following up on a lead in a homicide investigation," Kate said.

"A homicide?" He looked at her torn blazer and blackened loafers with skepticism.

"Yeah. My partner and I had gotten a tip from a local snitch that suggested our suspects in a homicide investigation were held up in a room on the sixth floor of the building," she replied, trying to keep her story simple yet truthful. "When we arrived, we found Chang had taken our suspects for himself and killed two potential witnesses. He also started the building fire to cover his tracks."

The Captain looked at her and grunted. "I've got two dead bodies with holes in them, a murder weapon, and a pretty good murder suspect, but you're trying to convince me that I'm all wrong."

"Your evidence will simply not hold up, sir." She coughed and wiped her soot-covered hand across her brow.

"No?"

"Besides you have no motive," Dawson added.

"Why would I kill either of these men? I'm a homicide detective."

The Captain didn't answer immediately, but stared hard at the two of them. She could almost see the wheels in his head turning as he thought, plotting his next move, figuring out how to best turn his suspicions about the two of them into cold, hard facts. There was an air of familiarity about him. He was not at all that different from her boss, James Roberts, a man who would rather shape the facts in a case around his own narrative than to find the real truth of the matter.

He hesitated a moment longer, then gave in.

"You've obviously been through a harrowing ordeal here this morning. I get that. But I also need your help in sorting out some of the inconsistencies in this case, also."

"We understand, Captain," Dawson answered for the two of them.

"Good," he replied, with some degree of satisfaction. "Why don't we meet in my office tomorrow morning, 9 am?"

Kate nodded. "Tomorrow morning, 9 am."

CHAPTER NINE

After a quick shower and fresh change of clothes, Kate Dawson climbed into her barely-drivable car, and drove to the Moscone Center. She crossed over the Embarcadero, and headed up Market Street, driving alongside the hundreds of other Bay Area commuters who drove into the City every day from the outer communities. Kate hardly ever used Market Street because it was one of the main thoroughfares that channeled most traffic into the downtown area, and soon found herself regretting her decision as she sat in bumper-to-bumper traffic. She hated the notion of having to inch her way there, but there just wasn't a shorter or faster route to the convention center.

She settled back into her seat, scanning the area, constantly glimpsing into the rearview mirror. First, she spotted the BART station for the Red Line at Montgomery Street, and wished that she was on board the Bay Area Rapid Transit train instead. Then, she clicked through the channels on her car radio, but every station seemed to have the same lead story with newscasters endlessly repeating details of the fire at the Regal-Majestic Hotel from that night. "You don't know shit," she chided the spokesperson. Disgusted, she rested her head back against the car's headrest, and looked up at the moving billboards.

No sooner had she changed focus, the one electronic billboard above the BART station played a jazzy tune, followed by images of flight attendants. Kate rolled down her window and pricked up her ears, listening: "It's all about you . . . a million dreams or more. It's all about you . . . at the heart of our world is you. It's all about you . . . excellence in flight. Korean Air." She stared dumbfounded. Five, sexy Asian women, dressed as flight attendants, walking slowly in slow motion down an airport runway in front of a Boeing 737. Each one of them real beauties wearing an egg-shell blue blazer teamed with a cream-colored skirt and white neck scarf that seemed to defy gravity. Even though it was just a simple commercial for Korean Air Lines, it suddenly all made sense to her. She made the connection. They were going to walk the girls right through the front door as these world-class flight attendants, and no one was even going to take notice of them, hiding in plain sight.

Dawson took out her iPhone, and dialed Jonathan Prinze, but the number rang over to his voicemail. "Jack, this is Kate," she said, speaking into the lower half of the cell phone. "I just figured out how they were getting the girls into the Moscone Center. They're going to be dressed as flight attendants for Korean Air. I'll send you an image or two. I should be there in ten to fifteen minutes. Traffic permitting. Bye."

At the next red light, Kate opened her Safari browser, and called up images for Korean Air. A thousand or so images appeared on the Internet, mostly of planes and corporate buildings in South Korea and businessmen. But as she scrolled through them, she refined her search criteria, and then selected only six or seven images to show him. They were individual images of the beautiful flight attendants in their distinctive uniforms. As she inched along in traffic, Dawson selected one after another, and saved them to her image file. She then entered Jack's cell phone number, and sent them off to him as one batch. Once he got her voice message, he'd understand what they were.

Like other great icons from the past, she realized the Korean Air flight attendants had certainly played a significant part in the company's 45th anniversary celebration and revitalization in 2014, with a series of memorable commercials depicting air travel as a sensuous experience. Kate clearly remembered them, and also the way in which ordinary travelers would stop and look at the flight attendants as they walked together as a group through airports and hotel lobbies. They seemed to have transcended the travel industry that had spawned them, and become an industry of their own design, not unlike the Dallas Cowboys Cheerleaders or the Radio City Rockettes. The Korean Air flight attendants were wanted everywhere, from half-time shows to parade marshals and now the G-20 Summit in San Francisco. Whatever they had planned for today's exhibition, it would be spectacular. If only Dawson had managed to figure it out sooner, she might have been able to do something well in advance of the conference. But now, it had come down to a matter of minutes.

She looked around—drivers in the other cars, pedestrians walking along the sidewalks, another eight or ten passengers who boarded buses and took their seats—all average people just like her; commuters going to work on this Thursday morning, each with their own fears and concerns for the future. As she looked at each face, she realized that they were all counting on her to do her job, expecting to return home that day to the loved ones that they held dear. No matter what happened, she had a responsibility to serve and protect.

Half-way between Montgomery and Powell Streets, the traffic finally opened up, and Kate gunned it.

She knew the streets in front and around the Moscone Center would be a big cluster fuck, so she turned right and followed the road directly into the Moscone Center Annex. Squads were parked there, as well as her fellow plain-clothed detectives. She waved at the cop directing her right into the parking garage, taking the first available spot. Within moments, she was scrambling down the long tunnel with others heading towards the convention center floor. As she moved along, Kate realized that she wasn't dressed at all like the others—comfortable pair of dark brown, gabardine slacks and loafers, a button-down blouse and tweed blazer she rescued from a bargain bin at Macy's—drab. She'd braided her hair into a ponytail and thrown on very little blush, just enough to hide the dark black circles under each eye. She carried her back-up piece, a .38 caliber Smith & Wesson, a six-shooter, that she kept secure in a small safe in her bedroom, and a couple of the quick reload cartridges in her jacket pocket.

Entering the Moscone Center, she stepped out of the tunnel into a bombast of light and sound. She paused for a moment to look for Prinze, and felt suddenly overwhelmed by what she saw. An overhead banner which ran the length of the entrance hall read: "G-20 Summit: Making Tough Decisions Today for a Better Tomorrow." Up until that very moment, for Kate, the G-20 Summit had just been an event on the calendar at the Hall of Justice, and all of the planning and preparation that had gone into ensuring the conference went off without a problem had boiled down to just a few moments in her life as a cop. Her actions, and her actions alone, would determine the fate of the world for the next fifty years to come. Dawson's head was spinning, and all at once, she found herself back in that training room at police headquarters . . . six months earlier . . .

"What's so damned important about the G-20 Summit?" Kate

asked the trainer, with her hand raised. The training room was small, but most of the detectives from the Homicide Bureau, including Clark and Jawara, Matt Balardi, Jorge Ramirez, Corcoran and Farris, were all there in attendance, under the watchful eye of Lieutenant James Roberts. "I mean, we know that it's coming. I guess, we just want to know why it matters so much."

Officer Mary Sparrow, the face of the San Francisco Police Department in all media-related matters, listened to Dawson's questions, and then paused thoughtfully before responding. "On Thursday, November 16, Mayor Gordon and Governor Brown are going to host the annual G-20 Summit at the Moscone Center for government leaders from around the globe representing twenty of the world's largest economies. At face value, the aims of the meeting are hugely ambitious and, with the world still suffering from the throes of a global recession, the organizers hope to create a long-term vision that could make a significant contribution to global economic recovery. Issues like political reform and climate change will also be discussed. It's also important domestically for the United States to demonstrate leadership at this summit meeting, and show the rest of the world that we have zero tolerance for any form of terrorism."

"Twenty countries," William Clark repeated, taking notes in his notebook. "Will we have a list to work from of those delegates from each country? It would be great if we had the chance to run the list against our database of known terrorists."

Mary Sparrow sighed. "Yes, Inspector Clark, I'll make sure you get a list of delegates," she replied. "But you should remember that the G-20 is an organization for finance ministers and central bankers, not terrorists."

Clark nodded. "Would you be able to tell a finance minister from a terrorist?"

"No," she confessed, losing some patience.

"Well, by cross-checking with the no-fly list," Clark explained, "we'll have a better idea of who is at the conference for reasons other than banking and finance."

"Leaders of all G-20 countries will also attend," she added, with a degree of concern. "We'll be expecting the new US President as well as representatives of the IMF and World Bank. It's also likely the UN secretary-general will put in an appearance. They will all require special handling. You just can't walk up to Bharat Mata, the Secretary-General of the UN, and ask to check her ID against a terrorist watch list."

William Clark grinned. "Don't worry so much, Sparrow. We know how to be discreet with world leaders."

"Which countries make up the G-20?" Ramirez asked, curious.

"G-20 literally means 'group of twenty,'" she answered, turning to Jorge and singling him out for his question. "There are nineteen countries who are members: Argentina, Australia, Brazil, Canada, China, France, Germany, India, Indonesia, Italy, Japan, Mexico, Russia, Saudi Arabia, South Africa, South Korea, Turkey, the United Kingdom and the United States. The twentieth member is the European Union, which is represented by whichever country holds the EU presidency; currently, it's the Czech Republic."

"Bueno," Ramirez returned.

Sparrow nodded at him. "I should also point out that two other countries will be there: Thailand, as chairman of Asean (the Association of South East Asian Nations), and Ethiopia, as chairman of Nepad (the New Partnership for Africa's Development). They are merely guest countries who have been invited this year."

"I can understand why you'd want to include the United States, Russia and China," Jawara said. "Most of the world's muscle lies with one of these three nations. But I can't imagine why you'd include Mexico or India. They seem so third-world. I'd be more inclined to add Norway or Iran."

"Inspector Jawara, the G-20 isn't a list of superpowers," she corrected him. "The countries in the 'group of twenty' represent ninety percent of global GDP, eighty percent of world trade, and two thirds of the world's population."

"Might does not always make right," Clark whispered, trying to correct his partner.

Jawara shook his head. "That is so lame, Clark."

"Has a G-20 Summit like this ever taken place before?" one of the other detectives asked for clarification.

Mary Sparrow kept her cool, with a smile. "Yes, detective, this is an annual event," she replied. "This is actually the 12th such summit. The first was in Washington D.C. in 2008, and last year, they met in China."

"With so many of the world's top leaders gathered together into one place, aren't you the least bit concerned with a strike from rouge nations?" Clark asked.

"Of course, that's why we're meeting today," she concluded, all perky. "For the next several months, I'm going to be meeting with each of the different bureaus and departments to plan out a comprehensive strategy that will ensure the G-20 Summit is not only successful but goes off without a hitch."

Dawson's head continued to spin around, until she was once again back at the Moscone Center, looking up at the sign. All the months of the planning and preparation that had gone into the G-20 Summit had boiled down to this moment in time and whatever actions she needed to take to prevent a disaster from happening. She glanced at one of the many monitors placed strategically around the room—the one closest to her was in

French—and read the clock in the lower right corner. It read 7:55 am. Prinze had instructed her to meet him in the entrance lobby at 7:45 am. He was late, and as the minutes ticked by, her level of anxiety increased ten-fold. She had to get in there before something happened.

The entrance to the Moscone Center was jampacked with people from various countries, walking, talking, and waiting to get into the main floor of the convention center. At each of the entrance doors, armed security guards stood watch, supported by dozens of police officers in uniform milling about, randomly checking identifications, and helping people find others from their party. Over her shoulder, she glimpsed the long, black limousines as they pulled to a stop at the entrance, and deposited additional delegates to the summit. Most men were wearing dark suits, with white or light blue shirts and colored ties. Some of the women wore traditional clothing that reflected the unique culture of their country, while others had eschewed that wear as old fashioned, and were in fact wearing business suits with skirts instead of trousers. As each of them walked through an entrance door, the delegates cued up in the long lines for metal detectors or broke off into small groups to chat among themselves. No one seemed like they were in a particular hurry to get into the main floor where the panels, workshops, speeches, and keynote addresses would take place. Everyone seemed to move at a very leisurely pace, even through the mandatory checkpoints and screening areas.

Security was tight, perhaps the tightest that Kate had ever seen. Once delegates had passed through the entrance, they were directed to one of several lines based upon their country of origin. Delegates from the United States, Canada, Great Britain and France, Italy, Germany, Mexico, Japan, South Korea, and Australia were sent through a PreCheck lane where they were permitted to keep their shoes on, and passed through a standard metal detector. Laptops, iPads, and other computing devices were scanned, and the delegates' credentials were authenticated with their identity by TSA screeners who were familiar with the process. Delegates from Russia and China, Saudi Arabia, Argentina, Brazil, India, Indonesia, South Africa and Turkey—those who theoretically posed the higher risk—were directed to the full-body scanners where advanced imaging technology screened delegates for metallic and nonmetallic threats, including weapons and explosives which may have been concealed under clothing. Screeners also tested laptops, iPads, and other computing devices by hand. And finally, credential authentication technology or CAT was employed to authenticate every identity document presented to TSA by delegates during the security checkpoint screening process. Some of the delegates beefed about two-tier process, but most accepted it as a consequence of the world in which they lived. Once they had passed through the security screening, delegates were permitted to enter the main floor of the convention center and move around at their own pace.

The clock on the monitor clicked over to 8 am.

Kate Dawson looked around, searching through the crowd for Prinze, but he was nowhere to be seen. She did find his company, Nexxus, under a sign which professed: "Bringing the Crossroads of the World Closer Together—Nexxus." There! Dead center, on a slightly raised platform, a bay of computers was open for delegates to check their email or confirm their dinner reservations. A few of the delegates had peeled off from the long lines, and were in fact engaged by some of his employees in computing. With her neck craned, she searched through each and every figure in the booth, but Prinze was simply not there. Maybe someone on his staff knew where he was.

She took a deep breath, about to start across the floor, as a figure moved up behind her and reached out.

Kate felt a man's large hand take hold of her arm, and yank her out of line. She turned, ready to run or defend herself. But by the time she regained her balance, Dawson was staring at Lieutenant James Roberts.

"Just what the hell are you doing here?" the Head of Homicide demanded. "You're no longer assigned to this case. You're on suspension, pending a full review. You shouldn't even be here, Dawson."

"I was invited by a friend," she said simply.

"What friends would you have in this crowd?"

Kate felt insulted by his words as she continued to look at her boss. "If you must know, he's the CEO of the City's largest and richest company."

"Jonathan Prinze? The Internet tycoon?" he guessed, flashing her a disapproving look. "You must be out of your mind, Dawson! Jonathan Prinze is a suspect in a murder investigation, the very one that you're investigating."

"Right or wrong, Lieutenant," she replied, "Jack invited me to be his guest at the summit, and I accepted his invitation."

James Roberts shot her one of his patented steely looks, and finally said, "Even though you'd been removed from the case and put on administrative leave, I never once thought about prohibiting you from attending the summit. Hell, the more police officers I got on the floor, the better I look. But I will warn you, I don't want any trouble. There's far too much at stake to let a rouge detective, like you, run wild and stir up trouble among the delegates. Just remember that my men will be watching you."

"You can't intimidate me, Lieutenant," she said.

"I wish someone would talk some sense into you," Roberts

mused. "You used to be such a promising detective. I'd even go so far to say that you were my top inspector. You certainly had an impressive track record of being right and solving cases. In fact, when you talked, the other detectives listened to what you had to say. I just want to know what happened to you. When did you become such a fuckin' *prima donna*?"

"I am still your top detective," Kate said proudly.

"It's just the way that I've done things lately has scared the shit out of you."

The Lieutenant shrugged. "Of course. You're reckless. You're undisciplined. You're unruly. I wouldn't be at all surprised if you had something to do with that fire last night. Had your handiwork all over it."

"And what if I did?" she asked rhetorically.

"What if I walked away from that fire with the information that would blow this case wide open?"

"I wouldn't believe you," Roberts replied, sourly.

Dawson glared at him. "I knew you'd say that."

Jonathan Prinze appeared out of the crowd of people, and approached them with caution, sensing the growing tension between Kate and her boss. He asked, "Is there a problem here, Kate?"

"Oh, Jack. Thank God," she cried, climbing into his arms.

Lieutenant Roberts shot a look at his female detective, and then, using the first two fingers on his right hand, he placed them on his eyes, indicating that he was going to be keeping a close eye on her. Finally, he lumbered away.

"What the hell was that all about?" Prinze asked, looking at her boss.

"Office politics," Dawson said simply. "I don't think we'll ever see eye to eye, and he resents the fact that I get results from doing things my way."

"He's got a lot of nerve," Prinze commented.

Dawson took a deep breath, and sighed. "I'm just glad you came around when you did. He can be such a fucking asshole."

"Just forget about him, Kate. He's not worth it."

"I know," she replied, nodding her head.

"I got your message and photos," Jack announced, taking advantage of a lull in the conversation to change subjects. "The flight attendants from Korean Air Lines are here as part of a very large contingent from South Korea. They arrived about an hour ago in three stretch limousines, and were very well-received by the crowd of delegates waiting to get into the convention center."

"Damn! I knew I should have gotten here sooner," she cursed. "Traffic was worse than I expected."

"You'll have plenty of opportunities," Jack said, looking at the schedule he had downloaded on his cell phone. "According to the official schedule, they'll make three appearances today, and will be part of closing ceremonies tomorrow. And of course the expectation is that they'll be out-and-about at panels and workshops."

Dawson craned her neck to look at his cell phone.

"Can you give me a run-down of today's events?"

"Sure," he replied, scrolling through the small print. "Right now they are making a brief appearance at the ribbon-cutting ceremony, which is already underway, and then, later this morning, they be featured in the Pan-Pacific tribute to Cho Yangho, the chairman and chief executive officer of Korean Air, and finally, late this afternoon, they'll be part of the parade of nations on the ballroom level."

"How accurate is this schedule?"

"Very accurate," he returned, as there was a "dong" sound on his cell phone. Jack scrolled through the settings on his phone, and clicked the alarm off. He then glanced at the message. "Do you mind if we walk and talk?"

She shook her head. "No."

They skipped around several long lines, and passed through the checkpoints at the front entrance of the Moscone Center rather quickly, with Jack nodding occasionally at individual TSA agents. Kate felt like she was getting treatment reserved only for kings and queens and statesmen, and not something afforded to the average delegates to the conference. When they reached the metal detector, Prinze took Kate's weapon and badge from her, and whispered something to the TSA official in charge, handing them over for inspection. The TSA official examined Dawson's identification and checked her gun before handing both back.

"What's with the VIP treatment?" she asked, retrieving her gun and badge.

Jack smiled. "I told each of them that I was madly in love with you, and that if they weren't nice to you, they'd be fired."

"C'mon, what's the real story?" Kate demanded.

"I'm the chairman of the committee, hosting this year's summit," he revealed with a twinkle in his eyes.

"You never told me you were the chair," she said, with surprise, as they continued walking, taking the steps down into the actual convention center.

"It's critical that the schedule be accurate," Prinze said, ignoring her comment. "Since there's a lot of business that must get done at these summits while all of the delegates are present, the host nation's executive committee must keep to within a couple of minutes of the published schedule."

"Which of those three events is most likely to draw the largest number of delegates in attendance?" she asked, pointing at his cell phone.

Jonathan Prinze thought for a moment. "Other than the keynote speaker's address to the conference delegates, I would guess the parade of nations and closing ceremonies. Both of those are scheduled for the largest spaces in the Moscone Center and traditionally have been favorite, crowd-pleasing events."

"What about this Pan-Pacific tribute to Cho Yangho?"

"It's scheduled in the smallest of our venues," Jack answered. "The Moscone Center Theater, which seats about nine hundred guests."

Dawson grinned. "I think we can probably rule that one out. With these five girls programmed to be weapons of mass destruction, General Chang is looking to maximize the number of casualties in this strike by scheduling them in a venue which holds the largest number of people."

"How do you know that?" he asked her.

"Because that's what I would do," she said, thinking like a terrorist.

Jack had a puzzled look on his face. "Something doesn't make sense to me."

"What's that, Jack?"

"We know these girls are carrying the deadly toxin inside of their bodies in some resin-polymer container," he stated the obvious. "How exactly are they timed or triggered to go off?"

"We don't really know," Kate confessed, with a shrug. "Based upon the results of his autopsy of Mylee's body, Dr. Brogan seems to think the body's naturally defensive amino acids and enzymes are eroding the containers, and that they will reach the core at a specific time and go critical."

"But you don't agree with his scenario?"

"No, I don't," she replied. "Everyone's body chemistry is different, and to think that one person's complex set of amino acids and enzymes are going to work in concert with another person's to achieve a specific goal at an exact time is naïve assumption. I'm more inclined to think they will be triggered somehow."

"How are they going to do it?"

"It's my guess that General Chang or his personal physician will give the girls a highly corrosive substance to ingest; in fact, they may have done that already, depending on the timing of their event," Kate said, with some thought. "They'll tell the girls it's a vitamin supplement, or something like that, and then in eight-to-ten hours, the girls will start suffering with cramps, collapse, and the cores will rupture. They will then become lethal weapons of destruction."

"What a horrible way to die," Jack remarked.

"Of course, Chang may have wired each of them with a tiny explosive, no bigger than a pin-prick, and plans to trigger the explosives from a remote location later. We just don't know," she concluded. "At least, there was no evidence of a wired explosive in Mylee's body when Brogan conducted his autopsy."

Prinze stopped walking, and turned to Dawson.

"What should we do?"

"I'm not sure," Kate replied, coming to a stop.

"The girls have been brainwashed by some of the best behaviorists in North Korea, and likely wouldn't respond to any of our commands, even if we found them in time. I'm also concerned that, if we start trying to pick them off one-at-a-time, the rest would resort to a fallback plan that includes self-immolation to avoid capture and detection. Self-immolation would result in the same dispersal of the deadly gas, perhaps with fewer casualties, but the end result would be the same, terrorists strike G-20 Summit on American soil."

"Doesn't look like we have many choices."

"I can think of only one," Dawson said, putting her hand to her head. "We pick them up all at once or we maneuver them into a containment room, and then seal it off from the rest of the convention center."

"A containment room?" Jack repeated, thinking aloud. "This isn't the Lawrence Livermore National Laboratory or NASA. We don't have anything even close to a containment room."

"Actually, I was thinking about the Theater. Particularly if there was some way that we could block off the vents."

"I think there is," he replied, as another "dong" sounded on his cell phone. Prinze glanced through his settings on the phone, and clicked the alarm off. "I've got to run. I'm actually already late."

Kate bobbed her head. "Where can I find the theater?"

"One floor up," Jack said over his shoulder, pointing upwards with his right hand, "and all of the way down."

When she reached the Moscone Center Theater, Dawson caught a glimpse of one of the North Korean army regulars at a door marked "No Admittance," and then he was gone, as if he had vanished into thin air. She ran up to the door, and tried the door handle, but it was locked, tighter than a drum. Kate looked around, and saw one of the armed security guards.

"Open this, please," she said, pointing at the door, while flashing her SFPD badge.

The security guard opened the door.

"Have you seen a cop on duty around here?" Kate asked.

"Sure," he replied.

"Get 'em," she concluded, going through the door. "And hurry."

Dawson walked down a dark corridor, moving very cautiously. She jumped, nearly out of her skin at a large shadow, but then realized it was part of the air conditioning system for the building. She continued walking along, and came to realize that she was actually in one of the large maintenance rooms for the convention center's heating and cooling system. Up ahead, she saw one of two men with his jacket off. He was dusting off his hands like someone who had just finished a job, while the other just stood around with a walkie-talkie in his hand.

She pulled the hammer back on her Smith & Wesson, sixshot revolver, and kept her finger on the trigger guard as she approached them with caution.

"Excuse me, gentlemen," Dawson said, her badge in her left hand, while her right hand aimed the sixshooter.

"This is a restricted area. Security personnel only."

They turned quickly; both of them surprised by her intrusion. The man in front raised his hands high in the air, as if surrendering to her, but his very broad movements made it difficult for Kate to see what the other man was doing. The man in front said in broken English, "Please no shoot. We work for Moscone Center."

"Yeah?" she replied, dubious. "Let's see some ID."

Instantly, the man in front dived for the floor, providing the other man who had a pistol a straight shot at Dawson. She had anticipated his move. For in the second or two that it took him to sight her up for a kill shot, she managed to fire her revolver at him, and jumped aside.

The bullet from his gun whizzed right past her, but her shot struck him right in the head. He went down, and was cold before he hit the floor. She moved forward expertly, gun ready, but by the time she had reached the spot where the other man should have been, he was gone. His walkie-talkie lay there in his place, next to his partner, the dead man's body bleeding out onto the concrete floor.

Dawson dropped down to one knee, and surveyed the large room, her eyes adjusted to the pitch darkness.

She moved along, quietly, and reached for the walkie-talkie.

She picked it up, glanced at it very quickly. As she put the walkie-talkie away, safely in her pocket, she inched her way along the floor, listening and watching for some sign of the second man. She must have been close because Kate imagined she heard someone breathing very hard, but as she moved toward the sound, she saw that it was only the large coolant unit. It seemed to be defrosting in much the same way that a home refrigerator defrosts when turned off. She wondered exactly what they had been doing when she arrived.

At the next corner, she continued to keep her head low, and made the turn past the spot where the coolant had been dripping down, onto the floor, which was actually slippery, making her keep her steps small and well-placed. Dawson held her gun out in front of her, as she rounded yet another corner. The other man had to still be there. She would have seen him run out the door, if he had left the large room, so he must have been hiding in the shadows, waiting to get the jump on her. She knew that she had no chance in a one-on-one clash with a North Korean army regular. They were far too well-trained in jujitsu and other forms of hand-to-hand combat. And besides, she figured that he had a two-to-one advantage in weight over her. The only way to beat him was to get the drop on him, first.

Dawson moved from shadow to shadow, like a predator stalking its prey. All at once, she saw a flash of light, glinting off the man's Makarov pistol, and she had him. He was a couple of yards away, his back against one of the large air conditioning units in the room. She crept closer, and closer, and then, the familiar strains of Eric Clapton's "Layla" blasted out of her cell phone, indicating an in-coming call or text. Instantly, he whipped his head around, and started firing at her. Kate returned his fire, as she leapt to the floor. She hit the slippery spot, a combination of water, ice, and coolant, and went sliding across the floor into the open. He felt emboldened as she lay on the floor right in front of him, and stood up, ejecting his spent clip and forcing in a new one. He walked toward her. She reacted by rolling to one side.

That's all she could do. She then pulled the trigger on her gun, and kept blasting away at him until she was out of bullets. He stood over her, his gun pointed directly down at her, frozen for a moment in time, and then went down.

Bullet-holes in his head and torso appeared as if, by magic, and started spouting blood.

As she slowly got to her feet, Kate found a gun in her face.

"Freeze!" the first police officer said.

"Christ almighty! I'm a cop," Dawson said, scared shitless. She handed her gun off, and raised her hands in the air. "That's one of the bad guys."

The second police officer was unimpressed.

"Yeah? If you're a cop, where's your identification?"

"Right here," Kate replied, handing the second police officer her badge. "I'm a detective with the Homicide Bureau—"

"Her name is Katherine Dawson, but I understand that she prefers the first name 'Kate,'" the Chief of Police said, as he and two of his senior lieutenants walked into the large maintenance room, and started looking around.

They found the body that was laying on the floor right off the bat, but had to keep searching until they found the open door to the coolant section. "Bloody mess."

The first police officer said, "We were just following up on a routine complaint from one of the security guards about a breach in the perimeter—"

"—and we found her standing over the two bodies," the second officer finished.

"Well, what have you got to say for yourself, Dawson?" the Chief asked.

"I think you'll find that both of the men are North Korean

army regulars," Kate reported, telling them what she knew. "They belong to General Ri Kyu-Chang, a North Korean hard-liner from the Cold War days. He is behind the plot to infiltrate five Asian women, who are booby-trapped with a deadly gas, into the G-20 Summit, and intends to cause an incident that will bring about economic chaos in the West."

The police officers looked at her, like she was completely insane, but the Chief of Police merely smirked, smiling broadly for his two lieutenants. The two senior members of his team had each been with him at the Fairmont Hotel that fateful day, and were still smarting from the whole fiasco. The media had been particularly brutal with them after the week-long "sick-out," and no one in the senior leadership seemed to be eager to open that can of worms again, even if it was the truth.

"I've heard portions of this fairytale once before," the Chief commented, biting down hard on his lower lip to keep himself from saying anything that might be perceived as being offensive—and therefore potentially grieveable to the Union—to Dawson. "Are you still maintaining this ridiculous story about five women who have had canisters of cyanide gas implanted in their bodies?"

"Sir, I saw it for myself," Dawson said, going on the record. "During the autopsy on Mylee's body, the chief medical examiner extracted a small, rectangular box, which was about the size of a credit card, from her lower abdomen. It was made of a polymer-resin plastic which contained a high volume of cyanide gas under pressure. It had been deliberately implanted in Mylee's body as a kind of booby-trap. We believe the other five women have similar implants, and they are timed to deliver their weapon of mass destruction sometime during the conference."

"Credit card?" the Chief of Police repeated, mostly for his men. "Are they able to 'charge' by simply shifting their body?"

Everyone laughed at the Chief's little joke, except Dawson.

"Sir, I didn't say that it was a credit card," Kate corrected him, angry. "I said that it was about the size of a credit card."

The Chief of Police stopped laughing. He stared at Dawson long and hard, and then thought to himself.

Finally, he said, "Have you ever heard of the story about the boy who cried wolf?"

"Yes, sir," she replied. "Everyone has."

"How many times did the shepherd boy cry 'wolf' and fool the villagers?" he looked at her for an answer.

"Twice, sir," Kate said, wondering what this had to do with anything.

The Chief nodded. "That's right. And the third time?"

"The third time, the villagers thought that he was trying to fool them again, and they stayed home. Of course, this time, there really was a wolf, and the wolf scattered the boy's flock."

"Dawson, the moral of the story is that 'nobody believes a liar, even when he is telling the truth,'" the Chief of Police concluded. "I'm inclined to believe you, and I'm going to give you a second chance."

"A *second* chance?" she asked.

"Tell me truthfully. Are those women here? Right now. At this summit," he asked her a point-blank question.

"Sir, I have reason to believe the five Asian girls have infiltrated or been placed in the contingent of flight attendants from Korean Air," Dawson said, getting straight to the point. "I glimpsed one early this morning being fitted for the uniform, and I saw two others dressed and ready to go."

"And you didn't try to detain them?"

"No, sir, there just wasn't enough time," Kate responded, truthfully. "My partner and I got caught up in the fire at the Regal-Majestic, and the two of us just barely got out of there with our lives."

"I believe you," he said, nodding his head. The Chief of Police paused another moment, and then turned to his two senior lieutenants. "Johnson, have all your shift commanders report in *now*."

"What? You're buying into this," Johnson objected.

"I want them to report anything out of the ordinary, no matter how trivial," the Chief replied. "You got that?"

Johnson looked pissed. "I got it," he acknowledged, reluctantly.

"Barnes, I want you to get me a 10-20 on those flight attendants," he barked, as he turned to his other lieutenant.

"Right away, sir," Barnes replied, taking out his walkie-talkie.

One of the police officers handed Dawson her badge. "I'm sorry, Inspector, for all the trouble," the second cop said.

"Thanks."

As Kate pocketed it, the other handed her the Smith and Wesson he had taken. "A lot of you old-timers like to carry revolvers," the first policeman said. "When you're ready to step it up, come and see us. We'll show you what a Glock or Sig Sauer can do."

"Actually, I usually carry a 9mm semi-auto Beretta," she replied, a bit miffed that she had been mistaken for an "old-timer." "I lost one in the fire last night, and have had to resort to my old service revolver." Dawson opened the revolver, emptied the spent round, then quickly reloaded her weapon with bullets from her pocket.

The Chief of Police couldn't resist the opportunity to talk shop, even with the world potentially crumbling down around them. He pulled a handgun from his shoulder holster, stepped right in between them, and handed it to Dawson. "I prefer the .357 Sig Sauer. It's got good sights, and is very accurate. The trigger pull is a little hard, but once you get used to it, you'll never use another pistol."

Kate took the Sig Sauer from him, and sighted the pistol up. "That's a very fine weapon, sir," she said, returning it to him.

The Chief took it in hand, and returned it to his shoulder holster. "Stop by the armory sometime, Dawson" he boasted loudly, "and I'll find you a real replacement for your Beretta."

"That reminds me, Chief," she replied, reaching into her jacket pocket. She took out the walkie-talkie, and handed it to him. "The second man that I shot was carrying this walkie-talkie."

"Well, it's Russian-made, but that's not unusual."

"He didn't try to call anyone, so it's my guess he and his partner were willing to risk exposure breaking into this room to reset the position of the vents in order to maximize the destructive power of the gas."

"That's an excellent point, Dawson," the Chief of Police said. He turned to the two policemen who had been assigned to patrol this area, and asked, "What do we know about this room?"

"Sir," the first policeman said, "this is one of three access points to the Moscone Center's heating and cooling system."

The second policeman added, "Generally speaking, sir, from this one room, you control the temperature and intensity of air-flow to approximately one-third of the space in the convention center."

The Chief nodded. "Are we talking about the exhibit halls? The ballrooms? The theater? The east and west conference rooms? The gateway annex?"

"Sir, there's no way of knowing without looking at the original architect's plans," the second policeman said.

"Just what the hell were they doing in this room?" the Chief asked rhetorically.

"I'm telling you, sir, they must have been physically trying to re-align the vents for airflow, adjusting the intensity from one room to another," Kate repeated. "The first man had his jacket off, and was dusting his hands off like someone who had just finished a job."

"I want you to pull the architect's plans," he ordered the second policeman.

Barnes ran up, with his walkie-talkie in hand. "Sir, the South Korean delegation is reporting that several of the Korean Air flight attendants are missing. Apparently, they were just about to do a run-through of their Pan-Pacific presentation, and the count came up five short."

"Johnson," the Chief of Police summoned.

"Johnson!"

"Yes, sir," Johnson replied, scrambling to attention.

"Get back to your shift commanders," he ordered.

"Tell them that we're looking for five Asian girls, dressed as flight attendants. They should detain them immediately, but warn them, the girls are dangerous and extremely lethal."

"Flight attendants?" Johnson questioned.

The Chief of Police turned to Inspector Dawson.

"Have you got any intel on what these women look like? Uniforms they're wearing? Distinguishing features? Really anything at all?"

"I know that all five are Asian, between the ages of fifteen and nineteen," she replied.

"So's my aunt Tilley," Johnson growled. "Do you have any mug shots? Police sketches? Surveillance photos?"

"Yes and no," Dawson said, taking out her cell phone. She saw there was a text message, stored in memory, from Lenny. She opened it, and read that he had sent her satellite images of those arriving at the Moscone Center.

Johnson grunted. "Well, what is it? Yes, or no?"

"Yes, but I've got to download them," she responded.

The Chief shot her an impatient look as she was fidgeting with her phone.

Dawson nodded her head at the Chief, and then said, as an afterthought, "Sir, if you plan on detaining those girls, I'd gather them all together in one place, like the Theater, and seal off the vents. They are programmed to kill, and will stop at nothing to fulfill their mission. I now suspect the North Korean soldiers were working to prevent us from containing that threat."

"That's good thinking, Dawson," he said, with a smile.

As she scrambled down the long hallway leading to the door, she tucked her cell phone into her right back pocket, and clipped her badge to her jacket. Just as she reached the exit, Lieutenant Roberts and two policemen barged through the door. He opened his eyes wide, but was not actually surprised to see her. The head of Homicide pushed her back against the wall, his physical presence towering over her like some great ogre that was leftover from mythology.

"I warned you about interfering in official police business!" Roberts shouted, his voice booming in the corridor.

"Sir, with all due respect, I don't have time for this now," she said, feeling bullied, trapped by him.

"Dawson, just what the hell did you think you're doing, running around here, playing James Bond?" he demanded an answer. "I've got a nice quiet cell, back at police headquarters, with your name on it."

The Chief of Police appeared around the corner, with his two senior lieutenants. "Roberts, shut the fuck up, and do something useful. Like seal off this whole section of the building."

"You can't talk to me like that," the Lieutenant complained.

"Oh, is that right, Roberts? Why don't you take it up with the Union?" he replied, fuming mad. "I suspect they're going to be eager to talk with you, too, about the way you bully female officers. In the meantime, Johnson, get this fat-assed bureaucrat out of Inspector Dawson's face."

"With pleasure, sir!" Johnson replied, hustling Roberts away.

Dawson breathed a sigh of relief. "I was wrong about you, sir. You're not an asshole, after all."

"No, you were right," the Chief of Police corrected her. "I'm just your kind of asshole, but I'd have you on my team any day of the week."

"Thank you, sir," Kate replied.

"Now, get me those images, and fast!"

Dawson found Jonathan Prinze on the floor of the convention center. She ran up to him nearly breathless.

"Jack, I need access to a computer in order to download some satellite images that are being sent to me by my 'eye-in-the-sky.' Have you got a place where I can go, and work in peace?"

Prinze nodded. "Sure, no problem. My company has set up a bank of computers in the lobby of the Moscone Center. I'm sure, you've seen it. There's a raised platform in the center of the room, just beyond the entrance. Mostly, it's for delegates who want to check their email or reserve a table for dinner at one of the local restaurants. But you'll have full access to the Internet and whatever apps you need."

"I saw those earlier today," she replied. "I thought they were just for delegates with special access."

"No, anyone can use them," he said simply.

"Thanks, Jack," she said, giving him a kiss on the cheek.

"I'm glad that I could help out," he added, genuinely interested in helping her.

Dawson paused for a long moment, and then said, "Well, actually, there is one more thing that you can do."

"Something makes me think I'm going to regret this," Prinze said.

"You know the monitors that are placed throughout the convention center?"

"Yeah, I do," he replied, somewhat anxious.

"We're renting those at a thousand dollars a pop from a company in San Mateo called System Source."

Kate shot him a sideways glance. "If I wanted to cut in and broadcast an image of my own, what would I have to do?"

"It depends on the image," Prinze responded, with suspicion.

"Lenny has sent me images from the arrivals this morning, and what I'm looking for is an image or series of images of the South Korean delegation, specifically shots of the female flight attendants," she revealed to him.

"The Chief of Police was hoping that I'd upload them for his watch commanders."

"If you think I'm going to help the police, after what they've put me through . . ."

"Do it for me, Jack," she pleaded with him.

Jonathan Prinze walked away from her, then returned immediately with his hands on his hips, shaking his head from side to side. "I can set it up for you," he said, his voice low as a whisper. "That's really not a problem—the connection's already there—but I don't want to know anything about what you're doing. My company contracted with the Moscone Center to provide the monitors and set up the network that connects them all together. We also agreed not to tamper with the preplanned programs that were going to run on them, so I don't really want to know what you're doing. Call it plausible deniability. Call it whatever you like. Just leave me out of it."

"No problem, Jack," Kate said finally. "I've got to be prepared to upload those files to him. What he does with them—"

"Fine. Just don't say anything more."

She didn't.

Returning to the lobby of the convention center, where she had entered the building a short time earlier, she found the Internet lounge on a raised platform in the center of the entrance, then climbed the set of stairs to the platform and sat down at one of the computers.

After two of his men failed to check in, General Chang and two others—all three dressed as delegates to the summit—moved through the Moscone Center, searching for the person or persons responsible. He had a gut feeling it was Kate Dawson, even though his rational mind reassured him that she had perished in the fire at the Regal Majestic Hotel. *But then again, maybe she had managed to survive? Maybe she had climbed free of the burning elevator car, and was now stalking him and his men?* Chang thought long and hard about this, and regretted the fact that he hadn't put a bullet in her head earlier that day instead of trying to orchestrate her demise in a burning building. He felt the Makarov PM in his pocket; primed and ready. They were careful, cautious, and unrelenting. They searched through the sea of faces near the entrance. Face after face blended into each other as he scanned through the crowd. Most of the delegates had already gone into their sessions for the morning, so that left only the few stragglers, the large contingent of police and security personnel and a handful of convention workers.

At that very moment, Dawson sat at one of the computers in the Nexxus lounge that Prinze had created for delegates to check their email looking through random video footage that Lenny had sent her of those entering the convention center. The footage was in ten-minute segments that were time-stamped, and she could run through the segments quickly by using the arrow keys to fast-forward or rewind. Finally, Kate stumbled across the first segment, that of the South Korean delegation entering the Moscone Center, with the Korean Air flight attendants. The group appeared to be a large one, and she could barely make out the images of the young girls, but it looked like the group that she had been looking for. She quickly hit the record button on the computer, captured and stored the segment on her desktop. Dawson continued to move forward with her review of the footage, hoping to capture General Chang and his men.

On the large monitors spread throughout the convention center, random images from the day's events played out in real time. First, the arrivals of hundreds of limousines dropping off delegates at the door to the convention center. Then, pictures of people in the crowd, talking and listening to others as they made their way through the long, registration lines. Next, shots of the delegates scrambling to their sessions, with audio in a multitude of languages, describing what was taking place.

And then, finally, coverage from the keynote speeches, also playing in a collection of foreign languages.

Back on the floor, Chang thought he saw something, her long blonde braid, and pushed a couple of French delegates out of the way. He and his men scrambled forward, running across the floor, towards the Nexxus platform. Several police and security guards warned them against running, and they reduced their speed by half. Relentlessly, they marched at a steady pace, closing the gap between them and the platform in a matter of moments. By now, General Chang could see her very clearly. *It's her! That bitch is mine!*

With the entrance floor nearly clear of delegates, Kate Dawson glimpsed them out of the corner of her eye, and knew she had run out of time. Perched at a computer atop the platform in the middle of the floor, she realized that she was a sitting duck. At any moment, they might start shooting at her. Kate figured she had two options: she could run away, leaving the video footage that she had compiled on the desktop of the computer, or keep working, until they were upon her. They wouldn't dare kill her right there in the open, or would they? She didn't know just how crazy Chang was. But just at that moment, Dawson got a clever idea, and decided that she was going to keep working. Her fingers sped over the keyboard, as the two North Korean army regulars climbed the stairs to the platform and moved quickly and quietly by a row of delegates who were seated near her, checking emails, totally oblivious to what was happening around them. The two soldiers flanked her on either side, while General Chang walked up the stairs, and took a position directly behind her.

"You are indeed a worthy adversary, Inspector . . . to have out witted your demise," Chang said, slowly taking the Russian-made Makarov PM out of his pants pocket. He trained the weapon right on the back of her head. "Twice our paths have crossed, and both of us have lived to tell the tale. There will not be a third."

Dawson ignored his remarks, and continued typing. She then struck the record button on her desktop, and as a last measure, stretched the computer's built in camera into an anamorphic format. Whatever footage the camera captured as standard 35mm film rendered as a widescreen image. The far corners of the widescreen display showed delegates now cowering in their computer chairs, bug-eyed, focused on Chang who stood in the dead center.

"Back away from the computer," the North Korean General ordered, "and stand up very slowly with your hands raised in the air."

"Are you going to kill me, General?" she asked.

Dawson had stopped typing on the keyboard, and turned from the computer, looking over her shoulder at him. She could see the Makarov PM in his hand, but she could also see delegates on either side, in the crossfire. He took a step back, keeping her at a safe distance, and glanced at the screen.

"Now, stand up very slowly, and raise your hands in the air."

Kate hesitated, and didn't move. Her legs felt like they were made out of jelly, and wouldn't support her weight even if she did manage to stand up.

"Why are you doing this, General?"

"The West is weak and corrupt," he replied, eagerly repeating his mantra. "Its leaders must be taught a valuable lesson in humility. Only when their people are suffering with disease, famine, and death will they understand what we have known for decades. Now, you will stand up, and raise your hands up in the air."

Dawson finally stood, her legs unsteady, and put her hands over her head.

"I'm begging you, General Chang," she pleaded with him. "Don't do this. The cyanide gas will kill thousands of people needlessly. There must be another way to achieve your political agenda without resorting to mass murder."

"Economic chaos in the West is the only way for us to succeed!" Chang shouted, sounding like a true megalomaniac. "You will see. After tomorrow, a new power will rise in the East as North Korea takes its rightful place as the supreme leader of all the great nations of the world."

"I don't think so," Kate replied, dropping her arms.

With that, she punched one last button on her computer. The screen lit up with a scroll of information, and then started replaying their conversation in a loop, with images she had downloaded earlier to the desktop playing at random in the background. In a flash, her screen replicated on the computers on the Nexxus platform, and the frightened delegates who had been cowering at their computer stations received the first images from her broadcast. Then like a tidal wave, every monitor in the Moscone Center started playing—and replaying—Dawson's conversation with Chang in a variety of languages. Soon, the whole place was buzzing with the broadcast.

"Have you any idea what you're doing?" General Chang cried out, raising his Makarov PM at her.

"I know exactly what I've done," Dawson replied, with a grin. "Congratulations, general, your first video is a hit. It may even go viral when it hits the Internet and is seen by billions of people worldwide. Hopefully, that's all I'll need to stop you from killing thousands of people with your deadly scheme." She stared at him, a shocked and bewildered look in his face. "You want to shoot me, shoot. But I'd advise against it. The hall is filled with cops from the San Francisco Police Department, and they'd like nothing more than taking down a cop killer."

Dawson walked past the stunned North Korean General and his men, who stood there for a moment transfixed by the images on the computer screen, as she headed to the stairs. To his credit, Chang tried pushing every button on the keyboard in an effort to stop the program from running, but he was completely powerless to stop it. As he looked around, panicking, dozens of computers continued to display his face and replay his words, no matter what he did to disable the program. In just a matter of moments, he had become Public Enemy #1.

When she reached the top of the stairs, she motioned to the exits around the room, signaling armed security guards to come to her location. Other security guards and police officers from the SFPD who had seen the broadcast on the monitors headed to the middle of the room where the platform stood with its banks of computers. They formed up into small groups, and the first group mounted the steps to the top as a handful of frightened delegates got up the nerve to leave their computer stations and scrambled by Chang and his men on the way down.

Suddenly, Chang turned toward Dawson, with his gun drawn, and yanked a young Asian girl, who had been hiding among the delegates, into view. Miao Yin was one of the original six girls that Wang Chi had brought to the United States, and sold in the first round of the slave auction. She had also been the one Kate saw through the keyhole at the Regal-Majestic being fitted for the flight attendant's uniform. She flashed a mouthful of pearly whites as Chang pulled her body in front of him as a human shield and pushed his gun into her abdomen.

Dawson had dropped to one knee, and was holding her .38 caliber Smith & Wesson revolver on him.

With six shots, she couldn't miss, but it also meant taking out his hostage, too.

"Let the girl go, Chang," Kate shouted.

Chang ignored her, and issued a demand of his own. "Miss Miao Yin and I have decided to leave the summit early. You are instructed to clear an open path between here and the exit door, and to have a vehicle waiting for us at the entrance. No police or fire or emergency vehicles of any kind will follow us, or try to stop us. Failure to comply with any of my demands, I will shoot Ms. Yin in the abdomen, and trigger the deadly gas that she carries inside her body."

"But you'll die, too," she reminded him.

"That's right!"

Dawson thought about it for a moment, then she said, "General, didn't anyone ever tell you the United States government refuses to negotiate with terrorists." At that, Kate fired her service revolver at Miao Yin's right leg, and instantly, she went down. With the General's human shield gone, Dawson pulled the trigger on her gun, and shot Chang high in the chest. The bullet passed right through him.

General Chang dropped his weapon, staggered back, and looked down at his own blood in complete shock.

"You know, you were right, General," she confessed as police officers raced up to take his men into custody. "You have to be ready to pull the trigger yourself, once in a while, if you want others to fear you."

Incredibly, Chang was still standing, his eyes filled with shock and disbelief. He started to reel, falling forward against the railing of the platform, starting to topple over . . . Then, from some inward place, he found the last reserve of strength, and grabbed Miao Yin's wrist.

She was yanked off her feet. Chang went over the railing, pulling the young girl with him. Dawson had no time to think. She simply reacted, by leaping forward and catching Miao Yin's inside arm near the elbow at the last minute. The North Korean general lost his grip on her, and plummeted to his death.

Kate held on tight to the young girl, like she was her daughter, until police officials could help Miao Yin to safety. They also treated her bullet wound, which turned out to be superficial.

As they marched Chang's men away, Jonathan Prinze walked up, and reported, "They've contained the other girls in the theater, and several delegates, who are actually doctors in real life, have volunteered to work with them in removing the deadly gas canisters from their bodies. Looks like we got lucky."

"That's really good news, Jack," Kate said, as she sat down on the stairs and began rubbing the sore muscles in her arm."

Prinze nodded, watching the mop-up operations.

"It won't be easy for them at first, but maybe, just maybe,

they'll be able to go back to being teenaged girls again, and live a happy productive life."

"They're the lucky ones, Jack," she replied, taking a big, deep breath, letting it out between gritted teeth. "But what about the millions of others who live in the shadow of slavery every day? What happens to them?"

"I don't know," he confessed. "Maybe the next time world leaders decide to hold one of these summits, they'll agree to do something about human trafficking."

"We can only hope, Jack. We can only hope."

CHAPTER TEN

Late on Friday night, Kate Dawson drove through the front gate at Bayside Village Apartments, and pulled into a parking spot near her building. As she walked across the parking lot, she spotted Lenny's late-model, two-door Mini Cooper, and smiled. His assistance with the satellite images outside the Moscone Center had made a world of difference with her investigation. She had decided to drop by his apartment and say thanks before continuing onto her apartment. Maybe she'd suggest they go out some night and catch dinner and a movie? She was feeling very good, and nothing was about to dampen her spirits.

As she huffed and puffed her way up the steps, Dawson thought she heard voices outside Lenny's apartment, and paused in the shadows. From her vantage point on the stairs landing between the second and third floors, she could just make out a beautiful young woman, dressed to kill in a short, black cocktail dress. She was holding a bag of groceries, which she saw included a box of Capt'n Crunch cereal, Peter Pan peanut butter, a quart of milk, and a bottle of Mountain Dew.

"Lenny, please open the door," Rebecca implored him. "After all we've meant to each other, I don't want to see our relationship end like this. You've got to give me another chance. You just got to—"

"Rebecca," he said, after a long, silent pause. "It's not you. I just need a little space right now."

"Just open the door, Lenny," she pleaded.

Lenny Provolone cracked the door to his apartment, and looked out at her through the three-inch opening. "Hi, Rebecca," he said meekly.

"You've been crying," she said softly, fighting the urge to reach through the crack in the door and wipe away his tears.

"A friend of mine died," Lenny replied to her. "A good friend. I think I may have been in love with her."

She was silent for a moment, and then asked, "The police detective?"

"No, she's okay."

"You never said anything about another woman."

Lenny nodded. "I know. I should have told you everything, but I was afraid if I had told you the truth about her, you would have gotten mad at me and never wanted to see me again."

"Perhaps," she said, feeling a little hurt, "but then don't you think that was my choice to make, and not yours."

"I suppose you're right."

"What was your friend's name?" Rebecca asked.

"Rosa," he replied, softly. "Rosa Romano."

After a moment's hesitation, Rebecca bundled up her groceries into one arm, and pushed her way through the door, moving across the threshold of the apartment.

Lenny closed the door behind him.

Dawson rushed up the rest of the steps, and walking on tiptoes, moved quickly to her friend's apartment door. She put her ear to the keyhole, and listened, her heart beating loudly in her chest. Normally, Kate did not think of herself as a voyeur, but she wasn't about to be cheated out of the rest of this scene. She just had to know if Lenny was going to tell her everything about Rosa or stand there in his dingy underwear.

She heard the plastic bags crinkling like they had been set down.

"Come here, Lenny," she said, tapping on the edge of the couch. "Sit down, and tell me all about your friend Rosa."

"Whatever you say, Rebecca," Lenny said, in full compliance.

"Why don't you start with how the two of you met?"

In the dark recesses of the corridor, outside Lenny's apartment, Kate tiptoed away, smiling. Maybe there was hope for him yet.

On Saturday, November 18th, San Francisco Police Assistant Medical Examiner Rosa Romano was laid to rest at Woodlawn Memorial Park in a section of the cemetery devoted to law enforcement personnel who had been killed in the line of duty. With the "sick-out" officially over, a record number of people, over three thousand, including law enforcement officials from all around the state, crowded into St. Mary's Cathedral, while another two thousand lined the streets outside, to honor her. The funeral procession down Interstate 280 stretched for miles, and took over two hours to reach the cemetery in the sleepy town of Colma, California.

Kate Dawson rode in the lead limousine with Rosa's parents whom she had known for years. She wore the Gold Medal of Valor that she had been awarded for stopping the terrorist group from detonating an atomic bomb in the San Andreas Fault, and thus triggering the mother of all earthquakes.

Later that afternoon, Dawson climbed into a rental from Enterprise Rent-a-Car, still dressed in uniform, and headed south on the Interstate to spend a few quiet moments with her friend, alone. She drove along the highway, with the moon-roof open and the windows down. The late fall sun felt warm on her back, and she enjoyed feeling the wind blowing through her hair. At the exit for Colma, Dawson pulled off the Interstate, and then drove several more miles to the entrance for Woodlawn Memorial Park. Other than a collection of groundskeepers who were planting flowers, the cemetery was deserted, a stark contrast from earlier in the day. She drove around the outer ring, and parked near the section that now had her best friend. Kate got out of the sporty coupe, and walked along a narrow path, reading the names and dates on the markers, thinking about Rosa and her old partner.

When she reached Miller's gravesite, she reached down, and brushed away the leaves, twigs, and grass clippings. The plain stone tablet read: "Frank Miller. Inspector. San Francisco Police Department. Killed in the Line of Duty. November 11, 1952– September 22, 2014."

She still felt responsible for his death, for if she had not convinced him to take on that one final case, Frank Miller would still be alive. Dawson felt all of the emotions of the last week that had welled up inside of her, but she fought to keep them all in check. In his forty years of service to the SFPD, he had never once been honored with a medal.

With only one thought in mind, she reached up and removed the medal from around her neck. She placed it on the grave-stone, and stepped back away. "I miss you, Frank," she said softly, almost a whisper.

Dawson continued around the circle to Rosa's burial site. The groundskeepers had already taken away the pavilion, collected all the chairs, and filled in the hole with dirt and a sprinkle of grass-seed on top. So, when she stopped to pay her respects, she stood alone, a single figure silhouetted against a beautiful back-drop of rolling hills and blue skies that stretched for miles. She thought about her friend, and sniffling back the tears, recalled some of her fondest memories. Then Kate stood at attention in her dress blues at Rosa's grave, and saluted her fallen partner.

After a few moments of silence, she turned, and walked away from the grave, without looking back.

Dawson climbed into her rental car, and drove back to San Francisco, thinking of Jack and the night that was to come.

Just after 11:15 pm on Saturday night, San Francisco's heart was still beating, thriving with nightclubs, restaurants, and live entertainment. A few blocks away, in nearby Chinatown, the restaurants were all full, the stores were still open and filled with tourists buying tacky trinkets, and couples walked hand-in-hand through the tacky, market stalls, under the bright, cheerful lanterns that illuminated every square inch of town. Down one of the side streets, a quaint bathhouse was also lit up warmly by lanterns, set out in the ancient style of traditional wooden chalets. The house was made modern only by a single, flashing neon sign which advertised reasonable rates for spa-tubs and soothing, private massage sessions.

The private spa room was quite large, considering its seem-ingly small exterior. Fashioned in the traditional Chinese style, it was lit by small, warm spotlights in the ceiling and on the walls. The polished, wooden floor gleamed with droplets of water, and was only partially covered by small, cream rugs. Two silk robes and several, big fluffy towels were hung along the walls, and two small leather sofas, plumped up with plush burgundy cushions, lined the rear of the room. The large, steaming hot tub built right into the floor took up nearly the center of the room. Two full flutes and a bottle of Dom Perignon champagne stood nearby, condensation dripping from the bottle. Jack Prinze sat directly behind Kate Dawson, gently soaping and rubbing her shoulders. She grinned softly as her neck went limp as Prinze's strong, wet hands massaged her tense muscles. The bubbles foamed gently around them, the steam rising softly, easing away the previous week's tensions.

"That feels heavenly, Jack," Kate purred, like a cat that was being stroked. "This is such a delightful surprise. After the horrendous week that I've had, you couldn't have chosen a better date for the two of us."

"Just sit back and relax," he whispered, tenderly rubbing her neck. "Would you like it harder?"

Kate giggled softly, "Jack, you are such a devil."

"Didn't I tell you that, once you got to know me, you'd discover I was a really nice guy?" he asked, really not looking for a response.

Dawson shook her head. "It's hard for me to believe we had that conversation on Monday, just five days ago."

"Yeah, I know. It seems like it happened months ago," he replied, smiling. "Do you still think I'm guilty?"

"I dunno. And right now, I don't particularly care."

She pulled some of the lavender and soft peach scented bubbles into her hand, rubbing them gently down her arm, her face glistening with the water, tanned and beautiful.

"Jack, do you remember that first night we made love?"

"Yes, how could I have forgotten it?" Prinze whispered into her ear, caressing her lower body with his hands, tending to her back.

"I was so angry with you," Kate confessed. "My best friend in the whole world had just died and all I wanted to do was to get back to my apartment, lay across my bed, and cry my eyes out. You know, feel sorry for myself. But you wouldn't let me go.

You captivated me with that sad story about being a responsible leader who couldn't take a day off from work to go sit out in the sun and smell the flowers, and then you quoted me lines from a song written by my favorite rock-n-roll group. You surprised me, Jack, and that takes a lot. I mean, here you were, this cold-blooded murder suspect—or at least that's what I had been told—and you were worried about me."

"When did you first realize you had fallen in love with me," Prinze asked softly, a sly grin hidden on his face.

"Well, it didn't happen all at once," she replied, bursting his bubble. "It just sort of crept up on me, and was suddenly there."

Jack worked up her back, using a large sponge to douse her neck in warm water, flowing down her body.

"C'mon now, tell me the truth."

"Ooohhhh, you're so impossible!" Dawson sat up, and tilting her head back, gave him a kiss on the cheek.

At once, the magical charm of their romantic interlude was broken by the shrill, unmistakable guitar riff of Eric Clapton's first five bars of "Layla." As the ring tone on her iPhone repeated, Dawson realized that she had forgotten to turn off her cell phone and set it to vibrate.

She pulled herself out of the warm tub, her naked body dripping water and bubbles on the carpet. Kate slid into a white robe, which clung tightly to her wet body, and walked into the changing room where she had left her clothes and her purse. The cell phone was still ringing when she picked it up.

"Hello, this is Kate Dawson," she spoke into the receiver. "Who is this? . . . What do you want? . . . How did you get this number? . . . I can't understand you. Don't call this number again."

Dawson came around from the changing room, dressed in her robe, rubbing her wet hair with a towel. As she approached the hot tub, she was still trying to make some sense of the call. Then she saw his body, and screamed, "Jack!"

Jonathan Prinze was lying face down in the water, his arms outstretched on either side of him, floating lifelessly, his chest flattened by what appeared to be a single blow, and his body crumpled nearly in half. Death from a single blow to the chest seemed incomprehensible to her, but there it was, right in front of her.

She reached over the side of the spa, and tried to gather his body into her arms, but his dead weight was nearly twice hers. Next, she tried to reach under his arms, and lift him from the water, but she couldn't manage the leverage that was required to maneuver him onto the floor. Finally, Kate just resolved herself to climb back in the hot tub and cradle him, pulling his arms around her and leaning her head against his.

"Jack, Jack," whimpered Dawson, as she began crying out loud.

For a long while, Kate clung tightly to Prinze's lifeless body, teardrops streaming down her cheeks. When she finally looked up from the body, she saw a single piece of paper stuck to the wall with a knife. Upon closer inspection, she recognized the image of three roses intertwined by their thorns. It was the symbol of the Morag Tong, an ancient guild of assassins, and a warning to stay out of Chinatown.

Angered, Dawson grabbed the slip of paper and crumpled it in her fist. She then shouted a warning of her own: "I'm coming for you!"

ABOUT THE AUTHOR

Born in Chicago, Illinois, in the 1950s, Dr. John L. Flynn is a three-time Hugo Award–nominated author, psychologist, teacher, and college dean. In 1977, he received the M. Carolyn Parker Award from the University of South Florida for excellence in creative writing. He received his Bachelor's and Master's degrees in English from the University of South Florida and worked as an English teacher in Baltimore, Maryland. He published his first book *Future Threads* in 1985. In 1998, he earned his PhD as a clinical psychologist from the University of Southern California. He has published nearly twenty books and dozens of articles. He currently resides in Lake Worth, Florida.

THE KATE DAWSON MYSTERIES

FROM OPEN ROAD MEDIA

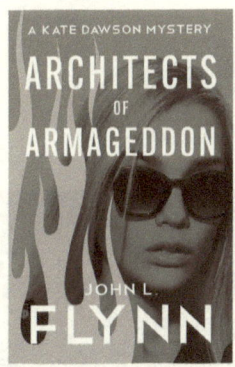